D1765230

WAITING FOR THE ANGEL

A Gorton Novel

by

Stephen Sayers

First published in 2016 by Ohm Books, UK

© 2016 Stephen Sayers
The moral right of the author has been asserted.

All rights reserved. This book is sold subject to the
condition that it shall not, by way of trade or otherwise, be
lent, re-sold, hired out, or otherwise circulated without the
publishers prior consent in any form of binding or cover
other than that in which it is published and without a similar
condition including this condition being imposed on the
subsequent purchaser.

ISBN: 978-1533592941

A CIP catalogue record for this book is available from the
British Library.

Whilst some aspects of this book are based upon true
events, all names and characters are fictional and any
resemblance which may seem to exist to real persons is
purely coincidental.

Dedicated to the people of old Gorton,
who didn't ask for much,
but who rarely got what they asked for.

Two Sisters

It was Saturday morning and Frankie Vaughan was on the wireless. Mrs Parnaby was whispering to herself, "*The Garden of Eden*? Yes – that's where it all started, right enough." She had almost finished polishing the brasses. They hadn't been done since Christmas, and looked a bit grubby. But they were nice and clean now, and the brass candlesticks on the mantelpiece had started to catch the firelight. Mrs Parnaby would set to every Saturday morning so she was straight for the weekend. There was an order to these things. After the fires had been lit and the fireplaces polished, the windows in the parlour were given a good cleaning with warm water, a drop of vinegar and plenty of elbow grease. It was easy; all you had to do was to use a sheet or two of newspaper and then buff each pane up with a clean cloth. Then came sweeping the carpets, the dusting and lastly, the polishing – furniture and brasses. It was eleven o' clock and she was nearly done. She was looking forward to having a cup of tea, but first she had one more thing to do. She had to clean the last and most precious of her brasses – the framed photograph of her daughters, Molly and Beau. There they were – with smiling faces and neat hair. It had been taken on the beach at Blackpool when they were both young. She polished the frame with vigour, and then used light strokes to dust the glass. When she had finished she held the frame and gazed at the photograph. "This one's Molly – well, she's Mary, really, but she likes to be called Molly, and she's the oldest by two years and this one's little Beau – well, she's Bernadette really, but she likes to be called Beau, and she's the lovely one." She stared hard for a while before positioning the photograph carefully on the sideboard. Then she went to make a pot of tea.

Mrs Parnaby was sitting by the fire with a cup of tea. Beau would be home soon. She worked as a Comptometer Operator at Bradford Gasworks; she had been there for three years. Mrs Parnaby sighed. It was a sigh of pride. "Bradford Gasworks – the biggest in Manchester. Aye, it's the biggest in Manchester, and I know the manager!" She adjusted her bosom. "Beau's done well there. She always does well. And she's got the loveliest face. She's got the face of an angel, a real Murphy face, like Mam had, God be good to her. No wonder Beau has so many boyfriends. Not like Molly – who never bothers with boys. She's always been such a mystery and such a disappointment. She took sixteen and three quarter hours of labour to come into this world! And the ginger hair doesn't help either. But you can say this for her – even though she doesn't have any boyfriends, she's a good Catholic. You can be sure of that. She's never out of the Monastery on a Sunday. She's not like Beau. She's got no time for it. When Old Father Rip Rap comes round asking for more money or telling folk that they haven't been to church, she soon sends him on his way." Mrs Parnaby sighed. The front door opened and Beau came in.

"By 'eck, Mam! Let's see that fire. It's blooming cold out there."

"Come on in, chuck. There's plenty of tea in the pot, if you want some."

"Ta, Ma. Brrrr!" She jabbed at the fire with the poker. Sparks spiralled up the chimney. Mrs Parnaby went to the kitchen to get Beau's tea.

"You'd better take your gloves off to do that, Beau. You don't want the fire ruining them."

"Aye, I've been glad of them today, Mam. I could have done with another pair on – and some on my feet, an' all!"

Beau took her gloves off and laid them neatly together on the arm of the chair – long black gloves that Aunty Madeleine had bought her for Christmas. Madeleine wasn't a real aunty. She was just somebody Mrs Parnaby had helped years ago, when Madeleine had been courting a man from Smithfield Market who had been in trouble with the police. She had never forgotten Mrs Parnaby's kindness, and had always given the girls presents at Christmas by way of a 'thank you'. Beau ran a finger over the raised seams. "They're lovely and fashionable aren't they, Mam?"

"Oh aye, they are!"

"You might say they're right up to the minute, because they come up well over my wrist and arm."

"That's Aunty Madeleine for you, Beau. She's a good Catholic woman, she is. She was high up in Lewis's! Oh, and she's got real style. She's a cut above everybody else, Aunty Madeleine!"

"Aye, Mam. I've always thought so."

"You've seen her in her fur coat and winklepicker shoes, haven't you? She's like a model, that one – she even wears *Electrique* scent."

"Aye, she's really with it for her age, isn't she?"

"And she always has plenty of fruit in the house, even when there's nobody ill. Mind you, she'd never entertain having such a thing as sterilised milk on the table. No, not Madeleine, she's much too sophisticated for that!"

"One of the best!"

"Do you know, I've even seen her kitchen floor covered with newspapers with joints of meat on them ready to sell cut price to all her neighbours."

"Did she, Mam?"

"You can't buy class like that, can you?"

Beau turned one of the gloves inside out.

"Ey, Mam, it says 'Empire Made' on the label. Does that mean that they're dead cheap?"

"No, Beau, Aunty Madeleine never buys cheap things. She's got them from Lewis's. She was a supervisor there, and she's still got connections."

"Oh, aye – she must have."

"Aye she has. If she'd have got them from somewhere like Henry's and it said 'Foreign' on the label it'd be a different story, but she'd never do that, not Madeleine. Those are good ones, they are. They're probably from Australia or New Zealand. Australia and New Zealand are in the Empire, aren't they?"

"Aunty Madeleine's dead kind, isn't she, Mam?"

"Of course she is, Beau. She's even got a pair for Molly and for your cousins Sandra and Mavis."

"Did she?"

"Aye, and you know she got me some gloves when I was young. White ones they were."

"Did she, Mam? Oh, I didn't know that!"

"And a long white frock."

"Did she?"

Mrs Parnaby brought Beau's tea in.

Beau took the hot mug. "Ta, Mam." She clasped it with both hands. "I'll take my stuff off in a mo, Mam. I need to get warm first."

"You're doing right, Beau."

It was early afternoon and Molly, Beau and Mrs Parnaby were in the kitchen. They were listening to Bob Miller and the Millermen on the wireless, and were making stew for that night. Molly was cutting celery into a pan. It had been a good day at Edgar Stone's umbrella factory, and now she was back home where she belonged. She liked working as a shorthand typist at the factory, but she liked being at home much more. She loved reading, and would spend hours in her bedroom with an eiderdown round her shoulders reading novels. Her favourites were by people like D. H. Lawrence, George Eliot and Iris

Murdoch. Somehow they satisfied something she knew life could never give her – or at least life in Gorton could never give her. Mrs Parnaby was peeling onions. She drew on a cigarette. "Are you going out tonight, Molly?"

"No, Ma, it's too cold. I'm going to curl up in front of the fire and read, then I'll probably put my new bedsocks on and go to bed early."

Beau looked at her sister. "Oh, listen to Little Miss Perfect! Go to bed early? What for? You should let your hair down once in a while, girl! You don't know what you're missing."

Mrs Parnaby stepped in: "How about you, Beau?"

Beau lit a cigarette. "Oh, I'm going out with Minnie and Theresa and Carol Bradshaw and that lot. We said we'd go to The Bessemer for a drink."

Molly looked across. "Are they the girls from the Comptometer Room?"

"Aye, they're the ones. They're a right good laugh, they are."

"But last time you said those three were... you know, a bit loose."

"Aye I did. But you can be a good laugh and still be lucky in love!"

"Lucky in love? You said that after a drink they were anybody's."

"Aye I did, but that's better than being nobody's, isn't it, Molly?"

Beau and Molly stared at each other.

Mrs Parnaby tapped Beau's glass bowl with a spoon. "Mix that flour well into the corned beef, you know, Beau, and don't forget the bicarb in the cabbage – put plenty of it in or you'll have it boiled white."

Aye, I know, Mam! I know!" Beau drew on her cigarette and then stubbed it out. "Eh, Mam, you know what happened today?

"What?"

"Your old boyfriend, Jimmy Wrigglesworth, came in. He doesn't come in very often. And you know what he said?

"No, what?"

"He said; "Tell your Mam,..." She laughed. "...Tell your Mam that while... while there's snow on the roof... there's still a fire in the boiler!"

Mrs Parnaby buried her face in the tea towel. "Oh, Gordon Bennett!"

Beau laughed. "Snow on the roof? More like a few flakes of snow on the roof, if you ask me!"

Mrs Parnaby lowered the tea towel and gave a chesty laugh.

"The silly bugger – look, the onions are making me cry now! And oh, and he used to have such nice curly hair, an' all!"

"Well he's got a big bald head now, Mam – and it wants a good polishing!"

"Well, I'm not going to polish anything of his now, girl, that's for sure!..."

Molly looked shocked. "Mam!"

"I haven't got the stomach for that sort of thing anymore!"

Beau scowled. "Don't be such a square, Molly."

"But they were lovely curls, they were – I always thought they were wasted on a man." Mrs Parnaby laughed; then she coughed, and became serious: "He was a caring man though – I'll give him that."

Molly got up and started rummaging in the vegetable rack for some potatoes. "Well there's still a fire in his boiler, Mam – and he might be able to light your fire!"

"He'll have a job, I'll tell you – that's all behind me now, lass – I'm too old now, thank God."

"Aw, Mam – you shouldn't say that!"

"No, no, I've had my fill. I'll leave that sort of thing to you and Molly from now on."

It was early evening. Beau was sitting in front of the dressing table in the girls' bedroom. She had just put her lipstick on, and was checking to see if it looked right. She pouted; yes, that peachy colour would do nicely. She blew a kiss to herself and smiled. When you go to The Bess you never know who you're going to meet. Vernon might be there. He didn't go in very often, but sometimes, on Saturday nights, he went in with Pete Bingham. Vernon was gorgeous. He was very mature: an engineer at Tether and Armley's. He used big words, and had letters after his name and everything. What a catch he'd be – but he was married, and that might make things difficult. Beau stared into the mirror. She could see sadness in her reflection. She knew Vernon would never look at her. Last time he'd spoken to her, she hadn't known what to say. He'd asked her about some Swedish film she hadn't heard of, and she'd felt stupid. When he talked to Pete and the girl Pete was with, she couldn't join in because they were talking about politics. Beau didn't know anything about politics, except that it was boring. And when she had talked about hand jiving nobody was interested.

Beau lit a cigarette, and then put the packet of cigarettes in her bag. She wouldn't take the lighter; she would ask men to light her cigarettes, and if she liked them she would cup her hands round theirs. She gazed into the mirror and blew smoke against her reflection. Maybe Molly could tell her about Swedish films and politics. Molly seemed to know about things like that. Beau would be able to talk to Vernon then, that's for sure. She patted her hair. It was well backcombed, and the waves looked just right. She checked everything else. The black jumper showed off those curves, and the yellow earrings went well with it. She stood up. Her black trousers fitted nicely. Mam didn't agree with women wearing trousers; she said they were unhygienic. What did she know? She slipped into her coat, and then reached for the bottle of *Soir de Paris* and dabbed it on her wrists and throat. Then she pulled the black gloves on. She looked at them this way and that, and kept looking as she picked up her bag.

Molly was sitting on a cushion in front of the fire. She wriggled her toes inside her new bed socks. What a good Christmas present they'd been. She got cold easily, and especially at the extremities – nose, toes and fingers – the 'sign of the cross'! Her bum got cold too. (Mam had always said that she had been blessed with a good bum.) It wasn't cold now, though. She was rubbing it gently when she heard Beau coming down the stairs – you couldn't miss her in those heels. The door opened and she came in: "Well look who it isn't – Little Molly Flinders, sat among the cinders!"

"Are you off to The Bess then, Beau?"

"Aye – tonight's the night!"

Phew! That's a strong scent you've got on!"

"It's *Soir de Paris*, Molly – that means 'Evening in Paris' and… it's deadly!"

"Yes, I've noticed."

"Cheeky little cow! But then we'll see what happens tonight, won't we?"

"Yes we will, Beau. Anyroad, enjoy yourself."

Beau struck a pose. "Right then. Bye, Molly. Don't do anything I wouldn't do!" She gave a little smile and went out. The front door closed behind her.

Molly wriggled her toes and whispered, "Better to be Little Polly Flinders than all done up like a dog's dinner!" She leant forward and felt her toes. "And Little Polly Flinders had 'pretty little toes'." This was going to be a cosy Saturday evening. She was glad she wasn't going out like Beau. It was far too cold to go out, and she never really enjoyed it anyway. There weren't many places to go in Gorton. Of course, there was always the dancing at Belle Vue. That was expensive though, especially if you were saving up – and you always got home far too late. She did go to the pictures now and then, when there was something good on, but that wasn't very often. And then there was The Bessemer. That was all right. The people she met there were nice enough, but she never knew what to say to them, especially the men. The men weren't interested in books or plays on the radio, or what her dreams were all about. They just drank, and drinking made her face go numb. But here, in front of the fire, Molly had everything she wanted – a good fire, a mug of hot Vimto and her library book – *The Virgin and the Gypsy*. Surely this was what life was all about.

Molly stared at the book. Reading was her salvation; her means to another way of being, where time would give way to timelessness and she would find herself in a familiar place. It was a place lit by angels, a shadow land where secret longings became conscious and where ideas gave way to the blood of life. The fire flared suddenly. She thought about Yvette and the gypsy, and she knew how much she would like to be loved; not just to be loved, but to be *desired*, and taken in the arms of a strong gypsy. What joy it would be to lie with that dark man. She put the book down and gazed into the flames.

January was always a lean month in Gorton; the days were short, money was short and in January, what you didn't have you had to do without. On a night like this, if people went anywhere, it was to their firesides – if they were lucky enough to have firesides. Beau knew that, and when she reached the end of Taylor Street and heard a din coming from The Bessemer. The sound carried on the night air like a hurrying prayer – conversation and laughter – but with mad shouting cutting through it all. She got to the step, pushed open the inner doors and went in. The place was full of people. She looked round the room, which smelt of fish and disinfectant. The girls were sitting at their usual table by the toilets, where they could watch all the comings and goings of the evening. Beau waved and made her way towards them. She felt a bit self-conscious, and moved with caution; she didn't want to be touched.

"Hiya!"

"Hiya, Beau. How are they hanging?"

Mrs Parnaby described Minnie and Theresa as 'dead common', and here they were at their smiling best. They were blonded sisters who smelt of hairspray, cigarettes and mint. Their friend, Carol Bradshaw, was a bit older. She was what you would call 'dead common' too – but she was steadier and quieter than the other girls, and they looked up to her. Beau took a cigarette from her bag and then put the bag down by the girls' coats. She kept her gloves on. She didn't want to take them off because tonight she wanted to be sophisticated. She signed to Theresa that she wanted a light; then she leant across to light her cigarette from Theresa's match. She lifted up her purse.

"Right, girls, four gills of Chester's Mild is it? Let's start as we mean to go on."

By ten o' clock, Beau and her friends felt drunk. They'd eaten meat pies and mushy peas with plenty of mint sauce, and had drunk as much Chester's as they could afford. They'd talked about work, clothes, records, men, dancing and more about men. They'd chatted to the landlord, George, and had a laugh with the regulars. When everybody saw Joe Molloy pushing his way through the crowd, somebody had started singing *Roll out the Barrel*. Joe had patted his belly and had given 'V' signs all round. Then he'd come across to where the girls were sitting, and had started shifting their bags and coats. He was looking for something underneath their seat. When they asked him what it was, he got all embarrassed. And then it came out. He'd lost his mother's teeth. He'd borrowed them so he could go out looking decent on Friday night, but somehow he'd arrived home without them. His mother had given him a good scutching and sent him back to look for them. So Joe had been on his hands and knees doing what he could, and after a lot of grunting and several sweeps of his hand, a smile had spread over his gaping face; he was on his feet, holding up a perfect set of teeth for all to see. A cheer had gone up. He'd bowed, and then he'd done a wonderful thing. He called for quiet, and then he'd given them *Danny Boy*. Joe had something special about him. Even without teeth he'd made people sit up and listen to that song.

Then Carol had started chatting to three young Teddy boys in their grey drape suits with black collars and cuffs and brothel creepers. They were from Openshaw, and had come to The Bess to see what the talent was like. Norman – the one with a ring on every finger – seemed to be very keen on Minnie. He kept whispering to her and she wouldn't stop giggling. Carol was paying a lot of attention to the one who looked a bit like Gene Vincent. She kept teasing him and touching his knee. He didn't seem to mind; he just smiled. He was good looking though, and when he looked round the room, the wall lamp behind him made his Brylcreemed hair shine thick and black, like a gypsy's. Theresa pretended to be shy with the one called Ray. He had a stammer and a rolled-up bus ticket behind his ear. He must have had an interest in ears, because he tried to nibble Theresa's ear every time George was out of the room. Beau didn't like the look of any of them; they were too young and far too common for her liking.

It was nearly time to have Elsie wheel out the piano. But John Clements got up and clapped his hands: "Eh, Minnie, do that turn you did on Christmas Eve! Go on, darling, give us all a treat!" Minnie smiled and just stared back at him. Other people started to shout. She looked at Theresa, who nodded and pulled her up by the arm. She stood up, picked up a circular beer mat from the table and folded it gently in half. Everybody cheered, and Minnie announced to the entire room in her husky voice that she was going to demonstrate the ancient art of talking out of your arse. She made a great show of holding the beer mat over her head and waving it backwards and forwards. She picked up an empty pint pot from the next table and held the rim to the side of her mouth. Then she turned her back to the audience and raised her leg gracefully until it rested on a nearby barstool. Down came the arm and she shoved her hand through her legs with the beer mat held between fingers and thumb. Everybody cheered, and there was a lot of chattering until finally it went quiet. Minnie took a deep breath, and in a trilling voice started her performance by making the beer mat sing the words "Nelly the elephant packed her trunk and said 'goodbye' to the circus. Off she went with a trumpety-trump, trump... thwwwww!... trump... thwwwww!... trump... thwwwwwwww!" She turned round and winked. "I won't take my coat off – I'm not stopping! The arm went up again, so did the backside and the beer mat went back through the legs. This time it mouthed, "The runaway train came down the track and she blew thwwwww!... The runaway train came down the track and she blew... thwwwww!... The runaway train came down the track, her whistle wide... peeeeep... and her throttle back... paaaaaarp.... and she blew-ooooo... thwwwwwwwww!"

The whole pub was in uproar. Beau was so impressed with how well Minnie's turn had gone down that she decided to have a go herself. So she got up and snatched the pint pot and beer mat from Minnie. "Give them me. It's my turn now!" Beau was ready to perform. She struck a more exaggerated pose than Minnie had done and pushed her backside out like a Salford prop forward. Then she shoved her hand between her legs and began to flex the beer mat, and with remarkable dexterity, she got it to mouth "Heigh-ho! Heigh-ho! It's off to work we go! With a thup, thup, therp and a thup, thup therp! Heigh-ho. Heigh-ho!" Minnie shook Beau's shoulder. "Beau!"

"Bugger off, Minnie. I've not finished yet!"

"But Beau, look who's just come in... It's Vernon and he's bloody seen you!"

Theresa came up. "You've just spoiled it all, Beau. You stopped our Minnie's doing her best one – *The Drunk in the Railway Carriage* – that's the best one!"

Everybody in the room was cheering, but Beau wasn't listening. She had her hands to her face. John Clements and his lovely wife came up. His blue eyes were twinkling. "Eh, that was dead good, Minnie! I've not laughed so much since I left the navy! Eh, Beau – I never knew you had an arse as good as Max Wall's!" Everybody laughed and then he said, "That was even better than last time, Minnie! You should try *Cherry Pink and Apple Blossom White* next!" He blew Minnie a kiss.

"Thanks, Clem!"

Then Vernon came up. "Hiya, Carol. Hiya, Minnie

– that was smashing. I didn't know you could do that."

Minnie laughed. "Thanks, Vernon."

Theresa came close. "She didn't do her best one, Vernon. You should see how she does *The Drunk in the Railway Carriage*. She's a picture!"

"I saw Beau's one though."

Beau went red. "I didn't mean to, Vernon... you know, it just happened. I must be a bit... you know, a bit tipsy."

"Don't be daft, Beau – everybody loved it. I could hear them laughing half way down Taylor Street."

Beau and Vernon stared at each other. Then people started calling for Elsie to wheel out the piano.

When Beau got outside she found her three friends up against the pub wall being kissed by the Teddy boys. This time Minnie's hand wasn't between her legs but between Norman's, and she was kissing him urgently and sloppily. Theresa had sunk into Ray's arms, and Carol had a firm grip on Gene Vincent. She broke away suddenly. "*Woman Love*, is it? I'll show you a woman's love!" And then she went back to the kissing. Beau turned round and went straight back into the pub. She stopped just inside the door, opened her bag and took a cigarette out. Then she walked straight up to where Vernon was sitting. "Eh, Vernon, give us a light, darling." Vernon looked at her and slowly reached for the box of matches on the table. He struck a match and held it up for Beau. She stared at him; then, slowly and deliberately, she cupped her hands around his. He smiled. She leant forward and lit the cigarette. She kept one hand on his whilst she blew the match out. "Thanks, darling."

"That's all right, Beau." They stared at each other for a few seconds, and then Beau leant forward and kissed Vernon full on the mouth. They kissed like they meant it until they heard George shout, "Eh, you two buggers – you can cut that out right away!"

They pulled apart. Beau put her hand to her mouth. Her cigarette broke awkwardly, and she felt a sudden burning between her fingers. She clapped her hands together and the cigarette fell to the table. Vernon picked it up and stubbed it out in the ashtray. "Are you all right?"

"Aye, but bloody 'ell, Vernon – I've just burnt a hole in my glove!

It was midnight when Beau finally got home. She was angry about what had happened to the glove. What a stupid thing to do. You could put your finger through the hole. You couldn't stitch that. But it wasn't just that she had ruined a perfectly good pair of gloves; it was the shame of how it had happened. How could she tell her Mam about kissing Vernon? She could hide the gloves away, but what would she say to Aunty Madeleine about not wearing them – and, even worse, what would she say to Molly? Little Miss Perfect would be all the more perfect then.

The house was quiet. Mam and Molly had gone to bed. Beau took her shoes off and crept upstairs. She undressed in the dark, and as she did so she heard Molly turn over in her bed by the window. She got into her nightie, and then switched the small bedside light on. She looked over at Molly and then walked slowly to the chest of drawers. She pulled out Molly's socks and knickers drawer and looked for her gloves. She found them, took them out and tried them on. They fitted nicely. Then quickly she put her own gloves in Molly's drawer, switched the light off and got into bed. She lay there breathing heavily. She felt good wearing Molly's gloves. It might be weeks before Molly discovered the hole, and then she'd have nobody to blame except herself; anyway, she didn't deserve them, the stuck-up cow! She lay there smiling in the dark. Then she took the gloves off and, as quietly as she could, reached out, opened her own drawer, put the gloves in and closed the drawer. Mmmm! Her thoughts turned to Vernon. He'd kissed her so nicely... so firmly... and he'd still be kissing her now if that George hadn't spoiled things. Then she sighed and fell asleep.

It was early in the morning. Mrs Parnaby was sitting on her bed with a shawl wrapped round her shoulders. She was holding a framed photograph of her husband. It was 13th January and the anniversary of his awful death. It was a death that had come too early to be just, and one that had broken so many hearts. It was a death full of fear, a fear that was belched up and spat out, spread red amongst holy bread and wine on the sheets. That was the way he had died. She had run a finger over his expressionless face, touched his hands, and whispered to God and to him about being sorry, so sorry, never forgetting and always being loved. This was the man who had worked so hard to keep the kids' arses in their pants, whose spirit was bent in half by what he did and how he did it. But you could still see the child in him. It was a kind of childlike grace that never really left him. You just had to hold him to find that out. And even in the lowest moments, he was brave and tried to be funny. He used to say, 'We'll be all right, Mam! We'll be all right. Always remember that we've got something that money can't buy – *poverty*!" But soon after that, he would cry. She would hold him and he would just lie there and cry.

And he'd cried when Paul had died that summer's day, when pitch bubbled as black as bile between the cobbled setts in Taylor Street, and kids chanted skipping songs outside the window. After that, he'd made his wife promise that if anything ever happened to him, she'd see to it that if nothing else, their little daughters would grow up to be good Catholic mothers. She felt such deep anguish now. There was guilt at the bottom of it. What of her promise? Why was it that Beau wasn't much of a Catholic, and Molly didn't look like she was going to be much of a mother? And why had she been so stubborn when Paul had said he had a headache, and she'd accused him of just not wanting to go to school? Why hadn't she realised that her trembling boy was falling breathless unto death? She'd failed as a wife and she'd failed as a mother; and that would never be forgiven. She crossed herself. In the name of the Father, the Son and the Holy Ghost. Amen.

The house was quiet. Molly was in the kitchen washing cups. She'd had breakfast, and she was now tidying up before going to the Monastery. She was going on her own this morning. Her Mam had got up early and had gone to the cemetery. She looked at the clock; there was plenty of time. She dried her hands, took the apron off and then went upstairs to get her coat. Beau was still asleep. Molly got her shoes and scarf, and put her coat on as quietly as she could. Then she went to her drawer to get her new gloves. This would be the first time she'd worn them, and she was looking forward to it. She put the gloves on, and that's when she found the hole in a finger of the right hand. She gasped and stared at the hole. It was a burn. It was clearly a burn. God, how had that happened? That's when she smelt cigarettes. "That's a cig burn, that is!" Then she sniffed the gloves: they reeked of *Soir de Paris*! "Beau, bloody Beau!" She went to Beau's bed, and was about to wake her up when she changed her mind and went to Beau's drawer. She opened it and found a pair of gloves. She took them out and was looking at them when Beau turned over and sighed. She left the room and went downstairs. She put all four gloves on the arm of the chair. Two of them had obviously been worn. There was a round burned hole in one of them, as well as a green stain on the seam. Beau must have worn them in The Bess last night, and the bitch must have ruined them and then swapped them for her own good gloves when she got home. Molly was furious. She bit her lip as she decided what she should do. She whispered, "These are mine and I'm having them back, and as for these – well if she's so fond on burning them I'll give the little bitch some help!" And with that she threw the gloves on the fire. She stared at them as they smouldered and then caught fire. They burned quickly and with a bright flame. "That'll show you – you little bitch." Then she went to put her own gloves on and discovered something was wrong. She had put one on but the other one wouldn't fit her right hand. Then she got it – there were two left-handed gloves! One of them was fine but the other one had a worn look about it. She had burned one of her good gloves and the one with the hole in it! "Bloody 'ell! What am I going to do now?" Molly thought for a moment, and then suddenly an idea came to her. She went upstairs and put the two gloves in Beau's drawer. Beau was stirring and so she left the room quickly, went downstairs, opened the front door and set off to the Monastery.

Molly was on her knees. All through Mass the saints had looked down on her, and she had felt the breath of martyrs upon her cheeks. Celestial trumpets had blazed like moonbeams as the memory of her impetuosity wrestled with the prayers of angels, flat-fingered and broken in their age, and her anger had turned into guilt. Why had she acted so rashly? She could have dealt with things in other ways and still have got her gloves back. There would be rows to face now, and she would never be forgiven by Beau, by Mam, by Aunty Madeleine or by God himself. What she had done was just wrong. She was afraid and then, without warning, she began to sob. She buried her face in her hands, and tried to control herself. After a while, she dared to look through her fingers. People in front of her had turned round. One of them was Mrs Pinkerton, who reached out and touched Molly gently on the shoulder. And whilst that warm hand remained firm she felt a comfort of sorts, like the comfort of being hugged.

Mrs Parnaby, back from the cemetery, was making a pot of tea in the kitchen. She'd already seen Beau when she'd gone upstairs, sat on her bed and asked her if she wanted breakfast. But now, it was time for a good strong cup of tea and a warm by the fire. Her thoughts were full of the pain of being at the graveside, and what she had whispered there in prayer. The door opened and Beau came in. "Do you want some tea, Beau?"

"Aye, Mam – that's just the job."

The tea was poured and they went into the parlour where the fire burned brightly. They sat down.

"How was it at the cemetery, Mam?"

"Well you, know how it is, Beau." There was a silence and then: "You just have to do it, don't you?"

"Aye, I suppose you do."

I don't know why you don't go, Beau. You loved your dad and Paul – you could go and see them sometimes."

Beau shook her head. "We've been through all this before, Mam. It just upsets me... and anyway, you know how I feel about religion and all that."

"Yes, I do and I really wish you didn't. It was just one or two things that brought you to this. I know they upset you when your brother died, and then your dad, but that doesn't mean to say…"

"Aye, I know."

"You can't blame the Church for all that, can you? It was one priest, just one priest. You can't blame God for that."

"Oh aye, you can, Mam. He was a Catholic priest! There's only two things you can say after things like that have happened to you – you can either say that God's a right sod for causing all the pain and be dead against him, or you can say that the priests have been lying to us. There isn't a God at all! They've just pulled the wool over our eyes."

"Oh, Beau! You don't know… you don't know how much that hurts me to hear you coming out with all that." Mrs Parnaby took her handkerchief from her sleeve and touched each eye in turn. There was a silence, and then Beau said, "Sorry Mam, but you've got to understand that I just don't believe in God any more!"

"Oh, Bernadette! God forgive you – God help me!"

"Mam, I'm old enough to make my own mind up now. Can't you see that? And even though I love you and I loved dad, I won't change my mind! It'll take a miracle to make me change my mind about it, and that's that!"

Mrs Parnaby got up, snorted violently into her handkerchief and went quickly out of the room.

Mrs Parnaby was sitting on her bed with a shawl wrapped around her shoulders. She was weeping silently. There was a knock at the door and Beau came in. "I'm sorry, Mam. I'm really sorry." She went across and put her arms round her mother. Mrs Parnaby put her hands on Beau's. "I'm just a bit upset, that's all."

"I know, Mam. I'm sorry."

"You know, Beau – they were mine too and I was

hurt when they went, an' all."

"I know, Mam. I'm sorry."

"They were mine too. How do you think I feel?"

"Sorry, Mam."

"Frank made me a woman and I made him a man. We were rich in all but money, and I lost him."

"Aye, Mam."

"And we had Paul. I carried him and I felt the first kicks of his little life here, in my belly. I gave birth to him, here, in this very room and I did my best for him even though we didn't have much."

"I know you did, Mam. Hush, don't get upset!"

"These things mean something to me, Beau. I suppose in the long run, everything means nothing, but when you care – when you really care – everything means *something*. Do you know what I mean?"

"It's all right, Mam."

"I feel like a failure, I really do."

"Why, Mam? What have you done wrong?" There was a silence broken only by the breathing of shallow breaths, until, finally: "Well. You see, Beau... Before Frank died, before he died, he made me promise." She stopped and composed herself. "He made me promise that I'd see to it that you and Molly would be good Catholic women when you grew up. Faith mattered so much to him, you see. That's all he had – apart from us – and he wanted to leave it to you."

"Aw, Mam! Hush, hush, hush."

"And when I hear you say you don't believe in God any more, well it's like, it's like I've broken my promise to him."

"No, you haven't, Mam. It's not your fault."

"You see, I know... I know that this life brings its share of sadness and happiness to you whether you're a believer or not, but when you are a believer, the sad things are a bit more bearable and the happy things are a bit more wonderful. Do you know what I mean?"

"Aye, Mam, I suppose I do, but you mustn't blame yourself. It's not your fault."

Father Richard Rack was waiting by the Monastery door as Molly came out. "Ah, there you are, Molly! Can I have a word?" He put his hand on her arm and drew her towards him. Molly avoided his eyes and tried to smile.

"Now you see, Molly, that Mrs Pinkerton is not so nearly such a big owd busybody as she might first appear. It's in her nature to be concerned, and that's why she came to me about you. She tells me that you've been having a few little difficulties just lately. Is that right, Molly?"

"Yes Father, it is."

"Life can be very trying at times, can't it, Molly?"

Molly couldn't hold back the tears, and she began to cry. Father Rack put his arm around her and they walked back inside the Monastery. Several people were lighting candles or praying. Father Rack found a place at the side where they wouldn't be overheard. It didn't take long for Molly to tell the entire story about the gloves, and to say how sorry she was for what she'd done. And all the time Father Rack had listened in silence, his grey head bowed. When she'd finished, she looked at him directly. "Please Father – what should I do?"

Father Rack thought for a moment and said, "Well, Molly, you can do no better than what you've done already – you've shown true remorse for what you've done, and you've been praying mightily for forgiveness."

"Thank you, Father."

"Now let me ask you a question, Molly. Molly – is your faith still strong?"

"Yes, Father, it is."

"Right, so. Well now, what you've got to do first of

all is to remember that you've been saved by your faith."

"Have I, Father?"

"Well you see, life's a funny owd thing. No matter who we are – believers and unbelievers, young or old, rich or poor, clever or not, we're all going to have to face the pain of it – you know, the losses we all have to bear – the loss of loved ones, our health, our jobs, our very selves, not to mention our gloves!" Father Rack smiled, and Molly did too. "We do what we can to get by, but it isn't easy and we don't always come up trumps. But when we believe in God and put our trust in him, we have a tried and tested way of dealing with it. Our faith is our light in the darkness! Our Lord showed us that. And when we live our lives according to faith we get a kind of God-given resilience that can overcome all pain, and then even the simplest of lives can be lived decently and in grace."

"Yes, Father."

Father Rack could see that Molly wasn't fully convinced by his attempts at eloquence, and so he tried again: "But this isn't the end of it, is it? We still have to sort out this glove business. What we need is a practical solution. Now then, Molly, you say that your Aunty Madeleine gave you the gloves, and that they were black and elbow length, didn't you?"

"Yes, Father."

"And did they have any… any sort of decorative markings or buttons or straps or anything else on them, did they?"

"No, Father – they were plain, just plain."

"Now that's very interesting, Molly. Wait a while here. I'm going to seek guidance and while I'm away you might say a few words to all them that listen to us in Heaven, and seek redemption from your sins."

"Yes, I will, Father."

Father Rack got up and walked away. Molly went

on her knees and started to pray.

In a few minutes Father Rack returned. He put his hand on Molly's shoulder. "Sorry to interrupt your prayers, Molly, but are these anything like the gloves your Aunty got you?" He held up a pair of long, black bri-nylon gloves. Molly stared up at him and then at the glove, and her expression changed. "Yes, yes! They're just like the ones Aunty Madeleine got me!" She felt the material with both hands.

"Well now, there's a surprise. I don't suppose they'd fit you as well, would they?"

Molly stared into his eyes. "Oh, Father – do you really mean it?"

"Try them. Put them on and we'll see!" Molly was excited and she fumbled to put them on, but they fitted beautifully. Father Rack could see that. "Oh well, you might as well take them, Molly. Ah sure, they don't fit me at all and black's never been my colour!"

"Oh thank you, Father, thank you!"

"It's a practical solution, that's all!"

"Where did you get them?"

"Don't ask, Molly – let's just say that God moves in mysterious ways."

Molly carried on playing with the gloves, lifting them up, laying them down, holding them to her cheek.

"But there's another matter to deal with isn't there, Molly?"

"What's that, Father?"

"Well, now you've got your gloves back, what's Beau going to say about her two left-handers in the drawer?"

"Oh, yes… There'll be trouble, won't there?"

"There will so, and if there is, you just take plenty of no notice – do you hear me now, Molly?

"I will, Father."

"Remember what she's like, the girl!"

"What shall I do, Father?"

"Well, you might try putting these in her drawer before she finds out!" He produced another pair of long black gloves just like the first. "Then she'll never know, will she?"

Molly gasped. "Oh thank you, Father!" Molly clutched his hand and kissed it.

"It's my Catholic duty, Molly. God knows it is, but it's one that she should never find out about. God knows, she doesn't really deserve it."

"What do you mean, Father?"

"Well you see, Molly, you're contrite of heart, aren't you? But she isn't. And the last time I asked her about coming to Mass she sent me packing. Sent me packing, so she did! Do you know what she called me? 'Father Rip Rap', that's what!" Molly smiled. "Half of Gorton calls you that, Father!"

"Ah sure, I know they do, but *she* started it – anyway, the half of Gorton that call me that are mainly *Prods*, so they are!" They both laughed.

"Thank you, Father. But why are you doing this for Beau when you don't like her?"

"I'm doing this for the whole family, because I *do* like them! Heavens knows, I've baptised three of you and I've buried three of you – and who knows, I might end up marrying three of you as well. I shall have had the complete Angelus then, won't I?"

Molly was taken aback. "Do you think I'll ever get married, Father?"

"Ah, now that's something for the Lord to decide, but you know, I wouldn't put it past him. Where girls are concerned, the Lord is a great one for marrying and for bringing babies home, so he is."

"I suppose he is."

"Your father always hoped you would. Did you know that?"

"Did he, Father?"

"Ah, yes. I liked your father. He was an honest man, a decent man, and a godly man who worked so hard to provide for his family. And he loved you and he was so proud of you, Molly!"

"Was he, Father? I didn't…"

"So he was, Molly."

"I didn't know that. I just thought Paul was his favourite; then when Beau came along, she seemed to be his favourite an' all then. I didn't know he had strong feelings for me!"

"Oh, you're right – he loved Paul, like any man loves his only son. And he loved Beau, like any man loves his youngest child. And he loved you too and he was so utterly proud of you!"

"Proud of me – why, Father?"

"Your father couldn't read or write – you know that, don't you?"

"I do, Father."

"I'm not breaking a confidence here, but I can tell you that he was ashamed of himself for, try as he might, he could never quite manage to get the hang of his letters and words. He just didn't broadcast the fact, that's all. He didn't need to, you see, labouring as he was in the factory. But he saw in you what he longed to be himself – someone who could read proper books, and use words as they should be used and make sense of things like other people do. You'd become what he'd always wanted to become himself. Frank felt he had succeeded with you – all his hard work in that factory had been vindicated, and you were his living proof of it!"

"I never realised that, Father. I always thought I was a bit of a nothing in his eyes, you know, a bit overlooked."

"Overlooked? Overlooked? How could anyone with any brains overlook a girl who has all the things you have – you're a sweet natured, intelligent, golden-haired girl, who, on top of it all, is as polished as an angel. You don't pick these things from off the bushes you know, Molly! These things are God given."

Molly didn't know what to say. Father Rack's words had shaken her beyond words. Once she had gathered herself she said faintly, "Thank you, Father. You've certainly given me something to think about."

"I have, Molly. I have." Molly reached out to him and held both of his hands in hers.

"God bless you, Molly Parnaby."

"And you, Father." Molly kissed his hands.

"And give my regards to Ellen, and let's not forget Beau as well."

"I will, Father." Molly turned quickly and walked away. Father Rack watched her go "Oh, and Molly, you know the kinds of delicacies and things a priest has to observe, so let's keep all this to ourselves." He gave her a wink.

Molly looked back. "Oh yes, Father. I promise, I will." And with that she left. Father Rack smiled. He knew he had done the right thing with Molly, and at the same time he had kept his promise to Madeleine Ellis. She'd sworn him to secrecy after her visit in November, when she'd given him a box of twenty long, black bri-nylon gloves as a 'donation to the needy of the parish'. Needy? These weren't the kind of woollen gloves that were needed by the needy; they were flimsy-whimsy gloves wanted by the stylish. But in this case, Molly was most definitely of the needy persuasion, though for reasons other than that of Jack Frost nipping at her fingers. He'd offered to write a thank-you note to Lewis's, but Madeleine Ellis said it wouldn't be necessary, because "it would be against Company Policy". But now he was beginning to see that when she'd given him the gloves, it was nothing to do with Lewis's or their policies. He had heard talk of Mrs Ellis before, and now that talk was beginning to make sense. Hers wasn't an act of kindness; it was more a matter of guilt, though it had been guilt that had finished up doing some good in the world. He knew that now there was rejoicing in heaven over the sinner who had repented, and on earth, fulsome repentance in hope of forgiveness had been rewarded by fulsome guilt in the hope of self-preservation. In the circumstances, he was happy to settle for that.

Beau was still in her nightie and fluffy pink slippers, and was sitting by the fireside with her mother. She'd been back to bed after her fraught conversations with her mother earlier that morning, and she'd just got up again. Mrs Parnaby sighed. "Molly will be back from Mass soon – I'd better think about making something to eat. Could you manage egg and bacon, Beau? We could have fried bread too, if you like."

"Aye, Mam, I'm hungry now."

The front door opened and Molly came in.

"Hiya!"

"Come in and warm yourself, Molly."

"Oh, I will – it's bitter cold out there." Molly went straight to the fire and warmed her hands.

"Oh, you've got your new gloves on, Molly! They look nice!"

"Oh thanks, Mam. It's the first time I've worn them."

"They go well with the brown of your coat."

"Thanks, Mam."

Beau stared. "Are they all right and everything, Molly?" Molly knew immediately that Beau was troubled. "Oh, yes, they're fine thanks, Beau."

Beau got up. "Let's have a look at them, then." She held Molly's hands in hers and turned them this way and that. Molly smiled.

"Do you want an egg and some bacon, Molly? There's plenty of fried bread an' all."

Beau turned suddenly. "I'm just going upstairs to get changed."

Molly sat down. "Yes, Mam, eggs and bacon would be grand."

Beau went upstairs. She knew that there wasn't a hole in the gloves Molly was wearing, and she was boiling with anger – the little sod must have switched the gloves back again! She went to the drawer and took the gloves out. She looked at them, and everything seemed to be in order. There were no holes anywhere, and they were in good condition She tried one on. It fitted perfectly and looked as good as new. Then she tried the other one and she couldn't get it on. It didn't take long to discover that it was a left-handed glove. There were two left-handed gloves! Beau stared straight ahead. She was stunned, and didn't know what to think or what to do. Then she remembered her mother's words: 'Everything means something… Everything means something.' What could two left-handed gloves mean? She sat down on the bed and tried to think. Left-handed meant bad luck didn't it? Aye, it did. Two left-handers must mean double bad luck! But how had it happened? Beau couldn't think straight. She was struggling with anger, with doubt, and memories of everything she had grown to hate and fear, but now it was guilt that she felt more than anything. And trapped within the guilt was a kind of scintillating light, a realisation of some deep aspect of herself that had been born and bred with rage, when the sweat-curled head of her brother laid in its death had brought her misery. And now it was the gloves that were haunting her – gloves that she had ruined for a kiss. What did all this mean? Her mother had said something about when you don't believe bad things happen. She couldn't remember her exact words, and wished she had listened more carefully when they'd had the conversation earlier that day. She thought she'd better go and see her, and find out what was happening. She got up, put the gloves in the drawer and went downstairs.

As Beau walked into the kitchen, Molly was just leaving. "I'll just go upstairs and take my coat off before my eggs and bacon." Beau walked straight past her. "Mam, give me a cigarette, will you?"

"Aye, Beau – just a minute." Mrs Parnaby wiped her hands on her apron. "Just let me put Molly's egg and bacon in the oven." She closed the oven door and took two cigarettes out of the packet. "There you are, Beau."

"Ta, Mam." Mrs Parnaby lit the cigarettes.

Beau inhaled deeply. "Mam, can I have a word with you?"

"Course you can. What is it?"

Beau sat down. "Mam, does God let you know about things?"

"What do you mean, Beau?"

"Well, does God let you know that he knows when you've done something wrong?"

"Do you mean does he speak to you about it?"

"No, not that, does he kind of show you when you've done something wrong?"

"Well sometimes he does, but he mainly does it through your conscience, you know, when you feel guilty about what you've been doing."

"I know, but when he shows you, how does he do it?"

"Erm, he shows you with little things like little signs – you know, unexpected things people say to you, or suddenly finding things you've not been looking for, or taking things away and that sort of thing.

"One way or another he lets you know, is that right?"

"Aye, that's about right, Beau. I mean I don't

34

understand these things like a priest does, but I do know that when you do things right, it usually comes right, and when you do things wrong – well there's usually trouble. But why do you want to know, anyroad? You don't even believe in God, you said so!"

Beau went red, but she didn't say anything.

Molly was in her bedroom. She took her coat off and put it on the back of the door; then she took her gloves off and held them to her face, smiling as she did so. She kissed them and put them in her drawer. Then she went to where her coat was hanging on the door, and put her hand in the pocket. She pulled out the gloves Father Rack had given her to put in Beau's drawer. She went to Beau's drawer, took out the left-handed gloves and put the new ones in. Then she put the two left-handed gloves in her coat pocket. She would get rid of those later. There was something right about all this. Father Rack was such a wise old man. What he had done was little short of miraculous. How had he done it? Molly smiled. She could see the humour in what had happened. It was mysterious, and somehow liberating too. She felt a kind of warmth beating in her stomach that she knew meant she was genuinely loved and so truly alive, but that didn't bury the sense of sadness and deep loss she felt when she thought about her father. For a while she just gazed out of the window; then she sank to her knees and started to pray. She prayed with urgency, an urgency born of deep longing for the love of her father. Why hadn't he told her that he loved her, and that he was proud of her? It would have made all the difference. It would have touched a life that was dead to love. The joy of it would have been made safe in her mind, and held there forever. And then, somehow in the silence that followed she found herself, her real self: the self she had known for many years in dreams, in her reading, and sometimes in the depths of anxious prayer. It brought a new awareness. The time had come. She was leaving one way of being, and she could sense another one coming. It was a way of being that was blessed by acceptance, and was filled with new life. She crossed herself, got up and then went downstairs to eat.

It was early evening when Molly came downstairs carrying her coat and gloves. She was wearing a beret on the side of her head. Beau looked up from where she was sitting, on a cushion in front of the fire. "You look nice, Molly! You've got make-up on, and everything!"

"Thank you, Beau – I thought I'd make an effort, you know."

"Your beret really suits you. It really does!"

"Yes, it's a bit like Lana Turner in *They Won't Forget*." She cocked her head to one side: "It's deadly, isn't it?"

"Aye... I'd noticed, Molly! Are you off to church?"

"Yes, I am. Wish me luck!"

"Wish you luck?"

"And Beau – don't do anything I wouldn't do!" Molly winked and then went out. The front door closed behind her. Beau looked back into the fire. She stared and wondered. Molly seemed to have so much. She'd looked so pretty – really pretty – when she left for church, but there was something more than that. There was a calmness about her, a confidence in who she was, and that made her even more attractive than the make-up and the film-star beret. Beau wished that she had what Molly had. Then she thought about the left-handed gloves and what they meant. She couldn't understand what had happened. It was something that made her fearful, and yet it felt exciting and mysterious – it was a hidden, unnameable pleasure, a dark gift of sorts. She wasn't sure if she could accept it.

She got up and went upstairs. It was cold in the bedroom, and she pulled a coat round her shoulders and sat on the bed. She stared out of the window into the gloom lit by the gas lamp on the corner of Gillingham Terrace. She thought about Paul in his final hour, the blotched face and neck, the skull showing through his poor fixed white face; her eyes filled with tears. She got up, went to the drawer and got the gloves. She went back to the bed, sat down and buried her face in the gloves. "Dear God help me..." She wept and then steadied herself. "O my God, I am heartily sorry for having offended Thee, and I detest all my sins, because I dread the loss of Heaven, and the pains of Hell; but most of all because I love Thee, my God, Who art all good and deserving of all my love. I firmly resolve, with the help of Thy grace, to confess my sins, to do penance, and to amend my life... God help me. Amen." She crossed herself and kissed the gloves. She was filled with sorrow, and without thinking she used the gloves to wipe the tears away. If only she could find reassurance; if only there could be genuine salvation. Minutes passed. A train thundered through the cutting. Beau tried to think. Then she looked at the gloves – the beginning and the ending of her recent sorrows, and the older, more painful sorrows they had brought to mind. She put one on and then looked at the other. Here it was, the other one she had found before and yet... and yet this time it fitted. It fitted the other hand! It was right-handed! How had they become a complete pair? "Holy God!" Beau stared out of the window and into the gloom.

Taylor Street was deserted. Everything was quiet. Smoke rose from the terrace chimney stacks;

children had left their chalkings on the wall and their shoes in the gutter. Molly walked with her coat open and her hands in her pockets. As she passed The Bessemer she could smell stale beer and cigarettes, and she thought about Beau and what must have gone on the night before. Beau seemed to know things she didn't know about Gorton life, and the people who would go to The Bess on Saturday nights. Perhaps she should go there one night just to see what it was like. She turned left into Gorton Lane. There on the brick wall was the wooden war memorial, with its carved sailor and soldier coming adrift from the frame that contained the names of the Gorton dead. Not that they mattered any more. Perhaps God remembered them, but nobody else did. Some people round here didn't even remember the living. She set off up the hill to walk over the railway bridge. When she got to the bridge she stopped and looked over the wall at the railway lines below. Everything was quiet. The lines shone silver in the dark. Railway lines: Molly had no idea where they came from or where they went. All she knew was that steam engines were never silent, and that they shook terraced houses to their foundations when they thundered through the night. She didn't really care. There they were: railway lines, fixed like the destiny in the palm of a hand. Molly felt in her pocket and pulled the left-handed gloves out and looked at them. Foolish bloody things! This was a good place to get rid of them. She rolled them one inside the other, stretched her arm out over the wall, and paused for a while. Then she let them drop. They fell silently and disappeared into eternal darkness. It was done. Nobody knew. It was something forgotten, along with all the rest.

Beau was sitting by the fire holding her gloves when her mother came home. Mrs Parnaby looked at her: "What's up with you, Beau? You've got a face like a fiddle."

"Mam, I need to talk to you – something very very strange has happened."

"Let me make a pot of tea first, Beau." Mrs Parnaby busied round making tea. When it was done, she sat down and offered Beau a cigarette.

"Right then, what's wrong?"

Beau poured out her story. She spoke with urgency, and left nothing out. Mrs Parnaby listened with her head on one side. Beau reached across to her and held her hands. "Mam, I'm dead scared." Then she cried.

"Hush, hush."

"What am I going to do?"

"Aw, Beau! Hush, hush, hush."

"It's a sign that's been given to me, isn't it, Mam?"

Mrs Parnaby smiled. "It is, Beau. It's a miracle, that's what it is."

"What am I going to do?"

Mrs Parnaby thought for a while. Then she said, "You need to go to confession, and get things straight with God and with the Church."

"And then what? Tell Molly what I've done?"

"No, Beau – you can't do that! You can't ever tell her what's happened."

"Why not?"

"Because that'll mean she'll know that you tried to do the dirty on her, and she'd never forgive you for that. There's been enough bloody trouble in this house. We don't want any more of it. God knows, we deserve some peace, don't we?"

"I suppose we do, Mam."

Mrs Parnaby smiled broadly. "Course we do. This is best left between you and me, Beau." She put her hand on Beau's cheek. "Just them as knows their own nose knows."

Molly stared at the Monastery. Its great stone face was lit here and there with lights from within. It was hers, and she never wanted to leave it. But then, as she looked round, she could see the long lit terraces, and the cobbled setts laid down hard against each other into the distance. She realised more than ever that all this was hers too. And she loved the life she had been given and what she was becoming. She went into the Monastery and walked over to the candle stand. She dropped a coin in the metal box and took a candle. The candle was for the father who'd loved her, and who'd been proud of her; she was going to light it, and bless the life that lived through the grace of God. She held it gently. When it was lit she stood it upright in the stand, and then crossed herself. She was concentrating hard. She wanted to pray, but she wasn't sure what she should pray for. She looked up to the vaulted ceiling and into the vacant faces of angels. Her breathing changed, and her shoulders began to shake with silent convulsions. As tears welled in her eyes, her strength gave way and she sobbed, "Daddy!" It was a cry that came from a frightened child. Old pain carried like droplets on the breath back through lost days, to the man with the mad hair who was her father – the daddy who was so disabled with shame that he couldn't speak his own mind. The word echoed round the Monastery and then, for a moment, there was an awful silence. Molly saw the need to control herself. She wiped her eyes and sat down, weeping silently. Then she waited for Mass to begin.

Miracles didn't happen in Gorton, but from time to time, strange unexpected events happened – the givings and takings that people sometimes encountered which made their lives change direction, and lent mystery to the way things were in the world. And just after Mass had finished one of those events happened. Molly stood up and looked towards the door, and there in the doorway was Beau, dipping her fingers in the Holy Water font and crossing herself. Beau looked over to where Molly was standing, and walked towards her. Her gaze didn't leave Molly's eyes for a moment – not even when she bobbed a quick genuflection in the aisle and then stood before her.

"Beau?"

"Molly – Molly, I've come back."

They hugged. For a long time they hugged, and when the hug had ended they grasped each other's hands. In that holy place, glove met glove and love was joined in the palms of their hands. The sisters smiled through daft tears, and smiled again. Beau whispered to Molly, "Sit down with me, please sit down". They sat together in the pew. Molly was about to say something when Beau put a finger to her lips. "Not now. I'll tell you later. Let's just pray together for a while." They knelt down.

"We'll pray for Daddy and Paul."

"No, Molly. There's been enough of that. Let the dead pray for themselves; we'll pray for the living."

They stared at each other for a few moments and then: "Let's pray for us, then – for the two sisters."

Beau smiled. "Yes, two sisters."

Father Rack was blowing his nose as he came through the door. He saw Molly and Beau in prayer, and a smile appeared on his face. He watched them carefully, and his thoughts turned towards salvation. It was clear that when Molly had buried her father she'd buried her trust in people, and when Beau had buried her brother she'd buried her trust in God. Beau's appearance in the Monastery wasn't exactly a miracle – but it was a racing certainty that her apparent change of heart had been tied up with the gloves in some way. He didn't know how, but he'd been a priest long enough to see the possibility. What mattered was that she seemed to have regained her faith. It would be something of an irony if that really were to do with the gloves. Think of it: Beau's newfound faith had arrived through dishonesty dressed up as kindness. But it didn't matter really. It had arrived. And its arrival might do Molly a bit of good as well. If it did, it would also be through some kind of dishonesty. But these things are always theologically complex. Poor Frank. He never did manage to get the hang of his letters and words, but no doubt the sentiments were there – they must have been there, it was only natural. In any case, as a priest, Father Rack had been taught 'to speak for those who cannot speak, and to act for those who cannot act'. To be sure, Frank could do neither. Father Rack decided that he would wait for Beau to come to him when she felt ready to do so. If she was serious, she would come. But he had a feeling that Beau was hooked, and when she did come, he would reel her in like a speckled trout from the Shannon.

Molly and Beau walked together in silence. When they reached the war memorial, Molly turned to Beau. "Do you fancy a gill of Chester's in The Bess, Beau?"

Beau looked surprised and smiled broadly. "Can you afford it?"

"Aye, come on!"

"Go on, then!"

They went inside. It was empty except for old Joe Molloy, who was sitting in the corner. He was alone, but he was talking – and he was using his hands to gesture with surprising grace. Beau nodded to him. "Hiya, Joe! Are you talking to yourself again, you daft bugger?" Joe stopped talking for a moment, looked over at Beau and flicked a 'V' sign in her direction.

Then he nodded to Molly and went back to his conversation. They went to the bar. "Two halves of mild please, George." The landlord started to pull the mild. "You've not been in here for a long while now, Molly?"

"Aye, I know, George. I've been busy."

"Hiding from me, more like."

"Cheeky bugger!"

"I know, but I'm right though, aren't I?

"Aye, maybe you are, George."

"Not like your sister here – she doesn't hide anything, do you, Beau?"

"Only my feelings about you, George."

"So you've got feelings for me have you?"

"Aye, I've got feelings right enough, but they're not the ones you're thinking about."

Everybody laughed, and then Molly and Beau sat at a table by the window. Molly couldn't contain herself any longer. "Come on, Beau – tell me what's happened. What's happened to you?" Beau stretched her hands across the table and held Molly's. "Just listen, that's all, just listen. I'll try, but it's not going to be easy."

"Go on, Beau. I'll be quiet, I promise."

Beau looked at Molly intently, and began to outline the whole knotty story. She told Molly about burning a hole in the gloves with a cigarette, and how angry she'd been about it. She described how she'd swapped her gloves for Molly's as Molly lay sleeping, and then afterwards found that they'd turned into left-handed gloves. "Honest to God, Molly, that was a sign – if ever there was a sign that was it!" Molly stared, but didn't say anything. Beau told of how she had felt such guilt – not just about the swapping the gloves, but about abandoning God for all that time. Then her face took on a most earnest expression: "And then... when I was praying for forgiveness, the gloves turned back into being left- and right-handed gloves again... They changed in my hands... as I was holding them, as God is my witness." She stared at Molly. Molly said nothing, but she enjoyed the moment. It wasn't just that she'd given Father Rack an undertaking that she would be discreet about the delicacies of being a priest, and what she'd done. It was more than that. She felt the joy of deception, and of the power she had made her own. She stared into Beau's eyes and said, "That was surely a miracle, Beau. You've been touched by the power of God."

"Yes, Molly. I know."

"Does our Mam know?"

"Yes, Molly – I told her and she said it was a sign, but that I shouldn't tell you about it. She said you'd never forgive me for being such a fickle bitch, but I had to tell you, Molly. I want to do the right thing. God knows, I've done enough wrong things in my life already, and from now on I want to do the right things."

Molly reached across the table and hugged her sister, and as she looked over Beau's shoulder

she smiled. The door opened and John Clements came in. "Well there's a sight for sore eyes."

Molly pulled away from Beau. "Hiya, Clem. You've not seen me for a while, have you?"

"No, Molly. Just let me get myself a pint and then I'll join you." He looked over at Joe and smiled. "Still at it then Joe, you fat bastard?"

Joe didn't even look up from his conversation, and just offered Clem a quick 'V' sign. Clem got his pint and then came to sit at the table. He brought a packet of Senior Service and opened it. "Do you want a gasper, Molly?"

"No thanks."

"Beau?"

"Aye, thanks Clem." She looked at Molly: "I'd best take my gloves off for this." Molly smiled.

"What brings you out then, Molly?"

"We've just been to the Monastery, and we thought we'd have a drink on the way back."

"I didn't know you were going to the Monastery, Beau. I thought you'd fallen out with that lot."

"Aye, I did, but I've just changed my mind about it all."

"Why's that?"

"Oh, you know… Things happen, people change."

"I remember you telling me that you'd seen through it all, and that believing in God was like believing in Father Christmas."

"I know, I know, Clem, but it's like seeing the same thing in a different way."

"What do you mean?"

Molly turned to Beau. "I know what she means, Clem. Do you remember when we were dead young and we had that row about The Hail Mary?" Beau blinked and tried to remember. "You know you thought the prayer said, 'Hail Mary, full of grace. Our Lord is with thee. *Blessed art thou a monk swimming!*"

Beau laughed and put her hand over her mouth. "Aye, I remember that."

"Well, when you're a kid you don't think about things, do you? You just accept them. Then, when you're a bit older, you start thinking about things, don't you?"

"And you realise that they don't always make sense."

"Aye, thinking can make you realise that some things can't be true. But you see, after that, when you really grow up, thinking can tell you that thinking isn't everything."

"What do you mean?"

"Well sometimes *feeling* is better. You know what I mean?"

"Like the head and the heart thing?"

Beau nodded. "Aye, that's it, Molly. Sometimes

what you feel in your heart of hearts is more important!"

Clem nodded. "Is that what's happened to you then, Beau?"

"Aye, I think so!" Everybody laughed.

"You know I've always felt like that about you two."

"What do you mean, Clem?"

"Well to me, Molly is always more head than heart, and you're always more heart than head!"

Everybody laughed.

Clem smiled. "One of the things I learned in the Navy – some of the Chinese lads taught me this – is that what you need is balance, like. If you're all one or all t'other you get a bit out of kilter with yourself, you know what I mean?"

Molly nodded: "You need to be an all-rounder?"

"Aye, that's it. So what you've got to do is to take a bit of Beau's heart and give her a bit of your head and then you'll both be right, won't you?"

Molly and Beau stared straight forward as they thought about what Clem had just said. Clem got up. "I'm just going for a gypsy's." He looked across at Joe, who was talking to himself. "Go on, you barmy bugger!" Joe turned and blew him a kiss.

It was Saturday morning, and The Dave Clarke Five were on the radio. Mrs Parnaby was whispering to herself, "*Glad All Over*? That's what we all are, right enough." She had almost finished polishing the brasses. They'd not been done since Christmas, and they looked a bit grubby. They were nice and clean now, though, and the knick-knacks on the mantelpiece had started to catch the light from the lamp on the television. Mrs Parnaby would set to every Saturday morning so that she was straight for the weekend. There was an order to these things. After the gas fires had been turned on and the teak surrounds polished, the windows in the lounge were given a good cleaning with Windolene and a soft cloth. It was easy. All you had to do was to spray it on and then polish the pane with a clean cloth. Simple! Then came the hoovering, the dusting and lastly, the polishing – furniture and brasses. It was eleven o' clock and she was nearly done. She was looking forward to having a cup of tea, but first she had one more thing to do. She had to clean the last and most precious of her brasses – the three framed photographs of her family. One was of her husband, Frank, with their three children – Paul, Molly and Beau – all of them young and without sin, and the other two were of Molly and Beau with their families. She looked at the photograph of Frank. There he was: tousled hair and sunken eyes, head turned downwards and to one side like a Christ, arms laid lovingly round his little children, spick and span in their nice summer clothes on the beach at Blackpool. She smiled and polished it gently, before standing it up on the sideboard. And this one was Molly with her lovely auburn hair and her husband, David, and their two children, Fiona, who was nine pounds and two ounces when she was born, and Francis. Molly had met David at a dance in the hospital where he worked. He was a Protestant, but he was a good man, and he was as fit as a fiddle. He did judo on Mondays and Fridays, and once a month he took them all rallying. And this one was Beau and her husband, Terry Hanley, who was a hod carrier with the Corporation, and their darling daughters, little Rosie, Mary, Róisín, who was a bit of a bookworm, and Ellen, who was sure to break a few hearts when she was older. Terry was a good man, an Irishman from Mayo, who had curly black hair, blue eyes and the voice of an angel. Beau had met him at a party in Bolton.

For a long time, Mrs Parnaby felt she was blessed. She had been mindful of how blessed they all were. Her two remaining children, Molly and Beau, had become what they had become. Frank could rest in peace – and when the time came, she too would rest in peace. It hadn't been easy, but the promise she'd made to Frank had been accomplished. Molly and Beau saw a lot of each other. They would often come round on Saturday afternoons; the children would play in the house and watch television, whilst the two sisters went shopping. They enjoyed going shopping together. They said it was just a simple thing, but it was a wonderful thing and nobody would ever know how much they enjoyed it. They had just been sisters at one time, but had later become friends; whether it was going to Mass on Sundays, or dancing at the ABC on Fridays, they were always the best of friends. Father Rack had once said, 'God made them sisters, but choice made them friends'. But what choices there were to be made.

And as time went by, some of those choices were difficult to explain. Nobody was expecting to hear that Molly had been killed in a car crash near Bolton. Nobody knew why she had gone there or what she had been doing. Her husband had been at home all morning. She had been in the bedroom reading *The Virgin and the Gypsy*, and then she had taken the car without telling him where she was going. It was a mystery. She had driven the car into a lamp standard. The police said that driving conditions had been perfect, and there was no obvious mechanical failure. Her husband said Molly had been a bit withdrawn earlier that day, but she wasn't so bad – and certainly not as bad as she'd been after Frankie had been born. He had no idea why she'd suddenly decided to leave. No idea. Nor did the rest of the world. She'd got what she wanted, and lost what she had.

Beau's choices were many. She survived Molly's death in the same way as she seemed to survive everything else in life, with seriousness and measured honesty. "It was an open verdict, so we'll never know why she died, but at least we know that she's at rest." Beau survived other troubles she met in life with growing faith: "I've always tried to accept things and carry on. I know I'm in God's hands. I was in his hands when I had my miscarriages, and that stroke. I was in his hands when Terry left me and went back to live with his sister's family in Ireland." But one of her choices had been difficult to explain. Beau had once asked Molly's husband if he'd give her something of Molly's to have as a keepsake. He'd agreed. He didn't mind what she had, so she'd chosen a book: *Revelations of Divine Love*, by Mother Julian of Norwich. She didn't really know why she'd chosen a book, and she didn't know why she'd settled for that one. She just had. It lay there by the side of her bed for months until, finally, she decided to read it. It was hard going and she didn't understand it. Yet, she still seemed drawn to it. She read it several times without getting much out of it, until one day she saw something in it that she hadn't noticed before. Towards the end of the book, she found a sentence that Molly had underlined. Molly never did things like that; she respected books, and was dead against writing anything in them. It was a mystery, but there it was, underlined faintly in pencil: '*This world is a prison, and this life is a penance.*'

These words didn't mean much to Beau, but they fascinated her. Why did Molly think that this sentence was of such significance that she'd broken one of her own rules and underlined it? It could have been underlined by somebody else, of course – her husband perhaps, or somebody who had borrowed the book. But that didn't seem likely. David wasn't at all interested in such things, and she couldn't think of anybody else Molly knew who would be either. No, this was Molly's doing, and that sentence meant something to her. Beau decided to think about it, and she made up her mind to try and find a way to understand it. And from that moment onwards, her life began to change.

It didn't come easily and she found it difficult, but she kept trying, and slowly began to make progress. She read as many books as she could find – proper books – and learned to use words as they should be used. She began to make sense of things. Through reading came understanding and the blood of life gave way to ideas – ideas that lit a shadowland and expressed her salvation. And that salvation led to a remarkable life. She became known as a wise woman, who would always help those around her if she could. Everybody knew that she had done so on many occasions. But although her life had been full, she rarely mentioned it, except when she wrote down her thoughts. So it was that through the printed word, she gave life to the people and events she had known. In *The Catholic Herald* a review of her book, *This Life as Penance*, said of it: 'This book examines in a startlingly honest fashion how the basic features of life – family, relationships, religion, morality and simple social expectations – can confine us to a life of pain. Parnaby's book is expressed with such direct and perceptive conviction that its truths are returned heavenwards like light from a diamond of rare quality.' Beau didn't know about that, but before she died she was heard to say, "It's been a struggle, an awful struggle, but thank God I'm beginning to see it for what it is. It's been a revelation… We were always in His hands and He was always in ours."

They were two sisters born into darkness, but their lives lit their way to heaven. They left everybody else behind in the place they'd known so well. They were two sisters, and now they are one.

Dancing in the Light: Ellen's Story

The spring sun streamed into the front parlour and set rainbow flames in the crystal vase on the sideboard. Ellen Gifford danced silently in the light. The sun touched the shelf, and lit the shell case from the trenches. It caught the face of Jesus and the oak rim of the biscuit barrel, and fell softly on the pot dog in the hearth. Ellen smiled and looked up to the photograph of Uncle George in his uniform. She lifted her arm and opened her hand to reveal a half-crown. She turned and raised a graceful hand through the sunlight. Dust swirled through her fingers. Ellen had found a half-crown down the back of the armchair. It was a half-crown which had been lost and then found, but it was much more than that. For the first time in her life, Ellen felt liberated. And there in the streaming light, amongst the rag rugs and polished legs and French leather armchairs, she danced in the joy of what that had given her.

The scullery was cold. Polly rubbed her hands together. "Aren't you cold, Ellen? I am! Look! You can see my breath!"

"No you can't! There's nowt there!"

"You've got nowt there! You're as daft as a goldfish!"

"Get lost!"

Mrs Gifford came in carrying a large brown metal tea pot and a crusty loaf under her arm. "Hey, c'mon now, no disputin'."

"Eh, Mam. Can we light the fire? It's perishing in here!"

"Maybe later. It's not too cold enough yet."

"But it's Saturday. There's going to be folk in all

day and there's ice on the windows."

"Maybe later. Anyroad, where's the lads?"

"Dudley's upstairs putting his trousers on and Joe's on the toilet."

"Are you having jam or dripping on your bread, Polly?"

"Er, dripping with a dead lot of salt on!"

"Now you – where's your manners? Say 'please' – and cut your own slice off that cake of bread!"

"*Please!*"

"Right, what do you want, Ellen?"

"Jam please, Mam."

"And don't forget to eat them crusts or you'll never get curly hair like your mammy, will you now?"

"Aye, Mam."

Mr Gifford came in with a cigarette in his mouth. He was buttoning his collar up. "Hurry up with that bottle of milk, Ellen. Pour me some tea, Polly. Mary, have you seen my shoes?"

"They're in the toilet on a newspaper."

"In the toilet on a newspaper? What are they doing in the toilet on a newspaper?"

"You came home with dog dirt on them, so I scrubbed them up and put them there."

"Go and get them for me, will you, Mary."

"I can't – Joe's still in there."

"Bloo-dy 'ell!" Mr Gifford shook his head. "Ellen, go and ask Joe to push my shoes under the toilet door will you?"

"Aw, Dad! It's cold out there."

"It's cold in here an' all. Can we light the fire, Dad?"

"Go on, Ellen. Mary, how about lighting the fire?"

"Maybe later!"

When Ellen came back with her father's shoes the fire had been lit and Dudley was sitting at the table. Mr Gifford had put some dripping on the coals to get the fire going. Blue smoke curled up the chimney and the fat was beginning to burn with a bright orange flame. The scullery filled with the smell of stale bacon. Polly got up from the table and took her bread and dripping and knelt in front of the fire.

"Don't hog the fire, Pauline. We'd all like to see some of it."

"I'm just trying to get warm, Dad."

"You'll be warm soon enough when you get in that kitchen."

"I'll be roasting, more like! You sweat buckets when you're next to the boilers and ovens. It's awful in there."

There was silence; then Dudley asked, "Erm, Dad, before you go, can we have us spends please?"

"Aye, Dudley. I was just coming to that." Mr Gifford reached into his pocket and produced a roll of pennies wrapped in newspaper. He unwrapped the roll carefully and took three pennies out and laid them on the table in a row. He touched each one in turn. "Dudley's, Ellen's and give this to Joe when he comes out the toilet."

"I wish he'd hurry up. I'm dying to go!"

Mrs Gifford nodded to Ellen. "Be a good child, Ellen, and go and tell Joe that his brother is waiting sore hard to go in."

Mr Gifford sighed, wrapped the newspaper round the coins carefully and put the roll in his pocket. Then he reached into his other pocket and brought a roll of shilling pieces wrapped in newspaper. He undid it and counted out two shillings. "And this is Polly's."

"Two bob!"

"Aye, Dudley, she's bringing a wage in now."

"Aye, and I have to sweat for it!" Polly reached across the table and picked up the coins.

"Why don't you give her all her wages then?"

"What – all her wages?"

"Aye, she's had to sweat buckets for them, she's just said!"

"Because sweat or no sweat, we need the money, that's why!"

Mrs Gifford came in carrying a dish cloth. "And besides, for years and years we've cleaned for you, we've fed you and clothed you and skivvied for you and we've fair worked our fingers to the bone for you! And we've…"

"Aye, Mary…"

"Ironed for you and made things spick and span for you…"

"Aye, Mary. We have. We've put food on the table and a roof over your heads and kept you. Now Polly's paying her way and when you're her age, you'll have to pay your way an' all."

It went quiet. Ellen reached across the table and took her penny. When she put it in her pocket, she felt the half-crown and held its silver promise firmly in the palm of her hand.

Woolworth's kitchen was full of steam. Wilfred Garside looked across to where Polly was standing by the row of washing-up sinks with Mr Pride and Mrs Bramble. He was butchering a side of beef. He'd done this a time or two before and he knew he had to be careful with the boning knife, but he couldn't help looking at Polly. There was something about the way she held herself, the nape of her neck, the soft curls from beneath the white scarf, her smooth arms and the way the apron fitted round her waist and swathed across those cradle hips.

Wilfred stopped. The boning knife had sliced awkwardly through the ribs. For a moment he was back in that trench at Passchendaele, where he'd thrust into tight belted flesh and felt the full force of steel cleaving upwards into bone. He remembered it. He'd always remember it. How could he ever forget that black, racked-back head and urgent eyes; and death's long groaned breath against his cheek? The triumph of it had roared darkly in the blood, but it was an affirmation that had soon given way to revulsion and then to shame. '*But ye that did cleave unto the Lord your God are alive every one of you this day.*' He looked up. There was Polly, the nape of her neck, her soft curls, smooth arms and those belted hips. Wilfred drew air between his lips as he watched her. She stopped washing, and looked round to see Wilfred watching her from the butchery bench. She didn't know that the light in his eyes was the light of his soul, but she did know that she liked his fair face and the way he was looking at her. She smiled at him and turned away, entranced by the expression on his face, and carried on with the washing up.

They arrived at the sweet shop and looked in the lighted window. Dudley waved his arm. "I bags all them lot and all them lot!" Ellen and Joe stood in front of the window and as they stared, they held hands. Dudley was remarking about this box of chocolates and that jar of sweets, and about things nobody else was listening to, whilst Ellen and Joe had become quite lost in the display before them. Boxes of rose and lemon Turkish delight and chocolate assortments sashed with scarlet and yellow ribbons were arranged on mirrored shelves. There were pictures of dark starlit nights, beautiful ladies with roses; men with hats and horses and mountains lit with red and green skies. Above them were rows of shaped sweet jars: sherbet strawberries; sugared almonds; marzipan fruit; oranges and lemons; damson drops and fruit rock. And below there were glass dishes and white paper doilies with dolly mixtures, cherry lips and floral gums, scattered in their kind like flowers of the forest.

Dudley whistled. He opened the door. "Right, I'm going in to get some toffees!" Ellen and Joe followed him. They stepped carefully over the moon-shaped doorstep, which was wet and looked like it had just been donkey-stoned. They wiped their feet on the doormat that marked the boundary between this world and the next; between hope and salvation. It was warm inside, and a soft sherbet perfume filled the air. They looked around them. Jars of sweets lined the shelves: red and white striped walking sticks, pear drops, rainbow crystals and chocolate limes. They went over to the till and looked in the trays on the counter. Joe was searching through his pockets. Ellen held her penny. Dudley looked at the door that led to the back room. "Shop!" He tapped a penny on the glass counter. "Shop!"

Joe looked round on the floor. Mrs Biddy Pinkerton appeared from the back room. "Hold on my dearios, hold on! Aunty Pinkerton is on her way!" She chuckled as she came. "Hello, my dearios, welcome and sweet welcome to the land of glittering bounty and confectionary heaven. We've got bagsful, we've got capsful and sacksful and they're a joy to the world! What can I get for you all this week? I've got lots and lots."

Joe was searching through his pockets. Mrs Pinkerton looked at him. "Have you lost something, dear heart?"

"Aye, Miss. I have."

"I hopes it's not your good looks!"

"No, Miss. It's my money I... I can't find my money."

"You can't find your money? We can't have that now, can we, eh darling? But then worse things happen at sea. My husband, Mr Pinkerton, should know. He lost the use of his ears at Jutland. He says he was standing too near the turret when it was blown off. He says it went 'BANG' – and bang went the use of his ears!" She chuckled. "Not that he's bothered, mind. He says he can't stand the sound of the human voice, which I think is definitely wrong. For how can you have a decent marriage if you can't speak your mind and get things off your chest? But I don't know. He says the only thing he misses is the sound of bacon frying in the pan, which is odd because we seldom have bacon and when we do it's flitch or rody and then generally we have it boiled with cabbage, because then you can make pea soup out of the water and everybody likes pea soup, don't they, except sometimes it can be definitely spoiled by those dark, tremulous after-vowels that often follows in the wake of when we takes it."

"What's a tremendous after-vowel, Mrs Pinkerton?"

"Well dearest, when I was at school, they were 'a', 'e', 'i', 'o' and 'u' and sometimes, and the longest one of all, 'y' but the less said about them the better, if you follow my meaning. So you've lost your penny have you, Joe?"

"Aye! Ellen, I've lost my…"

"Come here, let's have a look." Ellen started to search through his pockets.

Dudley tapped a penny on the counter. "Erm, Mrs Pinkerton can I have…"

"Now then, now then, bold soldier, where's your manners? It's ladies first. Ellen, what shall I get for you, darling?"

Ellen looked up. "Oh, can I have a ha'porth of yellow kali, please?"

"Yes you may, my handsome, of course you may. I'll get it directly." Mrs Pinkerton reached for the jar and started to unscrew the lid. Everybody watched as she weighed out the kali in the scales and then poured it carefully into a white paper bag. She twisted the top of the bag and put it on top of the counter.

Dudley cleared his throat. "And I'll have two black jacks and erm… a packet of Wrigley's… please"

"Black jacks and Wrigley's?

"Aye, that's right."

"Pardon me, I'm sure, for asking Master Dudley, but are you allowed to chews chewing gum?"

"Course I am, our mam said."

"Did she now?"

"Aye, she did, honest to God."

"Well if she does say, then that's all right."

"Aye, she does."

"Otherwise I'd be breaking a promise and we wouldn't want that now, would we?"

"No, we wouldn't."

"We wouldn't want Aunty Pinkerton struck down stone dead with a thunderbolt sent purposively down from heaven now, would we children? For, who would be here to serve you kali then, mmm?"

Ellen stopped searching. "When did our mam say that, Dudley?"

"Erm, this morning."

She pulled away from Joe. "No, there's nowt there, Joe. It's gone. You've lost it."

"Aw!"

Mrs Pinkerton took Dudley's penny and handed him the packets of chewing gum. Dudley put them in his pocket, and then he looked at Joe. "What's up, Joe?"

"I've lost my penny, Dudley! It's gone!"

Ellen felt the half-crown in her pocket. She looked at Mrs Pinkerton. "And I'll have a Wrigley's an' all please, Mrs Pinkerton."

"Well bless my soul! You too, sweetheart! Your dear mother must have had a real change of heart. It must be as bright and beautiful a conversion as that which attended St Paul on his way to Damascus."

Joe's eyes filled with tears. "Aw, it's not fair!"

Ellen gave Mrs Pinkerton the penny and then she put the bag of kali and chewing gum in her pocket. Mrs Pinkerton looked at Joe. "Oh now then, dear heart, don't take on so!" Dudley was going through

Joe's pockets. He held Joe's coat open and stared. Then he lifted Joe's jumper and put two fingers into his shirt pocket and smiled. He pulled a penny out. Mrs Pinkerton sighed. Joe's mouth opened. "Oh, Dudley, thanks!" Joe hugged Dudley and then went to take the penny. Dudley pulled his hand away.

"Haven't you forgot something, little brother?"

"What?"

"Have you forgot the deal we made over our mam's coat on your side of the bed?"

"But that was when I was cold!"

Joe made a lunge for the penny. "Aw, give it me!"

Dudley lifted his arm in the air. "You said that if you could have our mam's coat on your side of the bed for a whole week you'd give me your spends, didn't you?"

"But it was dead cold! Aw, give it me!"

"Aye, it was dead cold after you had mam's coat off my side of the bed and that's why I had to put the rug over me, didn't I?"

"Aw, Dudley! I'll give you a penny next week! Can I have something now?"

"No, you can't!"

"Aw, Dudley go on!"

Dudley turned his hand in a wide arc over Joe's head. "And two more packets of Wrigley's, please Aunty!"

"Dudley! It's not fair! I..."

Mrs Pinkerton handed Dudley the chewing gum, and Dudley put the packets in his pocket. "Thank you, Aunty. We'll see you next week. Come on, Joe."

"Cheerio, cheerio, my precious ones! Until the next time in Aunty's delicious toffee palace. I'll see you in my dreams, my dearios, in my sweet emporium of dreams!"

They went outside. Joe stopped and put his fists to his eyes. Ellen held him. Dudley unwrapped a black jack and put it in his mouth. "You've got to learn about these things, Joe. A bargain's a bargain, and if you break one you're for the chop, aren't you?" Joe was making a high-pitched hissing noise. Ellen ruffled his hair. "Come on, Joe. It's best we go home." Joe wailed. Ellen whispered in his ear: "Come on, Joe. I'll give you a dip of my kali. Would you like that?" Joe stopped crying and opened his eyes. Ellen took the bag out of her pocket, opened it and offered it to Joe. Joe looked at her. "Oh, thank you, Ellen, thank you." He put a finger in his mouth to wet it and then pushed it into the opened bag. He pulled it out and looked at it. It was covered with yellow crystals. Joe looked at Ellen and smiled; then he put his finger in his mouth. He was quiet now, and they walked home.

Mrs Gifford looked at the kettle on the trivet over the fire. It was boiling. She took hold of a dishcloth, wrapped it round the brown metal handle and poured boiling water into the teapot. Steam rose and disappeared up the chimney. The door opened and Polly came in. "You've timed that right, Polly! Come in and sit down. Will you have a cup of tea in your hand?"

"I could do with it, Mam. It's perishing cold out there – brrrr!"

"You're home early, girl."

"Aye, they sent four of us home. There was nowt doing after three o'clock."

"Come and warm yourself then."

"Ta, Ma! It's so good to be home and I can lie in tomorrow, an 'all!"

"You'll have to be up in time for Mass."

"I'll be up for Mass, Mam. You needn't worry about that."

Mrs Gifford poured the tea into cups on the hearth. She reached across and offered Polly the tea. "There, get that in you!"

Polly took the cup. "Oh, ta, Ma." She lifted her feet onto the sofa.

"Oh, that's so good."

"Are you going out later on?"

"I am! I'm going to the flicks – with a man!"

"With a man?"

"Aye, Wilfred. He asked me to go out with him yesterday!"

"Well, I just hope he's better than the last one!"

"Oh, Jimmy was all right!"

"I've told you before, girl – his eyes were too close together!"

"Aw, Mam!"

"You should never trust a man whose eyes are too close together – you should know that by now."

"But Jimmy was nice!"

"Did he ever ask you out after that first date?"

"No he…"

"Well he wasn't that nice then, was he?"

"Maybe not."

"What's this Wilfred like, anyroad?"

"Oh, he's dead nice. He's a Salford lad and he works with Ruby and Black on the butchery bench at our place."

"He's got a job then?"

"Aye, and he's dead good looking an' all! He's got these lovely eyes that look right into you."

"Eyes that look right into you!" She thought for a moment. "And what colour are this man's piercing eyes?"

"Green."

"Green eyes! Oh, God!"

"What's wrong with green eyes?"

"What's wrong with green eyes? You want to stay away from green eyes, Polly. Green eyes stand for deceit – everybody knows that!"

"Oh, Mam!

"I bet his eyes are too close together an' all."

"No, they're not, Mam. They're lovely!"

It went quiet and then Mrs Gifford asked: "What about his ears? Has he got anything between his ears?"

"Oh, aye, he's got plenty upstairs! He's a great one for thinking about things, and you should hear him talk. He makes me laugh. He's right funny."

"The man's funny, is he?"

"Aye, he says things like you should never turn your back on a Frenchman, and he calls posh people knobs! He makes me laugh!"

"So he makes you laugh, does he?"

"Aye, he'd make the cat laugh, that one! But sometimes, Mam, he gets dead serious, like when he talks about the war and politics and that."

"Politics?"

"Aye, he's a… what do you call it?… A socialist."

"A socialist? Dear God, the man's a socialist now!"

"I don't know what one of them is though!"

"I do! It means he's a damned conscie! A conscie, is he? Socialists always are, so they are. They're all lily-livered…"

"No Mam, he's not a conscie, he's only a socialist! He even lied about his age so they'd have him in the army – it was the Welsh Regiment, or some Welsh regiment, anyroad."

"Welsh is it? Well at least the Welsh don't hang monkeys."

"Aye, and he says that it's the war that made him into a socialist. He says it was all a deception, and the only people who ever gained from it were the rich."

"Dear God, I've never heard of such a thing…"

"He said the Germans were just ordinary men like our men."

"That's conscie talk, that is! God help and preserve us!"

"And he says he doesn't like the Australians."

"The Australians are British, aren't they? He must have said he doesn't like the Austrians."

"No it was the Australians right enough. He doesn't like them, but he won't tell me why."

"Don't tell Uncle George about him, will you, Pauline? He'll be mortified if he knew you're stepping out with a conscie!"

"I won't Mam, but Wilfred's a good man, honest to God he is."

"Are you sure, Pauline?"

"You don't know him, Mam!"

"I know I don't know him, but you've got a lot to learn!"

"What? What have I got to learn, Mam?"

Mrs Gifford took a gulp of tea and then stared hard at Polly.

"Well, Polly – for a start, men are not like women."

"Aye, I know men and women are different, Mam – course I do."

"They're not just different in the way you mean, they're different in other ways an' all, believe you me!"

"What ways?"

"Well like Granny used to say: 'Women are born to be mothers, and men are born to be lovers.'"

"Come again."

"Women just want what's best for their babies, and men want what's best for their inclinations!"

"Their inclinations?"

"Aye, as Granny used to say: 'When they're not after inclining towards their bellies, they're after inclining towards their ballocks!'"

"Mother!"

"So, it's true!"

"Why don't other women see it then?"

"Oh, they can see it as clear as a bead! They just don't like what they see!"

"That can't be right, Mam."

"Who said anything about right and wrong? That's just the way of it. Granny used to say that men are like dogs. Well, at first they're like puppies. You know type of style – they're clumsy and all over the place, so you've got to house-train them, as you might say. And if you do it right, by the time they're full-sized, they'll mostly do as they're told." Mrs Gifford gazed for a while into space and then said, "But you should never make the mistake of thinking that they'll always do as they're told. No, you mustn't. You've no idea what they'll get up to when they're out the house, no idea at all. Men are like that – they're always only a teardrop away from heartache."

"That sounds dead bitter to me, Mam!"

"Oh, but I haven't finished yet. There's something Granny never told us, though it's true. You probably won't like it, but the truth's the truth whether you like it or not, so listen hard." She lowered her head and whispered: "Some men are not like dogs at all, they can be more like rams!"

"Rams?"

"Aye, like big bold rams!"

"What do you mean, Mam?"

"You see, with some men – there aren't so many of them mind – if you treat them well, you can turn the animal out in them."

"The animal?"

"You see, dogs only follow dog-like, but rams command! They love like real men. And when you've been loved by a real man, you'll become a real woman. Aye, and you'll soon catch on with child and no mistake!"

"Mam!"

"Aye, if God made anything better than a man like that, he must have kept it to himself!"

There was a long silence and then Polly said quietly: "I need to think about all that."

Mrs Gifford smiled. "Ah, thinking is for geniuses, Polly. Just feel the truth of it, feel it and make sure you take it in deep into your heart."

Polly stared. "What's Wilfred then, Mam?"

"Oh, surely to God, I don't know, but I suppose he's a dog like the rest of them."

"When will I know if he's a ram?"

"You'll have to lose your innocence before you'll know that."

"You mean I've got to lose my virginity before I'll find out about him?"

"No, innocence and virginity are two different things."

"What do you mean?"

"When you lose your virginity... Well, it usually means disappointment, bitter disappointment, aye and some feel resentment an' all, but when you lose your innocence that'll mean you've seen the truth of it and you'll be free."

"Free?"

"Aye, freedom means life, doesn't it?"

"I'm just plain flummoxed now, Mam."

"You will be, child."

"I suppose I'll just have to wait, then."

"So you will, child, so you will, but then so will I."

"You won't have to wait that long, Mam – you'll be seeing him tomorrow at Mass."

"Oh, he's coming to Mass?"

"Aye, he said he'd come with me."

"Is the man Catholic?"

"No Mam, he's a prod, but he said he'd still go to Mass – for me."

Mrs Gifford stared into the fire. "He's going to do that for you?"

"He is, Mam. And you know how Protestants feel about Catholics."

"I do! Nobody knows better than I do, girl! The trouble it caused back in St Luke's when I converted over to marry your father!" Mrs Gifford spoke slowly. "Them Cork women were fierce vicious with me, so they were."

"What kind of animals are they?"

"Oh, those Corks are just she-wolves and I was just a poor wee lamb cast among them!"

"No, I don't mean that – I mean what kind of animals are women?"

"Do you really want to know, girl? Will it harm you half to death if I tell you?"

"No, Mam – tell me."

"All right then, I will." She cleared her throat and spoke carefully: "Women – now, when they're virgins, they're like cats, when they're mothers, they're like cows and when they're crones, they're like the screech owls of the night."

The moon lit the pale green window frame and filled the children's bedroom with wintry light. The tang of peppermint carried on the cold air in drifts that swelled and died on the senses. Dudley was chewing noisily. Joe's teeth were chattering. Ellen put the last piece of chewing gum in her mouth and crushed its sugar shell between her teeth. Hot peppermint oil spilled onto her tongue. She pulled the army greatcoat round her shoulders and gazed at the ceiling. The half-crown was in the palm of her hand.

Joe called out, "I want Mam's coat back, Dudley!"

Dudley increased his sloppy chewing. "You can't have it, Joe. It's my coat now."

Ellen turned her head. "You said Joe could have it 'til the end of the week!"

"Aye, I did! And it's Saturday now."

"But the new week doesn't start 'til tomorrow, Dudley! Sunday is the first day of the new week! You've already got your penny, so it's only right that you give Joe the coat!"

"That means I'll have to have the rug again!"

"I know, but you said at Mrs Pinkerton's that a bargain's a bargain and you're in for the chop if you ever break one. So give him the coat!"

"I'm not having that rug again!"

"If you don't, Dudley, I'll tell Mam about the chewing gum!"

"You've had some an' all!"

"Aye, I know, but I'm her favourite and she won't believe you anyroad, will she? I'll just play all innocent and she just won't believe you!"

Dudley went quiet. "Oh, all right then – he can have the coat."

Joe reached across the bed and pulled the coat over to his side of the bed. Dudley lifted the rug beside the bed and put it over his shoulders. The sound of heavy breathing followed and then chewing started up again.

After a while Joe said: "Can I have a chew of somebody's chewing gum?"

Ellen turned the half-crown round in her hand and then called out, "Give him yours, Dudley!"

"Sod off!"

"Give him yours, or I'll tell Mam – do you hear me?"

Dudley went quiet; then he said, "All right then, but we'll see about this!" He rolled onto his side and whispered, "Here you are, Joe – catch this!" Then he spat the chewing gum over to Joe's side of the bed. It went quiet.

Joe felt around for the chewing gum. "Where is it, Dudley?"

"Find it!"

"I can't find it!"

"Just keep looking!"

Joe carried on looking. Ellen said: "Did you really give it him, Dudley? You're not holding out on us, are you?"

"No, God's honour!"

"I can't find it!"

There was a long silence. Joe tried again, running his hands here and there patting the blanket gently. "Aw, Ellen!"

Ellen sighed. She took the chewing gum out of her mouth, got out of bed and went over to Joe. "Open your gob, Joe." Joe opened his mouth and Ellen pushed the chewing gum in. "There! Now, be quiet, will you?"

Chewing noises came from Joe's side of the bed and then it went quiet. Ellen was listening. "Is it good, Joe?"

"Aye, it was dead good."

"It was dead good?"

"Aye, it's gone now."

"Have you lost it again?"

"No, I've eaten it."

"You're not supposed to eat it. You're only supposed to chew it!"

"I didn't know! Anyroad, you only gave me a tidgy bit."

Dudley sighed. "What a pity our mam and dad are Catholics."

"Why's that, Dudley?"

"Because our Joe should have been contained in a condom, that's why!"

Mass at the Monastery brought anxiety and its balm. It was domination. It was submission, unyielding and unearthly. The unfamiliar would rise out of the familiar: like the Sanctus bell and cold air bearing incense and old words. It wasn't just the prayers whispered beneath the bent backs of men and women who brooded like ghosts in factory yards. It was something to do with the priests who stood above the world and beyond the people, and it was something to do with the people: the backs of their trembling heads and shirt collars and hair, and faces full of sadness; and all those impassive girls and serious men, and everywhere, signs of death hiding under scrubbed flesh. But sometimes, Mass promised life, as when eyes chanced to meet eyes and dared to send a smile into the listless air. Then it became the monastery of the world.

It was always the carvings that upset Joe – blind angels with books and harps, and the bare body of Christ, with its mouth yawning pain and lips reddened with communion wine. Here he was for all to see: a full-genitalled corpse hanging before the world. But in dreams, he became a pale-boned youth twisting in the heat of countless virgins, who were now cleaved to salvation, and delivered gently in their beds.

It was at times like this, below the crucified Christ, that Wilfred knew he was still alive, unlike so many he had known and some he had loved. He drew in a silent breath, stretched the toes in his boots and stared up at the roof beams. He was in a Catholic church and he was alive; he was alive and accepted by those around him, and even by those awkward girls who had just run the gauntlet of his eyes and who would have to do so again, because he felt good enough to do it now. Ellen was staring at him. He winked at her.

Polly could smell Wilfred – the boot polish and soap – and she could feel his presence, like a lilting warmth to her side. She could see his thick thighs, rucked and herring-boned in tweed. She longed to touch them, but she said the prayers and stared forward. Below the crucified Christ, warm wombs glistened with eggs, patient in their place, and drawn gently by the moon's great weight towards their blessing.

Mrs Gifford stared heavenly. Thoughts of her life in Cork drifted into mind: when little more than a baby she'd danced in her father's arms until she'd fallen asleep. She was Mary Murphy in those days, and they called her the 'Rose of Cork'. She was raven-haired and blue eyed, and she'd broken many a heart. And a time or two she'd had her own poor heart broken. What had become of him — that fine man in the trench coat with his cigars and Irish songs and him standing tall in all his glory? She remembered the flowers, his passion and how he'd made her laugh when he came out of the kitchen with a towel wrapped round his head like a turban. What had become of him? Some say he went to America. Some say he died in France. But then, some will say anything. You can never trust a jealous heart. But you can trust in God. And it was by God's grace that she became a nurse and went to Barringtons' and everyone was so proud of her, so proud of her that they'd taken photographs. That's when she'd met Albert. Albert Gifford, the travelling salesman, the man in a suit with money in his pocket and a fierce gleam in his eyes. Those eyes! They were eyes that pulled you up into their gaze. And she was pulled up, pulled up by the roots, enough to say goodbye to the tall terraces of St Luke's and go with him back to England and all the cobbles and carts and pounding hearts of Gorton town, where she loved her man and felt lonely for Ireland.

Father Immanuel Black was talking to Mr and Mrs Molloy, who were on their way out of the Monastery. He shook hands with them and then looked over to where Mrs Gifford and the others were standing. "God bless you, Mary… and the children! How are you all?"

"Well enough, thank you, Father."

"I take it that Albert is away on business again?"

"Aye, he's away to Limerick."

"Well, when he gets back I'll introduce him to Father Sollett. He's only just arrived in the Parish from Cambridge. He's an interesting young man. Tell your father that last year he represented St Edmund's at Bisley and that he has a most fascinating collection of Spode china. Albert will like that!" He turned to Wilfred and smiled. "And talking of fresh faces – who's this handsome lad with you, Mary?"

"Oh, this is Wilfred, Father."

"Ah, pleased to meet you, Wilfred." They shook hands.

"Good morning, Mr Black."

"You may call me 'Father'."

"I'd rather call you 'Mr Black'."

"Why's that?"

Wilfred stared. "Doesn't it say somewhere in the Bible: *Call no man your father on earth, for you have one Father, who is in heaven*?"

Father Black closed his eyes.

"I'm right sorry, Father! Please mind you, Wilfred's a Protestant."

"One of your relatives then, Mary?"

"No Father, he's... he's Polly's friend at Woolworth's."

He turned to Wilfred. "I know the passage in Luke you refer to Wilfred, but it's just as well that we don't set out to debate the meaning of it here and now..."

"Debating won't change a single word of it."

"... Because there are pressing things I need to attend to."

"Needs is must, Mr Black. Needs is must."

"Good day to you then, Wilfred. I do hope we'll see you in here again. And good day to you too, Mary!"

"Thank you, Father. I'll tell Albert about the new priest... and I'm right sorry about...."

"Oh that's quite all right, Mary. Try not to concern yourself over such things."

They got as far as the railway bridge, when Mrs

Gifford turned to Polly. "Go on ahead now, will you? Take the children. I want a word with Wilfred."

"Aw, Mam! Why have I got to go? What you can say to him you can say to me!"

"Just be gone with you, Polly! What I have to say isn't for your ears!"

Wilfred stopped and put his hand in his pocket and pulled out a packet of cigarettes. Mrs Gifford looked into his shining green eyes. "I've got to tell you Wilfred that I'm full of trepedition now you've said all that the Father back there. He won't forget what you said you know, and he'll blame me for it."

"Why should he do that?"

"I was a Protestant an' all once, and I don't think he'll ever let me forget it."

"I'm sure he won't forget anything. Men like that never do."

"Anyroad, if you've got such a bad view of Catholics, how come you're courting our Polly?"

"Oh that's easy, Mrs Gifford. It's not so much Catholics I'm bothered about, especially pretty ones; it's all the Jewish money-men that get me! They're the real danger."

"They're a danger?"

"Aye, they are. I'd get shot of the lot of them!"

"You'd get shot of all the Jewish money-men? I thought you were a conscientious objector."

"Who told you that?"

"I just thought…"

"Not me, Mrs Gifford! I did things in the war I'm ashamed of, but I'd do them things all over again to do away with the big Jewish money-men – them that own all the factories and that. They're the ones that caused the war and they're the ones that sent the lads out there to do murder!"

"Dear God, I've never heard of such a thing!"

"I've heard it said that that's what the crucifixion is all about: nothing good comes without bloodshed and

I believe in that, I do! There'll be no good in this world 'til we see the back of them money-men!"

"Polly said you're a socialist, is that right?"

Wilfred smiled. "She's nearly right, Mrs Gifford! I'm what they call a 'National Socialist'. That's what I am, and I'm proud of it! One or two of them at work are an' all and aye, they're proud of it!" His eyes burned. "I owe it to all them lads, young lads most of them – young lads, on their side as well as ours! What did they know? What did they know? What good did it do? We were just prawns, prawns in a bloody big game: them on one side and us on the other: boys against boys, our blood for their blood, their blood for our blood – and for what? When we came home we all had nowt! All we had was guilt – guilt and shame – but it should never have been left with us – no, not with us, but with all them fat bastards that started it. They should burn in hell for what they've done, they should, every last one of them."

Mrs Gifford stared at Wilfred. "I can see the fires of hell in your eyes."

"No Mother, them fires are in my heart."

"A National Socialist is it, Wilfred? Well at least we know now what kind of animal you are, then!"

Wilfred stared at her, and slowly his hand reached out towards her neck. "And at least I know what kind of animal you are, Mrs Gifford – you're one of them that chews!" He nipped the fur round the collar of her coat and pulled. Then he smiled and held aloft a twist of toothed chewing gum. "And I expect old Mr Black knows that an' all."

Mrs Gifford had a lot to say to Ellen, Joe and Dudley about chewing gum when she got back. It was made of old elephants' ears, it gave children bad stomachs and bad teeth, and chewing it would make them bad and mad and full of worms. It was just an uncouth, unhealthy and unnecessary habit that as she lived and breathed, she was going to stamp out. From that time onwards the coats would be put back in the wardrobe in their parents' room, and wouldn't come out again until they'd learned their lesson. That was followed by three long, cold nights of chattering teeth and angry whispers. It was his fault, it was her fault; it was everybody's fault. But on Thursday morning as they passed the canal bywash on their way to school, Dudley had an idea. "After you've had your dinner at school Ellen, say you've got the bellyache and then you'll get sent home."

"You what?"

"You'll get sent home and you'll be put to bed and Mam might let us have a fire in our bedroom."

"Why should I? Why not make Joe do it?"

"Because Joe's got no sense and besides, you're her favourite."

"Aw!"

"And if you don't... I'll tell Polly that you winked at her Wilfred at Mass!"

"But he winked at...."

"I'll tell her!"

Joe stopped and held her hand. "Aw, go on, Ellen! Cos then we'll all be warm."

The bywash gurgled and the wind blew Ellen's hair. She looked away and into the distance. "Oh, all right then."

Ellen looked round the room. It was warm and dark-panelled, and smelled of sweet boiled milk. A coal fire burned brightly in the hearth, and there was a large wooden radio on the desk next to a pile of registers. Mr Henry Ewing Sedgefield was sitting behind the desk, reading the note at arm's length. He rubbed his eyes and then looked at Ellen. "Miss Groombridge says you're unwell and that you wish to go home. Is that right, Ellen?"

"Aye, sir, it is."

"In what sense are you unwell, child?"

"I've got the belly ache, sir."

"Oh, belly ache is it? It could be…"

"It was after I'd had my dinner, sir."

"It could be the fatty bacon, Ellen. I didn't like the look of it myself!"

"Aye, sir."

Mr Sedgefield stared at her. "Though you look well enough to me, Ellen, so you'd better ask your mother about it." He stroked his jaw. "Is she at home?"

"Aye, sir."

"Well then, I'll have to take your brother, Dudley, out of Mrs Seabright's class and get him to accompany you home – not that he'll be able to do that without incurring some sort of mishap."

"You could send Joe, sir."

"Joe? Er, no, Ellen. He's far too young and you know as well as I do that he lacks common sense."

"Aye, sir."

Mr Sedgefield waved her away with his hand. "Off you go." Ellen went to the door and opened it, but before she left, she looked back and saw Mr Sedgefield with closed eyes muttering up to the crucified Christ who was impaled upon the panelled wall.

Polly lit a cigarette. "So it's smoking Woodbines now is it, Pauline?"

"Aye, Mam. I'm old enough now and it's time I got started."

"Does Wilfred smoke?"

"Aye, he does. He says smoking's good for his chest."

"Did you see the man today?"

"Aye."

"Well?"

"What?"

"Well, what did he say?"

"Not much, Mam. He kept his distance. He was talking to that young girl, Madeleine Ellis!"

"Who's she when she's at home?"

"She's just some floozy at work!"

"Does she smoke an' all?"

"Aye she does! How did you guess that?"

"Oh, I know the type!"

"All red lips and cheap scent!"

"And I bet she wrinkles and twinkles at Wilfred!"

"Aye, she does, but she's leaving next week, the little bitch – her boyfriend's got her a job at Lewis's."

"Maybe you'll get inundated with attention off Wilfred then."

"Aye, maybe, but I think he's gone off me since that to-do on Sunday."

"No! It didn't take long did it?"

"It didn't take much, neither."

"You see, I told you about them green eyes!"

"Fair enough, but at least they're not too close together are they, Mam?"

"We'll see, Polly. We'll see."

When they got to the canal Dudley said: "You can find your own way now, our kid. I'm going to the railway to see if I can get some pennies off the train drivers." Ellen stared at him. "You what? This was all your idea and now you're going to leave me here by the canal all on my own?"

"Aye, that's right."

"You right sod!"

He laughed. "And when I've got some money I'm going to see Aunty Pinkerton and get some toffees!"

"You bloody sod, Dudley!"

She watched him go. He looked back at her for a while and then turned and ran in the direction of the railway bridge. "I hate you, Dudley! You're always doing things like this!" She looked away and whispered: "Ever since I was little!" She put her hand in her pocket and felt the half-crown. Suddenly her expression changed. She held up the half-crown at arm's length. "That's what you call 'money', Dudley!"

Ellen walked slowly along the canal. The grey sky was stained with black. Steam hammers thumped in the factory yard and somewhere, far away, seagulls were crying like the dead. She got to the bywash. It streamed black beneath the great flat moss-greened stones, like the black blood of earth coursing through some opened vein. She shivered and walked to the edge. This was where Dudley had often left her before. He was just like the other big kids; he was big enough and daft enough to jump over to the other side of the bywash. She had never dared to do it and so she always had to go the long way home along the tow path. It was just like that time when Dudley had climbed over the railings into the park. She hadn't been able to get over them; she'd just had to wait there and look through the bars until he'd finished on the swings. It was always the same. She'd been the littlest before Joe was born. They used to laugh at her at night just because she was afraid of the duck under her bed, which had turned out to be a rolled-up shirt. They didn't seem to understand how frightening that was, or how helpless she'd felt, but she still remembered it all and it felt like that now.

She'd had enough of being the little sister, the girl who could never do things. She was going to show God and all his angels that she was as good as any boy. She looked at the bank opposite. It looked close enough. It didn't look all that dangerous. She looked around. There was nobody there to see her. Nobody was there to stop her. She stepped back and then walked forward to the bywash and stepped down onto the exposed cobbles by the water's edge. For what seemed like a long time, she stared forward. She saw the past: sitting with the faded pink band round her head; the golden fires in the scullery lit with blue, the glinting rings on the fingers of her mother's hands, the music she'd heard when she'd had scarlet fever. She felt the future: black shoes and handbags; the smell of boiling thick brown broth, the heat of tears through the night and the skin of a wet-haired baby upon her breast, backwards and forwards, rocked with love. This was the moment; the coming of age, the eventual triumph she always knew would be hers. She began to rock backwards and forwards, backwards and forwards. Then she took a step forward and jumped. Dear God! The moss on the cobbles turned her foot and she moved sideways and fell into the water. Her hip hit the cobbles. The water was cold and bubbled in her nose and ears, popping and glugging in the roll of hair. Strange tendrils and soft surfaces touched her hands and legs and held her body like a water baby borne in sweet redemption's arms. She felt her hip and groaned. Then slowly and awkwardly, she sat up at an ungainly angle in the water. All her clothes were wet. What was she going to tell her mother now? Somehow she got to her feet and struggled onto the bank, with pounding heart and teeth rattling like a ratchet full of old bones. Then she set off, walking clumsily along the towpath in the direction of home, sobbing as she went. After a while, she put her hand in her pocket to see if the half-crown was still there. It was. She held it firmly in the palm of her hand and it went through her mind that she should go straight to Mrs Pinkerton's shop and spend it all on sweets.

Polly lit a cigarette and stubbed it out immediately. "It's no good, Mam! Fags taste horrible."

"And I thought you said it's time you got started."

"Oh, I suppose it's only to do with that Madeleine

– if she can do it I can do it an' all!"

"And of course, Wilfred smokes doesn't he, child?"

"Aw, Mam!" She sat down suddenly. "I really like him and I want him to notice me."

"And you think he's more interested in Madeleine just because she smokes?"

"It's not just that... It's... it's, oh, I don't know."

"You've got an itch that you can't scratch, haven't you, darling?"

"What can I do to get him, Mam?

Mrs Gifford stared at her. "I didn't realise it was that bad with you."

"Help me, Mam. You know about these things. Help me, will you?"

"You want me to help you to catch a man who's made a fool of you?"

"Don't say that, Mam. I just need to understand how I feel, but oh – I think I love him."

Mrs Gifford sighed. "I didn't think I'd take to him at first, but when I saw him stand up to old Father Black on Sunday, I started to change my mind."

"What do you mean?"

"All right, I know I'm a daft old woman, and his political ideas seem a bit mad to me, but I've seen passion in him and that counts for something."

"Passion?"

"Aye, it's in his eyes! Have you not seen it in his green flame eyes? That says something rare about the man."

"What do you mean?"

"The nearest most women get to passion are the times when their husbands get amorous. But amorous is just polite lust. It's boyish and it's like having something in a cage. I know that sometimes you get ordinary lust like when it comes after a row, or on a Saturday night when you've had too much to drink. But lust has its eyes closed, it's selfish and it never gets you anywhere. You survive lust, but you can't live on it. But then there's passion, and it's passion that makes sense of everything else. Passion is love with life in it. It's life getting more life. It's the dance of life, and that's all we can ever hope for."

"I don't know what to say, Mam."

"Aye passion – if God invented anything better, he must have kept it to himself!"

Polly stared into her mother's eyes as she began again.

"Ah, but passion is dangerous an' all! I've seen it often enough, for when passion burns, it creates new life and then as sure as night follows day, it turns against itself. I've seen it breaking hearts. It can cremate the very soul that's cradling it."

"I don't know what you're talking about, Mam!"

"As sure as death, you will!"

"Don't be like that, Mam. You've got Dad and you just don't know how I feel!"

"I don't know how you feel? Can you hear yourself, Pauline? Oh, I know how you feel all right. I've been in love an' all! I've been in its grip. I well remember the pain of it and that's what it was – real pain. Love isn't love until it hurts. And it pained me sore hard, so it did!"

"You've still got him, though! You've still got Dad, haven't you?"

"Who's talking about Dad, Pauline? You know I love Albert, and he loves me back. To be sure, I'd never do him any harm, but when love, real love, arose in me, it wasn't with him." She stared into the fire. "I was young and you might say 'impressionable' – not that it mattered much. I knew love, so I did, and then he went away and abandoned me and he... then he took a big part of me along with him."

"You've never told me that before!"

"No, but it's always been there to tell – always."

"So what did you do?"

"What could I do? Sometimes second best is all there is. And then all you can do is cry and wait for the dreams to come." She searched through her apron pocket for a handkerchief.

After a while, Polly broke the silence. "Is that what's going to happen to me, Mam? Is all I can do is just wait for my dreams to come?"

Mrs Gifford stared at her. "I don't know, darling, I swear I don't know." She blew her nose and then put her hand over her mouth. "I never thought I'd get to this, I never thought it, no, never in a hundred years – but you've reminded me so much of…"

"What?"

"There's something you could do, but if I tell you, you must promise me never to speak of it."

Polly gazed at her. "What is it, Mam? Tell me."

"Never to Wilfred, or your father, or your brothers, nor Father Black, nor any man…"

"I won't Mam, honest to God, I won't!"

"This is for the ears of women only, but only good-hearted women." She came close to Polly, then sat down beside her and stared hard into her eyes.

"I'll tell you a question: Pauline, will you swear to God you'll remain silent?"

"I will, Mam. I swear on the Bible. What is it?"

"There's a love philtre."

"A love philtre?"

Mrs Gifford's voice lowered to a whisper. "Aye, Granny told me about it. It's like a… it's like a kind of spell."

"A spell! Aw, Mam, I don't want to get mixed up with things like that! It's against the laws of God!"

"How can the getting of love be against the laws of God?"

"Aw, Mam!"

"Besides, my people have heeded the old ways since time out of mind, and they've all feared God and they've all followed the laws of the Church like the good Christian folk they were."

"But spells and all that are just superstition, Mam!"

"Superstition is it? Aye, well if it is superstition, it's the exact same superstition that turned water into wine and then wine into the holy blood of God that Father Black lets us drink from the communion cup to save our souls!"

"It's not like…"

"Ah well, you just think I'm being blasphemous, don't you, child? Well surely I'm not, but if that's your view on the matter, I'll let things lie and I won't say no more, so I won't. But if you want my view, you either do nowt to try and get him or you do something, something that's been tried and tested by our good people through the ages – and I know which one of those *I'd* do!"

There was a long silence. Polly picked up the packet of cigarettes and then put it down again. She looked at her mother. "Does it work then, this love spell thing?"

"Oh, it works all right."

"How?"

"Well that's a mystery, child – one great big mysterious mystery. Granny used to say that it was as much a mystery as Mary Mulligan's black baby."

"Who's Mary Mulligan, when she's at home?"

"Ah sure, I don't know the woman, but I know this: the power of dragon's blood can no more be denied than the smile on her piccaninny's face." There was another silence; then Polly sighed and said, "All right, Mam, what exactly have I got to do to make this spell work then?"

Ellen stumbled down the back entry towards the yard door. When she got there she stopped and looked around. There didn't seem to be anybody about. She peered through the hole in the door where the latch went through. Nobody seemed to be in the kitchen. She lifted the latch and pushed the door. It opened slowly. She closed it behind her and glanced into the kitchen window. Then she went to the drainpipe that ran down the wall and climbed it until she was able to haul herself up onto the toilet roof. She looked around. Lines of washing stretched in the yards beyond, and the sight of whitewashed yard walls and clean clothes hanging there made her feel even dirtier. She walked to the kitchen wall, took hold of the drainpipe and began to climb up to her bedroom window. It wasn't as easy as usual, because she didn't want to make a noise. The window was closed, but she was able to ease the frame up and when she had enough space she went in head first. Once she had righted herself, she listened. It was quiet. She stood up and closed the window gently, and then set to work on removing her shoes and socks, and her jacket. They were still wet, and were stained green with muddy patches. She did her best to clean them up, but it was no good; soap and water were needed. Then she went to the chest of drawers and took out a handkerchief. She spat on it and tried to wipe the mud from her nose, hair and hands. When she felt she'd done all she could, she put her jacket back on and then her shoes and socks. She looked round the room, took the half-crown out of her pocket and pushed it under the lino near the window. Then she went to the bedroom door and opened it. She listened and carefully made her way down the stairs. These were stairs where the living met the dead, and where memories arose and fear entered the blood. Ellen could hear voices, and saw that the scullery door was open. She moved slowly and deliberately, and soon reached the door. She listened and heard her mother say. "The main thing to remember, Polly, is that if you ever tell anybody what you've done, the magic will be broken – now have you got that?"

"Aye, Mam – I won't say nowt. I've written it all in my diary and nobody even knows I've got a diary."

"Keep it out of sight, then."

"I do, Mam. I keep it hidden in my secret place."

"So! Now read back to me what you've got to do." There was a short silence and then Polly read in a flat monotone: "I've got to get some dragon's blood from the chemist's, and then I've got to sprinkle it on the fire at midnight on a Friday and then... er... I say the words."

"Have you got the words right, girl?"

"Course I have. I wrote each line down just as you said them:

> *'I do not wish this blood to burn,*
> *But my love's heart I wish to turn.*
> *May he neither eat, sleep, or drink*
> *Until he comes to me.'* "

"And then what?"

"I've got to leave the room without turning or looking round or speaking to anyone."

"Aye, and then what?"

"Then... then, Wilfred will come to me!"

"He will! He'll be compelled to and he'll come at once, believe me – he will!"

Ellen's mouth opened. She felt sure they would hear her breathing, and moved quickly to the front door. Her mother and Polly started talking again, and a cup of tea was mentioned. Ellen opened the front door as carefully as she could, and then slammed it shut. She walked clumsily down the hall and into the scullery. "Mam, I've been sent home from school because I've got the belly ache."

Mrs Gifford and Polly looked up. "For the love of... What's happened to your good coat and... and your skirt?"

"I fell in a big puddle, Mam."

"A big puddle?"

"Aye, in Slack's Brewery."

"Slack's Brewery? What were you doing in Slack's Brewery?"

"I took a short cut! They sent me home because I've got the belly ache!"

"Belly ache is it? Maybe you're starting your monthlies!"

"Ah-ha! Little sister's growing up! She's starting flooding down there!"

"I'll have to have words with her…"

Polly laughed. "Like the words you had with me?"

"What words?"

"All I got was: 'When you're having your monthlies, don't wash your hair and keep away from men'."

"Well, what's wrong with that? That's what Granny used to say, so she did."

Ellen put her hands on her hips. "No, I'm not getting my monthlies! Mr Sedgefield said it was the fatty bacon, the fatty bacon we had for us dinners! It was all tied up with string."

"Fatty bacon all tied up in string? Well, I'll just have to get the gripe water out then, but first it's into the kitchen with you."

Polly picked up the packet of cigarettes and stood up. "If you believe all that blarney about fatty bacon, Mam, you'll believe anything! Right, I'm going to get ready."

"Aye, go on then, but mind what I've told you. Come on, Ellen! Let's get your clothes cleaned and dried. Pick that old newspaper up – you'll need something to stand on – and it's into the kitchen with you. These clothes will take ages to dry, and look at the state of your hair – it's blacker than the hobs of hell! We'll have to get some carbolic on that!"

Flames flickered gently in the hearth. Even the moonbeams that lit the lino and filled the bedroom were warm. Dudley was chewing sloppily. The sweet, dark smell of liquorice drifted on the air. "See, I told you it'd work, didn't I? We're nice and warm now, all because of me!"

There was a silence; then Joe said, "Can I have some liquorice, Dudley?"

"No, you can't, Joseph. I've worked hard for this."

Ellen hugged the hot oven shelf, which was wrapped in a sheet, and sighed. "You shouldn't have left me on my own by the cut, Dudley, you big pig."

"Sticks and stones…"

"It'll take days to dry my clothes out."

"Well, you shouldn't have tried jumping over the bywash – you're still only little."

"Aw, Dudley – let's have some liquorice!"

"No, I won't, Joe. Go to sleep."

"You should share it, Dudley."

"Why should I? I bought it with my money."

"Well, because you should!" There was a long silence; then Dudley said, "I'll tell you what, Ellen, I'll give you some liquorice if you go downstairs and tell them that you need to go to the toilet, and then get some more coal from the yard and bring it up here so we can keep the fire going."

"Will you give some to Joe an' all?"

"Course I will, if he brings some more up afterwards."

"Will you do that, Joe?"

"Aye, I will if he'll give me some!"

Coal for liquorice, liquorice for coal – lesser exchanges of redemption held to lighten the darkness.

It was Joe's turn to go downstairs to get more coal. The fire was glowing red and the children were sleepy, but Dudley had insisted that he should go and keep his part of the bargain by bringing up some coal. Ellen told Joe to do as she had done and put the coal down the neck of his pyjama jacket, and hold it steady at the waist. Joe closed his eyes and crept down the stairs. He tried to think of the liquorice that would come his way if he managed to get the coal. When he reached the bottom of the stairs, he heard Polly's voice. He opened the scullery door and went in. Polly was sitting by the fire with Mrs Gifford. They looked round. "Joe! Why are you up?"

"I've got the belly ache, Mam!" He held his stomach. "I must have caught it off Ellen."

"In the name of… Polly, go and get the gripe water! Dear God, I forgot to give Ellen her dose tonight, but I'll make sure you'll get some in you, Joe!"

"No, Mam! I don't like gripe water. I don't like it!"

Polly hurried away and came back shaking a bottle. "Give me that spoon, Mam. I'll do it."

"No, Polly!"

She poured the gripe water out, walked to Joe and stuck the spoon in his mouth. "C'mon now, swallow it all up, Joe. It'll do you good!" Joe swallowed it and then pulled his tongue out. "Ugh!"

"Now then, you're best off to bed right away. Go on and I'll come up and tuck you in in a mo."

"But I want the toilet, Mam!"

"You're always on that toilet, Joe! You must have the worms or something!"

"I want to go, Mam!"

"Go on then!"

Joe went outside and opened the coal shed door as quietly as he could. He felt on the ground for coal. There wasn't much of it, but what he was able to pick up he put down the neck of his pyjama jacket. When he thought he'd got enough he closed the coal shed door, opened the back door and went in. Mrs Gifford called him into the scullery.

"Don't go up just yet, Joe – let me feel your head to see if you've got the temperature."

"No, Mam. I'm feeling miles better now! It must have been the gripe…"

Mrs Gifford guided him to her and as she did so the coal fell from Joe's pyjama jacket and scattered over the scullery floor.

"In the name of sweet… ! What's all this?"

"It just a bit of coal, that's all!"

"What have you taken all this coal for?"

"Dudley made me do it, Mam! He made me, honest to God, he made me!"

"What for?"

"For some liquorice!"

"Right! Upstairs, now! I'll soon sort this out. Just watch me, so I will!"

The railway line ran in gravelled earth. It was Saturday morning and there weren't many people about. Ellen held a bucket and walked on the sleepers between the tracks. Her clothes were still wet and she was cold. Dudley and Joe followed behind, carrying the tin bath that was kept on the backyard wall. Through tears Joe had told Mrs Gifford everything. So she had sent them out to collect coal from the railway cutting. She'd told them that it was sinful to steal, they were short of coal, and it didn't grow on trees; they'd have to find some more to make up for it. They could get it on the railway lines, and they weren't to come back until they'd collected a good bath full. Good, black, Welsh steam coal it was. They'd better do a good job, or else she would tell their father when he got back from Limerick and he'd soon give them what for.

It wasn't easy, but they did what they could. Whenever an engine passed by, they chanted: "Coal down, coal down!" Sometimes, the firemen would shovel a few large cobs out of the cab and onto the side of the line for them to collect. Sometimes their blackened faces just stared down without a word.

When Ellen was close to the bridge where Gorton Lane led to the Monastery, she found some lumps of coal scattered about the track. She put them in the bucket. And then she picked up what she thought was a lump of coal, and found that it wasn't coal at all. It was soft and light. Ellen put the bucket down and looked at it. It was black cloth material, which unravelled as she examined it. She soon realised that there were two bits of material, one rolled together with the other. She held them up to the light. They were gloves! They were black elbow-length gloves. She stared at them and then began to put one on. It fitted. She held her arm in the air and opened and closed her hand. Dudley and Joe put the bath down and came up beside her.

"What's that, Ellen?"

"They're ladies' black gloves! Finders keepers, losers weepers!" She put the other glove on. It didn't seem to fit. No matter what she did, she couldn't get it on. Then she realised that they were two left gloves. "They're both left-handed," she said in a flat monotone. Dudley laughed. "What sort of lady would leave two left-handed gloves on a railway line?"

It was like being in a dream. A mood arose. There was a time; there was a place, fixed like destiny in the palm of a hand. There were faces, words – lots of words, muttered as a hurrying prayer in a changing tense. There were words and faces in time and space, forgotten and then remembered, brought forth and made new by their telling. In this mood, old dreams carry new life.

Ellen struggled to put the other glove on her right hand. Her fingers were small, and although the glove was left-handed it went on. She held her hands up to the pale sun. The eternal veil descended. She stood like a sinister bride outside of time. The past and future elided with the stars, and granted her all the grace of a godly marriage. She picked up the heavy bucket and walked back along the line.

Polly lit a cigarette. "He's only going out with her now, isn't he?"

"Going out with who?"

"That Madeleine Ellis – the common cow!"

"How do you know that?"

"Mr Pride told me. Apparently, Wilfred took her to the Corona!"

"That's bad news."

"I just don't know what to do about it."

"Well you know what they say: 'Bad news always comes with a chance wrapped up inside it'."

"Aye, but Mam, what chance have I got against her? She's dead good looking and I'm just, just plain Jane!"

"Eh, eh, eh, you can stop all that now, girl!"

"Well, I am, aren't I?"

"Let me think about this."

"What's there to think about?"

" Have you burnt the dragon's blood yet?"

"No, Mam. It's all just superstitious malarkey, isn't?"

"Holy God, it's not!"

"Aw, Mam! It's a waste of time, all that!"

"No, it isn't at all, child. You have to put your full faith in it. If you don't, it won't work – I'm telling you."

Polly ran her fingers through her hair and then sighed. Mrs Gifford touched her hand.

"And besides, I've got a little idea of my own that I might try."

"What's that, Mam?"

"That's for me to know and for you to find out."

It was cold. But even on the coldest of days in Gorton, you didn't see many children wearing gloves. Sometimes the girls had knitted mittens. Sometimes the bigger boys shoved their hands into striped football socks and pretended they weren't soft, and it was only all a joke. Some of the little ones sucked their fingers. More often than not, children just blew into their clenched fists or pulled their arms as far as they would go up their sleeves. So it caused quite a stir to see Ellen in black ladies' gloves. By the time she'd reached the school gates, a crowd of excited children had gathered round her. Mr Jarvis Bamford was standing by the main entrance, watching the children in the playground. He saw the group at the far end, and decided to stroll across to see what the fuss was all about. When he saw Ellen, his eyebrows rose. "Oh, it's Ellen Gifford, is it?"

"Yes, Mr Bamford."

"You'd better go and see Mr Sedgefield. He told me to tell you that he wants to see you the moment you return to school. You'd better go and wait outside his door. No doubt he'll deal with you right away."

Ellen stopped and stared at him. Mr Bamford pulled a face. "All right! All right! Be gone with you then!" Ellen looked at the children's staring faces and then made her way to the main entrance. She went in and walked down the empty corridor until she reached Mr Sedgefield's door. She hesitated and looked around and then knocked gently on the door. Nothing happened. She knocked again, a little louder this time and Mr Sedgefield answered: "Come!" Ellen turned the handle, pushed the door open and went slowly into the office. Mr Sedgefield looked up from his desk as Ellen closed the door. He got up and walked to the window, keeping his back to her.

"Oh, I see. It's you."

"Yes, sir."

After what seemed like a long time, Mr Sedgefield said: "Ellen, do you agree that there's only one God?"

"What, sir?"

"Is there, or is there not, just one almighty God?"

"Yes sir, one God."

There was another long pause; then he asked, "Well tell me why, then, are there two religions?"

"Two religions?"

"Yes, Ellen, the one true God, the one true faith, 'The Faith of Our Fathers', the one holy, catholic and apostolic church and then… and then, there's the so-called Protestantism, but what exactly it protests about is quite beyond my understanding – unless of course, they're concerned about their own inadequacies and shortcomings!"

"Yes, sir."

"And your mother was a born Protestant, wasn't she?"

"Aye, sir."

"And she still has, shall we say, a certain Protestant air about her, doesn't she?"

"I don't know, sir."

"I mean she seems to have difficulty… how shall I put it… sometimes recognising the truth?"

"Does she, sir?"

"Take this letter, for example." He reached inside his jacket pocket and brought out a folded blue piece of paper. He began to read in a raised monotone: "Dear Sir, Our Ellen is away illy sick with the belly ache off the bacon tied up with the string that you gave her for her dinner today and Joe got it also and so it's not the monthlies and the bacon is surely at fault and also she fell in a big pond behind the Slacky Back and all the suit is wet, sir." He turned round and looked at Ellen. "Well, girl?"

"What?"

"You know that's not the truth, don't you?"

Ellen bowed her head.

"She's covering up for you, isn't she?"

"Er, no sir. It was all Dudley's fault… He…"

"It's Dudley's fault that you fell in the bywash?"

"Oh that?"

"Yes, that, Ellen. It wasn't a 'big pond' at the back

of Slack & Cox Brewery, was it?"

Ellen clasped her hands together and said nothing.

"She's covering up for you, isn't she? You know you've been strictly forbidden to go anywhere near that bywash. We've told you over and over again, haven't we?"

Mr Sedgefield stared silently at Ellen; then he said slowly, "What on earth have you got on your hands, girl?"

"They're my gloves, sir."

"Gloves? Gloves? They're not gloves! They look like something sported by a common woman, and a Protestant one at that!" He came towards her and breathed: "Take those things off right away! Take them off!"

Ellen took the gloves off as quickly as she could. "Now hand them over and come with me, young lady!" Mr Sedgefield held her by the ear, pulled her towards the door, opened it and marched down the corridor. The children were lined up in the corridor waiting silently to go into their classrooms. They stared as Mr Sedgefield strode by, with Ellen following on behind, towards Miss Groombridge's classroom. As the children filed in, Ellen looked into their guarded and downcast eyes and saw amusement and fear fleeting through their gaze, then hiding in deadpan expressions. The children sat down behind their desks in perfect silence. Mr Sedgefield had a few words with Miss Groombridge, who nodded her head. Mr Sedgefield looked round the room before taking hold of Ellen's wrist and pulling her fully into view. He lifted his head and took a deep breath. "Now, children, I want you to look at this, this child. You all know her, or you might think you do. Ellen Gifford, daughter of a difficult family – a difficult family that has produced a difficult child. This child is not only disobedient, but she is also incorrigibly wayward. Do you know what she has done? Mmm? Well, two of you know, because you saw it happen and you told me. You might well bow your head, Ellen. The shame is upon you. What this child did was to disobey all our instructions and instead of going home like a good Christian, she went the way of sin and took a shortcut to Taylor Street by way of the canal! By way of the canal! I'd say that's by way of the devil! Look at her. Look at her tremble! As well she might, for boys and girls, for she almost paid a high price for her rank disservice to the school and her resistance to Christian instruction. She fell into the black bywash and was close to losing her life! She was close to losing her short, irresponsible life! Let her lack of judgement and faithlessness serve as a warning to you all. Not that many of you have to contend with Protestant mothers who are constant strangers to the truth, but let it be a warning nevertheless. Do not go near the canal! Do I make myself clear?" The children replied in one voice: "Yes, sir."

Mr Sedgefield looked at Ellen. "And where there's one sin there's always many. For when she returned to school this morning she did so wearing these!" He held up the gloves for everyone to see. "You might ask yourselves: who does she think she is? She's a schoolgirl and not the whore of Babylon! She's just a schoolgirl!" There was silence; then he said in a breathy monotone, "So don't let me see any of you wearing this sort of nonsense! Christian gloves will do! And now, I'm going to take this girl round every single classroom in the school and I'm going to tell them exactly what I've told you so that there's absolutely no excuse, no excuse whatsoever, for people from this school not knowing how to behave properly in future. Thank you, Miss Groombridge." He nodded to Miss Groombridge, took Ellen by the arm and walked briskly out with her.

The sun streamed into the front parlour. Ellen was sitting alone with the half-crown in her hand. It had been some time since Mr Sedgefield had hauled her round the classrooms. She had felt angry and humiliated, but from an early age she had learned to endure things, to wear them out and still be there at the end of it, and that's what she'd done. She hadn't been able to tell her mother everything that had happened at school that day, but she'd explained her tears by admitting that Mr Sedgefield had forbidden her to come to school wearing her black gloves. Her mother had only said that the gloves were far too big anyway, and she never mentioned them again. That seemed to be that, and there were other things in Ellen's life. And she still had the half-crown. She lifted it up to show Uncle George in his uniform. Nobody else knew about it. There was power in its secret, and one day she would use it. She couldn't imagine how she would use it, but she knew the time would come when she would find the right way.

As Ellen mused about the future, she heard footsteps and voices outside in the street, and then there was a knock at the front door. She stopped and opened it, and there was Wilfred with a strange, but attractive, young woman. Wilfred smiled at her. "Er, hello Ellen. It's me, Wilfred. Do you remember? And this is my friend, Madeleine. We've come to see your mam. Can we come in?"

Ellen opened the door wider and then stepped back. "Aye, all right. Come in. I'll call her. She's upstairs dusting the bedrooms."

"Ta!" They went into the front parlour and sat down.

"Mam – Mam! Wilfred's here to see you."

"All right, Ellen – I'm on my way down!"

"How's school then, Ellen?"

"Oh, it's all right, Wilfred. Thanks."

Madeleine cleared her throat and then spoke nervously: "I went to your school, Ellen!"

"Did you?"

"Aye. It was a while ago, but I remember it. How's that Mr Sedgefield?"

"Oh, that old sulk – I don't like him."

"Why not?"

"Because he doesn't like me!"

"How do you know?"

"He shouted at me for wearing the wrong gloves."

Mrs Gifford came in. "Hello, how are you?"

"Oh grand, Mrs Gifford. This is my friend, Madeleine from Lewis's."

"Hello, love."

"Hello, Mrs Gifford."

"We've come about your letter." Wilfred reached into his jacket pocket and pulled out a folded blue letter.

"Right so, but Polly's not here. I want her to listen to what you have to say an' all."

"I can always come back."

"No, you'll have some tea with us. I'll go and put the kettle on." She bustled out of the room.

Madeleine coughed and then said, "Eh, Ellen, I can tell you something about that Mr Sedgefield.

Did you know that he used to be a priest in Exeter? My aunty lives in Exeter. She told me all about it."

"A priest?"

"Aye, it was some years ago now. He got sacked for having an affair with one of his parishioners. She was married an' all. It was in all the papers and everything, and it caused a right scandal."

Wilfred nudged her and asked, "What didn't he like about your gloves then, Ellen?"

"Oh, he said they were dead common, but they're not common at all – it's just that they're a bit big and they don't fit me, that's all. I'll go and get them and show them to you." Ellen went out just as Mrs Gifford came in with a tray full of tea things. She put it on the hearth and then looked at her guests.

"Now then, we'll just give that a moment to brew. She looked Madeleine up and down. "So you used to work at Woolworth's then, Madeleine, did you?"

"Aye, in Confectionary."

"But you're not there now?"

"No, I work at Lewis's in Ladies' wear now."

"Ooh, that's a good job. How did you get that?"

"My boyfriend got it for me."

"Oh, your boyfriend?"

"Aye."

"Oh, so Wilfred here isn't your boyfriend?"

Madeleine and Wilfred looked at each other. Madeleine smiled.

"Well, he is now."

"Oh, I see."

"Two weeks!"

"Anyroad, Mrs Gifford, I can call again next week if you want me to talk to Polly an' all."

"Aye, that'll be good. Friday's a good bet. She'll be washing her hair then. I'm sure she'll be interested."

"Right oh, then. I'll bring some leaflets so she can study them."

The door opened and Ellen came in. "Here they are!" She held up the black gloves.

"Oh, they're nice! They're not common at all. I'd wear them."

"No, you wouldn't." Mrs Gifford's eyes sparkled. "Not unless you've got two left hands!"

"They're both left hands?"

"Aye, strange isn't it?"

"Where did you get them, Ellen?"

"On the railway line there, just by Gorton Lane bridge."

"Did you know that they were both left-handers?"

"Aye, but I don't care. I just put them on. And as long as I don't go to school in them I'm all right. I'm not bothered."

"She says she's going to wear them for the Whit Week walks. And I think she should, an' all. Mr Sedgefield will see her, but she won't be in the school, will she? She'll be walking through the streets, so he can't touch her, can he?"

"Have you got a nice frock, Ellen?"

"Aye, I've got the white one I had last year. I'm going to make a headdress and a train out of curtains."

"Black gloves with a white frock?"

Ellen stared and said nothing. Mrs Gifford cleared her throat. "Tell me about these National Socialist leaflets then, Wilfred."

Madeleine waved her hand. "No, Mrs Gifford, just a minute. I work in a place where we can get girls' clothes cheap. I'll get you some long white gloves to go with your white frock, Ellen. They might be a bit on the big side, but I should be able to get you some for the Whit Week walks."

Mrs Gifford pursed her lips. "I'm not sure about that, lady. We don't want your charity, no we don't, dear. My husband's got a good job. He's a traveller with Mather & Platt's and he goes everywhere."

"This won't be charity, Mrs Gifford. It'll just be a present. It's like a Christening present or birthday present. It's not charity, they're just presents. Gloves don't even cost anything. We get them off mannequin parades. They're only worn once and then they get thrown away – so it's only fair that we get them, isn't it?"

"It's such a shame to see them wasted, Mrs Gifford."

"Aye, and you've got to stand up for yourself in this life. You're not going to let that Mr Sedgefield get away with treating Ellen like that, are you? Don't you want to see his face when she rolls up with posh new gloves on?"

"It'll be a picture!"

"Aye, there is that, I suppose."

"Well, he's got it coming to him!"

"Did you know that Mr Sedgefield is chummy with Mr Black, Mrs Gifford?"

"Is he? I didn't know that, Wilfred."

"They went to the same seminary together, and neither of them takes kindly to Protestants."

"They've got it in for you and your family – you realise that, don't you?"

"To be sure they have, haven't they?"

"Well, then, let me bring you some good white gloves so you can show them what's what!"

"Needs is must, Mrs Gifford. Needs is must."

Mrs Gifford thought for a while, and then she smiled. "Aye, go on then! Half as much is often twice as many! We'll learn those damned devils, won't we?"

"Good lass!"

Madeleine turned to Ellen. "We'll get you some really nice gloves, darlin', and turn you into a princess!"

Wilfred stared at Ellen and smiled. Her gaze met his. It never left her. He spoke softly: "Aye, lass, we'll bring some magic into the world. We will, I promise."

Ellen gazed into his unfaltering green eyes, and at that moment she knew how she would spend her half-crown.

They walked hand in hand as children before the tide, and as rich as summer's setting suns down Pine Street and beyond into Taylor Street, where windows framed homes and gave away secrets: fancy lamps, bottles, empty vases, radios, photographs, burnished brass, gleaming hearths and sleeping cats. Then hand in hand by Aunty Pinkerton's sweet shop with its glowing lights, and on to what was left of Parker's old smithy and down as far as the corner until they reached The Bessemer. Then Mr Gifford stopped and bowed to Polly: "After you, dear lady!"

Polly hesitated; then she smiled and went in. The bar was full of smoke and in one corner, a hurrying conversation that rose into laughter, followed by groans of mock indignation and somebody shouting: "Fair play to you then!" Mr and Mrs Molloy were laughing and pushing the piano round. Mrs Clements blew a kiss, and waved at Mr Gifford. After they had been to the bar and Mr Gifford had bought a pint of Chester's and Pauline a gill of orange juice, they found a table and sat down. Mr Gifford looked at Pauline. "I'm dead glad you've come out with me, Polly. It's been a long while, hasn't it?"

Pauline stared at him. "Aye Dad, it has."

"Aye, we used to go everywhere together."

"Aye. We did, Dad."

"We did. We went to Belle Vue Zoo and that, and Stockport canal catching tiddlers in a jar, and do you remember when we went see the rose-coloured swans in Sunny Brow Park?"

"Aye Dad, the white ones!"

Mr Gifford laughed. "Ee, you fell for that one right enough, didn't you?"

"And you won't let me forget it, will you, Dad?"

"We used to talk and talk about this and that. It was all chitter-chitter-chitter, wasn't it?"

"Aye, it was."

"But somehow, it's not the same now..."

"Well, you're away all the time, Dad, and I'm working and..."

"No, it's nowt to do with that, Pauline. I don't know...'

"Aw, Dad!"

"Nowadays, you kind of... you know... hide things from me a little bit, don't you?"

"I don't. It's just that…"

"I mean you don't tell me things no more. You just keep things to yourself, and I don't know…"

"Don't be like that, Dad!"

"But it's not right to do that to your own father, is it?"

"Aw, Dad!"

"I mean you've been a bit funny lately, and you haven't told me why, and me and your Mam are a bit… you know… flummoxed. We just can't fathom it like, you know what I mean?"

"Is that why you've brought me here – just to shout at me?"

"No, lass! I just…"

"You're all the same, you lot – you go round treating me like a daft little kid! But I'm not a kid – you should know that!" Pauline stood up. Mr Gifford held her wrist gently. "No, lass, no, I'm not treating you like a kid. It's just that I fear I'm losing you and I couldn't bear that, that's all."

"Aw, Dad – don't say that!"

"I'm just a bit… you know, upset." Pauline sat down. She put both her hands over his.

"Don't be upset, Dad. It's all right. You're not losing me – you'll never lose me. I'm your daughter, your Polly, and I will be for ever and ever. And you're my dad, my funny-haired father, who will always be my best man in the world."

Mr Gifford stared at her. "Sweet Pauline."

"I love you, Dad."

Mr Gifford pulled his hands out from underneath hers, and shook his head. "Well, what is it then that ails you?"

Pauline looked down. "Oh, it's nowt really."

"Pauline."

"Oh it's just to do with me and Wilfred, Dad. Things are not right between us."

"Oh, I'm sorry to hear that, love. Is there owt I can

do?"

"It's complicated, Dad and there's nowt you or anybody else can do to sort it out."

"Does your mam know?"

"Aye, she does. We've talked about it."

"And what did she say?"

"Oh, she just said that's all you can expect from a man with green eyes, and then she told me about a love philtre."

"Oh, one of her old Oirish spells was it? Oh, Lord! Did you try it?"

"Of course I didn't! It's not spells I'm after, Dad, it's passion – passion and commitment."

"You'll likely be disappointed, then."

"Why? What do you mean?"

"I mean where there's one, you rarely find the other."

"I don't get that."

"Passion is love that's on fire – it's urgent, it's the yearnings of the flesh – but commitment is more like giving something up and putting something else in its place. It's got nowt to do with passion."

"You've always been dead committed to Mam though, haven't you?"

"I've always been committed to her – she's my wife."

"But does that mean you don't feel passion?"

"I never said that."

"Well, what then? I don't get it."

"I know passion right enough. There's been times when I was so driven by it that I couldn't eat, I couldn't drink or sleep, but that's... that's when a man feels best alive! I've been filled up with passion. It's like being filled with life itself."

"Aw Dad, and did you ever tell Mam that?"

Mr Gifford looked down. "Who said anything about your Mam?"

"You what? I never knew you've... Who..."

Mr Gifford held up his hand. "There's a lot you don't know about me, Polly."

For a long time neither of them spoke; then Polly lifted her eyes and held her father's gaze.

"And there's things you don't know about me neither, Dad."

They finished their drinks in silence, and then they left.

"Close your eyes and then give me your hand, Ellen."

"Why, Mam? What's going on?"

"Just a little surprise for you. That's all, child."

Mrs Gifford guided her into the front parlour. "Now then, open your eyes and let them delight on what they can see!"

Ellen opened her eyes and saw Wilfred leaning forward in the armchair. He smiled at her. Mrs Gifford turned her by the shoulders. "No, not him, you eejit – look what Polly's got!" Ellen looked. Polly was holding up two long white gloves. She gave them a little shake and smiled. "Wilfred's brought them for you. Aren't they beautiful?"

"They're from Madeleine."

"Oh, Wilfred – thank you!" She ran to Polly, took the gloves and held them to her cheek.

"Oh, thank you, Wilfred! They're dead good!" She went over to where he was sitting and hugged him.

"They're from Madeleine, Ellen – she said she'd get them for you, didn't she?"

"Aye, but I never expected owt like these! These... these are just belting! Where is she, anyroad? I want to hug her an' all!"

"Oh, she had to stay behind at work, but she'll be along soon. She wants to see you in all your finery!"

"Ooh, come on, Ellen – try them on."

Ellen smiled, and struggled to put the gloves on. Then she held her hands in the air, opening and closing her fingers for everybody to see, and twirled them in the light.

"These are all right, aren't they?"

"They're just a size too slack for you, girl – but sure, you'll soon grow into them."

Everybody watched as Ellen danced for joy around the room. There was a grace about her angular arms, a radiance about her blank face that betokened enchantment.

"Ellen, Ellen!"

"My pretty arms!"

Ellen, we haven't finished yet!"

"What?"

"Close your eyes again, Ellen."

"What, again?" Ellen closed her eyes. She stood in the middle of the room all fixed and angular, and with a grin on her face.

"Come on in, Dudley."

The door opened and Dudley came in.

"Over here, Dudley. Now then, Ellen. Take a deep breath and… open your eyes."

Ellen opened her eyes and there, draped over Dudley's trembling arms, was a dress of purest white, full-embroidered and frilled to the hem. It caught the light from the window: lovely in its satin aspect and soft folded shapes. Slowly her grin disappeared and she stared, expressionless, at the dress over Dudley's arm. Then she whispered, "O, sweet…" before shouting, "For me?"

"Aye, lass! Aye, it's for you! It's for you!"

"Madeleine got it for you, Ellen!"

Ellen went to the dress and ran its long folds through her fingers.

"Take it – go on, take it!"

Ellen smiled and lifted the dress gently from Dudley's arms, and held it to her cheek whilst her hands ran this way and that way over the embroidery. She lifted it by the shoulders and held it awkwardly to her body, kicking a leg and swirling round with it. "Oh, it's… it's dead beautiful!" She went to Wilfred. "Thank you, oh thanks, Wilfred!"

Mrs Gifford got up. "It's from Madeleine Ellis, Ellen – she'll be here in a bit. You'll be able to thank her then."

Ellen turned the dress around and looked at the buttons. "Oh, sweet!"

Mrs Gifford turned to the door. "We're not finished yet! "Come on in, Joe!"

Joe appeared at the door. Smiling broadly, he lifted aloft a delicate headdress of white flowers with a long, flowing veil. He walked quickly to Ellen; she put her arms round him, and stared at the veil. Joe put it uneasily on her head. "Oh, Joe – that makes me feel just like a princess."

She adjusted the headdress and pulled the veil over her face. Everybody laughed. "Come here, child, you daft ha'porth! I'll make it right for you!" Mrs Gifford lifted the veil and pulled it gently over Ellen's head to reveal her smiling face. Ellen looked round the room and curtsied to the right and left. Everybody clapped. This was joy, pure timeless joy: that uplifted sense of life that gladdens the heart and makes secure a moment of childhood repose. There was a knock at the door. Mrs Gifford went to open it.

"Oh, hello, Madeleine! Come in! We're just trying on all the things."

Wilfred got up. Madeleine strode in, and the room filled with her perfumed presence. "Hiya, darlings! Oh, just look at you, Ellen Gifford! You look like a… like such a beautiful…"

Wilfred went across to Ellen. "Like a beautiful and proud princess!" Ellen put the headdress down and held out her hands to him. Wilfred grasped them. "We did promise that we'd turn you into a princess, didn't we now?" Ellen embraced him. "Oh, Wilfred!"

Mrs Gifford cleared her throat. "Now get along

now, child, and we'll put these on so we can all see what you look like. C'mon, upstairs with you! C'mon you boys, an' all, and follow us up. You too, Dudley – and stop looking at Madeleine. C'mon!" They hurried out of the room. Polly shifted in her chair.

After a while Wilfred said, "Your Mam wrote to me, Polly, and said you wanted me to tell you more about National Socialism, so I've brought you a pamphlet that will tell you one or two things about it."

"Did she? I didn't… Thanks."

"But we can talk about it now if you like."

"Well… er… I don't really…"

"Never mind all that stuff now, Wilf. She doesn't want to talk about all that stuff now, does she? Don't you think Ellen looked nice, Polly? She was a picture, wasn't she? I said I'd get the stuff. It took ages to ask around and get her size. Well, they're all different sizes actually – but we can alter things a bit, can't we? And I'm trying to get some matching shoes an' all. That's where I've been just now as a matter of fact – seeing a mate of mine in the loading bay who's got a good few connections you might say, if you follow my meaning." She started to whisper. "It's a bit, you know… a bit like claiming overtime." She winked.

Polly opened her mouth and then closed it again. Then she said: "Aye, she looked bonny – real bonny, our Ellen."

There was a silence.

"Erm… have you told Polly our news yet, Wilf?"

"No, not now, Madeleine. It's not…"

"Go on, tell her – she'll be right pleased."

Wilfred stared at Polly and then looked down.

"Oh, I'll have to tell her, then! Polly, Wilf's asked me to marry him! Isn't that dead good? We're going to get married, aren't we?" She looked at Polly: "Aren't you happy for us?"

Polly's mouth opened and she stood up slowly.

Then the door opened and Mrs Gifford and Joe came in. "Ladies and Gentlemen, here she is – our lovely Princess Ellen!"

"Oooooooh!"

Everybody came in. Polly put her hands to her face, turned and went quickly out the door.

"Where's she gone?"

"What do you think, Wilfred?"

"You look even lovelier than before, Ellen."

"You do your Mam proud, Ellen. You're such a bobby-dazzler!"

Ellen did a twirl. Her face was expressionless; then she stopped and looked at Wilfred. "There's only one way to thank you, Wilfred." She went across to where he was sitting, and kissed him on the lips.

Polly lay on the bed and cried silently.

You should have died unto my love
And lain pale as a rose, my hand in yours
To hold onto until my own ending
Remembering your breathless words
Holding faithfulness to what you said
Holding faithfulness unto death
Without bitterness or cooling love
You should have died unto death
And made it easier for me to meet my own
You could have cried with me before you left
And denied all others the softness of your breath
Before those wild briars are drawn through my
heart
Leaving me no more, and spiked to the test.

Being abandoned is the cruellest of fates. You can understand it and yet you can't accept it. Try as you might, you can't understand why the one who loved you, the one who said he would die for you still lives on without you. What sense, what purpose does that serve? What God would ever sanctify that? Why should it happen? Where is happiness now? So give me my aloneness. Take me to a place where there is only me. Please – give me peace, for without it there can be no end.

It was Friday morning. Gatherings of people were in the street. Dudley and Joe were standing outside their house, with their father. They were in their best trousers. Joe's hair was parted down the middle, and Dudley wore a pink rose in his lapel. Mr Gifford was dressed up in his suit, and his highly-polished brown shoes. His black, unruly hair shone in the sunlight. He was holding his new camera, and showing Joe and Dudley how to use it: "It's like firing a rifle. Hold it steady, breathe in, hold your breath, aim and fire."

"When Ellen comes out, can I take a picture an 'all?"

"Let me take one first, Dudley. Then both of you can have a go – but just one each mind. Film doesn't grow on trees, you know."

Wilfred came up carrying a bunch of white flowers. "Hello Joe. Hello Dudley, and you, sir, must be Mr Gifford."

Mr Gifford looked hard at Wilfred. "Aye, that's me – Alfred, Alfred Gifford. It's young Wilfred, isn't it – our Polly's fellah?"

"Your Polly's fellah as was, Mr Gifford."

"Have you come round to see our Polly?"

"No, sir – I'm waiting for the princess! I suppose you are, an' all!"

"Me? No, I'm waiting for the angel!"

"Well, you've got a fine day for it."

"Aye, I'm glad it is. I'm going to take some photographs. It'll be a proud moment to see our Ellen, all done up to the nines, walking in the Whit Week walks."

"It will for me, an' all."

"And I hear that it's you and your friend from Lewis's that we've got to thank for that!"

"Aye, Madeleine's a good 'un."

"Will she be coming to the school with us?"

"No, she's got to go to work – she's got some business to sort out."

"That's a pity, lad."

"Needs is must, Mr Gifford. Needs is must."

The sound of excited voices and clapping came from the other end of the street. A little girl appeared in a doorway wearing a lacy pink frock. Mr Gifford smiled and turned to Wilfred.

"You served in the war didn't you, son?"

"Aye, many of us did."

"Where were you?"

"Flanders. I was in Wipers and one or two other places before the finish."

"Don't you feel proud? You know, you took part in the defence of all this, didn't you?" He waved his arm and looked down the street.

"What we did in Flanders was nowt to do with defending the realm, sir. It was about killing other people's sons. It was dirty and without mercy. We killed thousands and thousands of them. Some couldn't bear it. Some enjoyed doing it. Some even got rich out of it. You should have seen them Australians taking the Germans' gold rings. It was butchery, and none of us deserved it. Me? I'll never forgive them that sent us, them who stayed at home and prospered while young lads were sent to them awful filthy places."

"Oh, I didn't know…"

"Most folk don't know, do they?"

The door opened and Madeleine put her head round: "Are you ready?"

"Aye!"

The door opened further and Madeleine came out, followed by Mrs Gifford and then Ellen.

Everybody clapped. Ellen's face was expressionless, but everybody could see that she was trying hard to suppress a smile. Wilfred went to her, lifting her hand and kissing it before presenting her with the flowers.

"These are for you, your majesty."

Ellen took the lilies gently, and smiled. "Nobody has ever given me flowers before. I don't know what to say. They're lovely. You're lovely. Thanks, Wilfred. They'll always remind me of you."

Wilfred looked away.

Mr Gifford came up. "Go over there, Ellen. That's it, by the wall. That's it! Smile!" He covered the viewfinder with his hand, took the photograph and handed the camera to Dudley.

"Remember, just take one apiece. Then I'll stand next to her so Joe can take one of both the pair of us."

Mrs Gifford went up to Wilfred and whispered, "Oh, I wish you hadn't done that, young man – lilies always remind me of death."

Wilfred was calm. He looked her full in the face and after a while he said, "Well, they remind me of life, Mrs Gifford. They remind me of life here and now, in these streets with these people, where it's safe, and where the tea doesn't taste of petrol and where I don't wake up with shit in my pants. They remind me of soft grass and new life and clean sheets and food, and girls. That's what they remind me of, Mrs Gifford!"

Mrs Gifford stared at him. He turned away and then looked back.

"Oh aye, and they'll always remind me of the Blessed Virgin."

Polly watched them go from the bedroom window. They walked slowly towards Taylor Street. Ellen held her father's hand on one side and Wilfred's on the other. Mrs Gifford and Madeleine followed, holding the boys' hands. It was like a wedding party: Ellen was the bride and Wilfred the groom, and Polly's father was there to give the bride away. It was too much for Polly to bear. It seemed the only bride she would ever be was a Bride of Christ. She turned away from the window. *And the Spirit and the bride say, Come. And let him who heareth say, Come. And let him that athirst come. And whosoever will, let him take the water of life freely.* Polly went to get her coat.

Polly reached Gorton Lane and stopped at the bridge. She looked over the blackened wall. There they were: railway lines, fixed like destiny in the palm of a hand. It's easy to believe in destiny – those mysterious powers that fashion lives. It's easy to believe – and yet, when something like this happens, certainty fades and nothing seems to make sense any more. She was overcome. Her heart couldn't beat fast enough. Her breaths couldn't come soon enough. Cold yearnings ran in her blood. Everything was hanging on one thing, and that was Wilfred's love. Nothing else mattered. Nobody else could help. This time, Christ and all his angels couldn't soothe her driven heart, a heart that was so full of love and purpose. Polly raised her eyes to heaven and whispered, "Nothing's ever as it seems, is it? There's deception at the heart of things – dark dealings, lies, betrayal, abandonment. Please, please, help me. Please. Amen."

As they came to the school gates Mrs Gifford turned to her husband. "Are you going to have a word with Mr Sedgefield about the way he treated our Ellen?"

Mr Gifford shook his head and frowned. "Mary – you know I don't like kicking up a fuss. It's least said soonest mended, isn't it?"

"Well I think you should – the man's a damned disgrace!"

"Aw, don't spoil it, Mary. It's a good day today."

Wilfred said, "I think you should, Mr Gifford. The man's a bully. And he's got it in for you and yours. You should see to it."

"Nobody asked you, son. I'll deal with it, thank you very much."

"I just hope you will, that's all!"

"You just don't understand, so leave it be will you?"

"That's a very weak argument, Mr Gifford. What is there that wants understanding?"

"Look Wilfred, this is family business, so just mind your own."

They walked in silence and then Mr Gifford said, "I can't wait to see his face though, when he sees what Ellen's got on!"

"Aye, it'll be a picture!"

"I've got my camera an' all!"

Everybody except Ellen laughed.

The girls' playground was full of people: boys in shiny white suits, big men with big banners and poles held steady in leather harnesses, cigarettes, tasselled cushions, trilby hats, red roses pinned to lapels, painted wooden trumpets, girls with bouquets, women with fur stoles and babies in prams. Joe held one of Ellen's hands. Ellen held Wilfred's hand with the other. Some girls waved to Ellen. She let go of Joe's hand and waved back. Wilfred turned to her: "You look really pretty, Ellen. Remember that, won't you? Be proud! You're a proud princess!"

"Am I really like that, Wilfred?"

"Aye, that you are, kid."

Ellen smiled.

Dudley went over to some boys who were trying to comb their hair. Mr Gifford chuckled.

"There he is. Can you see him – old Sedgefield –

standing over there by the main entrance with all them teachers?"

Mr Sedgefield was talking to the teachers, who were listening intently to him. Then he turned and held his hand above his eyes to view the people in the playground. He paused before raising a whistle to his lips. He blew it several times and gradually, conversations stopped and people turned to listen to him.

"Welcome everyone. It's good to see so many of you here this morning. We have a good day for it and you all look perfectly splendid in your new clothes." Everybody laughed. "Now, I want all the children to line up according to their classes here in the yard – just as you do to enter the school. Your teacher will sort you out into four columns, girls first: youngest at the front and the older ones at the back. We'll be following on behind the Fathers, so you'll have the honour of representing the children of the school in this year's Whit Week walks. Your teachers will take you to the gates, where you'll wait for the parade to arrive – and when you're told, you'll join the end of it as it passes and then continue with them down Gorton Lane. It's just like in other years, so please don't worry about a thing. I'm sure it'll be a great success. God bless you." Then he turned to the parents. "And I do know that you somewhat older children won't need me telling you what to do!" Everybody laughed. "As ever, those of you who are going to walk, please kindly form three columns behind the children. The parade won't be long, and… in fact… I think I can hear them coming now!"

Several of the parents moved to the back of the columns of children. There were nods and smiles and pointing fingers, and adjustments made to ties, hats, buttonholes, skirts and hair.

Mr Gifford looked at Mrs Gifford. "Doesn't our Ellen look bonny, Mary?"

"Aye, she's as proud as punch, isn't she?"

"Aye, and I bet you two are proud of her an' all!"

"Aye, we are, thanks to you and Madeleine, Wilfred!"

As they turned to look at Ellen, they saw Mr Sedgefield cross the playground with Miss Groombridge. They stopped and spoke; then they went up to Ellen, and began to talk to her. Miss Groombridge held Ellen by the wrist and lifted her arm. Mr Sedgefield shook his head. He said something to Ellen, and bent his head to listen to her reply. Ellen looked round and pointed to Mr and Mrs Gifford and Wilfred. Mr Sedgefield took Ellen by the arm and pulled her out of the column. She cried as she trailed rather awkwardly behind Miss Groombridge and Mr Sedgefield, who were striding across the playground towards the Giffords. Mr Gifford went to meet them.

"What's up?"

"Dad, he won't let me walk!"

"Why not?"

The sound of bugles was getting louder. Mr Sedgefield kept hold of Ellen's arm and came close to Mr Gifford, who knelt down and put his arms round his daughter. "Why not? Why won't you let her walk?"

"Have you no sense at all? Can't you see? She's dressed up like a... beyond her years. She's representing the school! People will see her, and they'll think the worst of the school!"

"Why, what's wrong with her?"

Mrs Gifford came up with Wilfred. "What's going on, Alfred?"

"He won't let me walk, Mam!"

"He says he doesn't like her clothes!"

"Why, what's wrong with them? They're brand new, they are."

"Aye, she looks like a princess."

"She looks like an angel!"

"An angel, you say. Oh, I see – an angel! Well, I have to say she looks more like a fairy to me – a Piccadilly Fairy! What do you think, Miss Groombridge?"

"Oh, I agree, exactly like one."

"What do you mean?"

"She's dressed beyond her years: her gloves are much too big and showy, her dress is too long, and quite frankly she looks... rather common!"

"Bloo-dy 'ell, Mr Gifford – don't stand for that! Tell him!"

"You keep out of it, Wilfred. I'm sorry you feel like that, Mr Sedgefield. We just did our best for her, that's all."

"Tell him, Dad! Tell him I want to walk!"

Mr Gifford turned away. "I thought she was the prettiest thing I'd ever seen in my life."

Ellen was twisting in her father's arms. "Oh please let me walk, Mr Sedgefield! Please!"

"No, I'm afraid not, Ellen. That wouldn't be suitable at all."

"Aw, please let me. I could walk on my own... right at the back behind all the others."

"No, I think it best that you go home with your parents, Ellen."

"Aw, Dad, Mam, tell him! I just want to walk. Get him to let me walk, please, please."

Mr Sedgefield looked at Ellen. He had a look of sorrow about him. "It's regrettable, for it's not so much the little girl who's at fault here – although I have noticed a certain sullenness on her part from time to time – but indeed, it's yours, her parents', for allowing her to comport herself in such a manner as this." He waved his hand.

The band stopped playing. All that was left was the steady 'tick-tick-tick' of the kettle drum; then the man at the front shouted, "*Victoria*!", and the bugles and big drums sounded. The columns of boys and girls walked forwards and started to join the parade. Mrs Gifford struck a pose with her hands on her hips, and pulled a strained expression:

"Oh, com-part herself pabically in sech menners as this? Is that all you've got to say, you… you big, holy bastard?"

"Mary! Mary!"

"Well look at him – he is! He's all froth and ballocks!"

"Well said, Mrs Gifford!"

"I've heard tales about the man!"

Miss Groombridge pushed Wilfred away. "No you haven't. He's a… he's a very, very, nice man!" Her exertions made her choke, and she turned away and went into a coughing fit. Mrs Gifford stiffened. "And as for you, you love-struck Jezebel; you should be hung up by the heels for all your jig-a-jigging up to him and not letting our poor darling walk! Look at her! Look what you, and that… that feckin' lizard, have done to her!"

"How dare you say that about him, you dreadful, awful, miscreant?" Miss Groombridge carried on coughing.

"Oh, mixcrement is it? Well then, let me tell you what you are, will I?" She threw back her head. "You're a black enamel, hairy-arsed, puss-faced, contagious old cow – that's what you are, Mrs feckin' Bumbridge!"

Mr Gifford took her by the arm: "Please, that's enough, Mary! Come away now, please!"

"Well, she had it coming to her."

"Wilfred, please go and take the boys out of the parade and tell them we're going home."

"Aye, Mr Gifford!"

"Her eyes are too close together an' all!"

"I'm sorry, Mr Sedgefield. Mary's like this sometimes. She's not been herself just of late, you see. She's Irish and it's her age – she's going through the change, like, you know. She doesn't really mean it! Please forgive her. It was just a remark – just a funny remark, that's all it was, do you see?"

"Sure I bloody mean it! The man's stopping our wee girl from walking. If I was a man... sure I'd give him a good scutchin,' so I would!"

Mr Sedgefield straightened himself up to his full height. "In which case, and in view of your wholly disrespectful attitude, you leave me no alternative but to ask you to report to me in my office first thing on Monday morning, so we can discuss your children's withdrawal from this school."

"Oh, Dad – please stop him. I'm dead sorry I wanted to walk."

"Oh, surely there's no need for that, sir. You'll give us one more chance, won't you? We've not really done anything wrong. All we've done is to do our best!"

"No, I think it best in the circumstances, Mr Gifford. Withdrawal is all I can offer. Shall we say 9.00 a.m. on Monday, then?"

"Oh, sir, please keep me here. I want to stay – a dead lot!"

"Please Mr Sedgefield, don't do this to us. Think of the shame it'll bring to our family."

"It's a pity you didn't consider that when you decided to parade your daughter through the streets of Gorton dressed like a painted moll, to witness her faith – isn't it, Mr Gifford?"

"But sir, I beg you!"

Mr Sedgefield shook his head, then for a moment he hesitated.

"Listen to me, Mr Gifford. I'm not an unreasonable man, but can't you see – you leave me no alternative."

"But surely just this once you could... Look at her. She's dead upset now."

Wilfred came back with Dudley and Joe. "Here they are, Mr Gifford. I've told them what's what."

"Thank you, son."

Mr Sedgefield looked at Wilfred and the boys and then said, "Look, I'm not entirely without sympathy for what your daughter must be feeling in all her innocence."

"Help her, then."

Mr Sedgefield thought and then said, "I suppose I could telephone to Mr Cheape at All Saints and have a word with him. He might be able to help."

"Is that your last word on the matter, Mr Sedgefield?"

"Yes, it is. I've been perfectly reasonable in the circumstances."

"If that's all…"

"That's all I'm prepared to do. Is that clear?"

Ellen fell in her mother's arms.

"Now, this is all rather embarrassing, Mr and Mrs Gifford. I think we should terminate this conversation forthwith."

"But surely…"

"There's nothing more to say, Mr Gifford. Now is that clear?"

Mrs Gifford nodded her head. "Aye, it's as clear as a bead, Mr, but there'll be no need for us to come in on Monday."

"Oh, and why not?"

"Because we'll be taking out all our children from the school right away. Is that clear to you, Mr Sedgefield?

"Yes it is. Fine, Mrs Gifford."

Dudley turned to his father and rested his head on his shoulder. Joe began to cry.

"Right so. That's that, then." She held out her hand to Mr Sedgefield, who stared at her. "But being good Christian men, we shouldn't part on a sour note now, should we, for it'll shame us all?"

Wilfred stared at Mr Sedgefield. "Now's your chance to show what Catholicism is all about, Mr Sedgefield. Doesn't it mean we should behave without malice to each other, and forgive those who would test our patience?"

"We should always behave like Christians of the one true faith, sir."

Mrs Gifford waited a moment and then said, "Well let's do it properly anyroad, will we? I don't expect you'll want to shake me by the hand, Mr Sedgefield, me being such a common woman an' all." She sniffed and wiped her nose with her hand.

"So I'll just have to take the bull by the horns, and leave you with something else instead."

"What's that?"

"Well, it's just as righteous in its own way, that's for sure."

"What is it?"

"Well it's a sort of… how can I describe it?… It's a sort of an Irish saying, you might say. We say it just to clear the air when somebody like me departs from somebody like you, in circumstances not unlike our own, Mr Sedgefield, you know sir – just to make things right between us, so to speak."

"Yes, I understand. What is it?"

Mrs Gifford bowed her head and then looked him straight in the eye. "Are you ready now?"

"Yes, I am."

"Are you listening?"

"Yes, I'm listening."

"Are you listening, Mrs?"

"Oh, well yes, if I must. I'm listening, Mrs Gifford."

"Well, hear this." She took a breath and then whispered with a deep and sincere conviction, "*Póg Mo Thóin!*"

There was a long pause, with the only sound being the children's crying. Then Mr Sedgefield looked at Wilfred and said, "Well then, I suppose that er… in the spirit of true Catholic amendment and reconciliation, I should say 'Amen' to that."

He cocked his head to one side and smiled. "And if I might say so, Mrs Gifford, 'Bag Malone' to you too, and I hope you'll write to Mr Cheape at All Saints. I think you'll find him to be a fair man."

Then he turned, and taking Miss Groombridge by the arm he hurried away towards the main entrance. Mr Gifford's eyes widened and he blew out his cheeks. He took Ellen's hand, Joe took the other and they all went out of the gates. They turned into Gorton Lane and Mr Gifford said, "What did you have to say that for, Mary?" She said nothing. "I don't know if I'm on this earth or Fuller's Earth now. What are we going to do?"

"Oh, we'll do what we always do – as good Catholics, we'll leave it all unto God." They walked slowly towards the bridge, with Ellen and Joe still crying, and Mrs Gifford smiling every step of the way.

Pauline wasn't there when they arrived home. Later that day, at 4.21 p.m., some boys found her on the railway line just beyond Gorton Lane bridge. She had died from multiple injuries. At the funeral, Madeleine was inconsolable. It wasn't just that Pauline's death had affected her so badly, but she had also felt abandoned. When Wilfred Garside had heard about what had happened to Pauline, he'd moved out of his lodgings in Ardwick Green and had left work without collecting his wages. Nobody knew where he'd gone.

There was an inquest, and the coroner returned a verdict of death by misadventure, saying that he had been exercised by the circumstances leading up to the tragic event. When Pauline was a child, she had been sent out regularly by her parents to collect coal from the railway lines, and although this practice was commonplace in Gorton, it was one that was dangerous and wholly unacceptable in today's world. He also referred to a contributory factor recorded in the post mortem report: at the time of death, Pauline was three months pregnant and might, consequently, have been confused.

Ellen was standing in front of the mirror. She adjusted her hat and turned her head this way and that, before puckering her lips and looking at her teeth to make sure she hadn't got lipstick on them. Then she ran her hands down either side of her skirt, and turned to pick up her coat. She put it on and did up the buttons. Then she gathered up the letters on the table; she'd post these on her way to the bus stop. She opened the front door and went out. It was a lovely early spring morning, bright with clear skies and just right for her mood. She saw Mrs Bamford shaking a rug at the front door, and waved to her. "You can come and do mine after that, Mrs Mop!"

"And you can go and take a running jump, Mrs Parnaby!"

"It's going to be a nice day again today."

"Aye, I think we deserve it after the weather we've just been having!"

Ellen waved again, and turned into Church Lane. She hadn't gone far when she saw a man wearing a brimmed hat pulled well down over his eyes and a dark coat, collar turned up, walking slowly up the lane towards her. She looked down at the pavement and continued on her way. When she glanced up again, the man was standing still and was staring at her. It was a gaze that was steady and intense, and it made her feel uncomfortable. She came to where he was standing. The man put his arm out and stopped her.

"Get off me – what the 'ell do you think you're playing at?" She looked at him. He was breathing quickly.

"Princess!"

Ellen stared, and as he raised his head she caught a glimpse of a twinkling green eye. She took a closer look.

"Wilfred?"

He didn't speak at first; then he said, "Aye lass, it's me!"

They embraced. "Oh, Wilfred! Is it really you?"

"I just wanted to find…"

"Where have you been?"

"Are you all right?"

"Hush, hush, hush!"

They held hands at arm's length. "My, you've grown up, lass! You're beautiful, really beautiful."

Ellen let go of his hands. "You shouldn't say that! I'm not a little girl no more – I'm a respectable married woman now."

"I'm sorry. I didn't know. I just…"

"What are you doing here, anyroad?"

"I've come to find… to find you."

"Find me?"

"Aye, I want to say 'I'm sorry' and… and to say 'goodbye'."

"What for? Why? What's happened?"

"Look, Ellen – can I meet you? I need to talk to you. I need to explain."

Ellen couldn't think straight. "What for? I've got to go to work. I'll be late!"

Wilfred took her hands in his. "Just meet me, that's all. Just meet me."

She looked into his eyes – those eyes that had once met hers all those years ago, with lilies at the front door; those eyes she had looked into and found something beyond words, beyond all reason and beyond conscience; eyes that meant so much. She felt a turning of conviction and a flood of passion, and she said slowly and calmly, "I'll see you in Gorton

Park on Saturday afternoon, at half past two. My husband, Frank – he'll be at work then, on a two-ten shift."

"Make it six o'clock and meet me on the opposite side of the road to the park gates, near Sharple's shop. It'll be going dark then, and what with the blackout it'll be less obvious. There's too many people round here that I don't want to meet."

"All right then. I'll be there, Wilfred."

"Aye, be there. It'll be good to see you, but don't tell no one will you, Ellen?"

"No – I won't."

She held him, and he kissed her on the cheek. She returned the kiss on his lips before hurrying off down the lane towards the factory gates, without looking back.

It was getting dark. They walked slowly away from the park gates and down Crossley Street.

"Let's hope no one sees us."

"They won't if we walk close to the walls and we keep looking down."

"I'll link you an' all." Ellen took his arm, and looked at him. "Please tell me, Wilfred, what have you come back for?"

"They're sending me away, Ellen."

"Where?"

"I can't tell you that, but I can tell you it might be dangerous."

"Why will it be dangerous? Who's sending you?"

"It's war work, Ellen, I can't tell you what. I'm down in London and they've given us four days' leave to say our goodbyes."

"You've come to say 'goodbye' to me?"

"Aye, in case it's the last time I'll see you. I want to put things right between us."

"Why me?"

"There's nobody else. I've only got my brother,

and he's in France with the army. There's only you, now – only you that I care about, anyroad."

Ellen didn't quite know what to say, but she couldn't help feeling flattered, and proud to be treated so gallantly. She smiled and then frowned. "Why did you go away when our Pauline died?"

"I knew they'd all blame me. I had to go."

"You could have told us first. You could have said something to Madeleine, couldn't you?"

"Madeleine didn't need me, and I didn't need her. She was just out for what she could get."

"Did you know Pauline was pregnant?"

"Course I did. She told me."

"Didn't you think you should have stayed to look after her? It was your baby, wasn't it?"

"It wasn't mine! I never went near her! That's why I left her and started courting Madeleine."

"Who did that to her, then?"

"Don't ask me! I don't know. She said she was a virgin when I met her. And I knew, when she told me, that they'd all blame me – so I left and went to stop with my brother in London."

They walked without saying anything; then Wilfred said, "And that's when I met Miriam, Miriam Reissmann. I fell for her, I did, and I went to live with her in Germany."

For a long time Ellen didn't speak; then she asked, "What's happened to her, then? Have you said your goodbyes to her an' all?"

"I can't! I stayed there with her for years, and then the bastards took her from me. They took her, and she's gone now and she won't be coming back. They were after me, an' all. I had to get out. But I haven't forgotten what they did to her. That's why I'm going away."

Ellen didn't quite know what to make of this, but eventually she said, "When you left I was just a little lass. I wasn't a woman or nowt. What was I to you?

Why did you like me then?"

"I thought you'd have known better. You weren't just a little lass. No! You were Ellen, Ellen Gifford, just as you are now and just as you'll be when you're dead old. That's who you are and what you are, and that's what I saw then and what I can see now – only, only more so now. That's why I had to come back. I had to come back because of you." They stopped and turned to one another, and in the darkness that held them they kissed.

They got to the wire fence where it had come away from the metal stake that held it. Ellen pulled it up, and Wilfred ducked down and climbed through the gap onto the railway embankment. Ellen followed. They made their way down to the red and white signal.

Ellen whispered, "Are you sure you're all right? This is the same line, you know."

"There's nowhere else, is there? Better here than nowhere. Needs is must, Ellen."

Ellen took off her coat and spread it on the grassy slope. Wilfred took his coat off too, and they draped it over themselves as they lay down. And there, by the gully, they lay in shrouded silence, searching for each other and sensing the mystery of what they had become.

Ellen cleaned her coat in the sink, and never told Frank about Wilfred's visit. She never told him about the passion that had been Wilfred's, and that now was hers. But she did tell him that she was pregnant, and Frank had cried. Frank often cried; he was easily moved, but not so easily inclined to do anything other than cry when he was. They'd wanted a child for some time, and Ellen had always said that if their first child was a girl they would call her 'Pauline'. But in the event it was a boy, a weak little boy, and they called him 'Paul'. Ellen never heard from Wilfred again. Nobody ever did. His last words to her as they climbed the railway embankment had been, "I'll come back again some day, lass – you know that, don't you?" But he never did come back. She'd wanted to tell him so many things. She'd wanted to tell him about the way he'd changed her life forever, and about Paul. She'd wanted that more than anything.

But there was something she could never have told him; it would be her secret for ever. She'd never tell anybody about the half-crown, the dragon's blood, the whispered words and all the brightness of Irish magic that had brought her incarnation into the world.

Lilies in a Briared Wreath: Paul's Story

On mornings such as this, if Paul Parnaby wasn't sitting alone on the railway embankment he was in the backyard, sitting alone on the roof of the coal shed. Today, the sun was shining and he was sitting on the roof with his arms around his legs and his head resting on his knees. His mother had told him to sit in the sun because it would do him good. She said it might put some colour in his face and dry the sores on his arms. Paul had forgotten about the sores and didn't know why the sun would make them better, but he believed her and besides, it was good to sit on the coal shed roof. He was safe there, and he could dream. He knew that he wasn't clever like his sisters. He didn't know much and he wasn't happy at school, but he could dream – and dreaming was like a friend.

The breeze smelt of hot oil from Tether & Armley's factory. It blew over the brick walls and played gently with his hair. Paul thought about his mother and how she used to stroke his hair, so gently, so very gently. That was a long time ago. Things were different now; so much had changed. But there were some things that had stayed the same, like the steam hammers pounding in the factory yard. They were like friends. Paul knew each one of them. They struck the hours in Gorton and gave it life. Boys had learned to make the sound of them, girls had learned to skip to them and everybody knew their names. This one was called 'Bimbo'. You could hear him all day – bim-bo, bim-bo – the beat of Gorton's heavy heart.

Mrs Parnaby was making a pot of tea. She could see Paul through the kitchen window. She stared at him and whispered, "Poor little mite – he looks like something out of Belsen." Mr Parnaby came in winding a ball of green twine. He followed her gaze. "What's to do, Mam?"

"Have you seen our Paul, Frank? He's as thin as a lath."

"Aye, I know. He's like a little monkey, isn't he?"

"Oh, don't say that!"

Mr Parnaby laughed. "I just meant that he's a funny little thing."

"It's not funny, Frank! You could strike matches on them ribs!"

"But what can we do?"

"We can do nowt, Frank – nowt at all."

"We could maybe try an' build him up a bit."

"Aye, I know that! Doctor Hardwicke said I've got to get some meat inside him, but meat doesn't grow on trees, does it? It's rationed! If it wasn't for Madeleine and that Jimmy Kidd from Smithfield Market, we'd be... well, I just don't know."

"I do my best to provide, Mam. It's just that...."

"I've tried though, I've really tried. I've tried him with everything – stewed tripe, luncheon meat, ox cheek and boiled ribs – but he won't touch any of it. He just won't touch it."

"Well, maybe it's just a phrase he's going through, like."

"I've tried him with oxtail, liver, jellied brawn, sheep's heart, pig's trotters, meat paste..."

"He likes savoury ducks with plenty of gravy on though, doesn't he?"

"Well he did, but he doesn't any more – not since he found a row of blond eyelashes in one of 'em."

"What were they doing there?"

"Don't ask me, but he won't touch savoury ducks now. He just won't go near them."

"I've always liked neck of mutton with pearl barley myself. Maybe…"

"Oh, I've tried him with that. He won't have it. The only thing he'll have is corned beef. Aye, corned beef, beans and mashed potatoes – oh, and tinned soup. That's it, and there's nowt in a tin of soup to stick to his ribs, is there?"

"I've never liked corned beef, myself."

"We seldom have it, Frank."

"It's a good job. I'd never eat it!"

"You do – it's in your potato 'ash!"

"It's in our potato 'ash?"

"I just feel rejected, Frank. He doesn't like what I make for him and it's like, it's like… he doesn't like *me*." Mrs Parnaby sniffed and searched in her pinny for her handkerchief. "What have I ever done to him to deserve all this?"

"Nowt, Mam. Nowt at all! It's all right. Hush, hush! Don't upset yourself."

"He just sits up there… He doesn't do anything. He just sits there. He makes me dead sad. He really does! He doesn't even wear socks or nowt on his feet. He says he can't bear owt on his feet!"

"Aye, he makes me dead sad an' all – he doesn't even play football. He's got no interest in it. What kind of son is it that doesn't even play football?"

"Never mind bloody football – he doesn't even play with his sisters!"

"What can we do?"

"I don't know what we're going to do, Frank – but we'll have to think of something, that's for sure."

The sun was strong. Paul could feel its warmth on his skin, and it set pink light under his eyelids. His mind was drifting. His thoughts followed the dull beat of the steam hammer, and slowly its rhythm became the crash of oars on a Saxon longship surging through heavy seas. He'd seen a picture of something like it at school. There was a man at the helm. Paul watched him. His face was turned towards the sun, and the wind lifted his hair. It might have been a vision of pure light – streams of solar yellow, a Saxon's hair gently feathered in the morning freshness. Then, without a sound, the oars lifted and the longship disappeared into the blinding light of heaven's plane. Sometimes things don't make sense. Sometimes things don't even *have* any sense. Sometimes there's emptiness at the heart of the world.

Paul imagined things he'd seen in books: open skies, and waves breaking upon purple shores. He saw cottages along lanes that led to forests and beyond, to apple orchards and perfumed hay meadows, where flowers grew like scattered dolly mixtures: pale blue, pink and white petals lightened by the sun. Then, from a scalp prickling in sweat, there arose buds of blood: hard black beads pushing upwards through the flesh and into the light. Dark stems trilled from his mouth, and opened delicate white flowers blushed full damson in the throat. And all the while, the breath of heaven carried on the wind. Sparrows chirruped in the yard, and his family circled round him in an inane dance.

He imagined that somewhere beyond the factory rooves, barking dogs had set off stiff legged in rotating steel wheels. He could feel his washed and bleached body being shunted along railway lines to unknown places. It was like being driven out of the past, and being drawn towards the future – a future that was beyond all imagining. A dark future pulsing with unconscious blood: a future that was on fire. Where would it lead? Suddenly a girl's voice called, "Paul, our Mam says you've got to put your boots on and come down and get your dinner!" It was his sister, Molly. "It's tongue butties." Paul opened his eyes. There was Molly looking up at him. She was surrounded by the clutter in the yard: beyond the clothesline and prop, there were ladders, a mop and bucket, paraffin cans, tins of paint and a tin bath hanging on the wall. Somehow it all seemed different. Things looked coarse. Things were not things. Words were not words. Names were empty, like bubbles on the breath. It was as though he didn't know the world any more. What had happened to it? What was happening to him? He climbed down the drainpipe and followed his sister into the darkened house.

Mrs Parnaby came into the bedroom and sat at the bottom of Paul's bed. Paul looked up from the book he was reading and stared at his mother.

"Paul, I want to talk to you."

"What about, Mam?"

"It's about your food, Paul – why won't you eat your food?"

"Aw, Mam!"

"Don't 'aw Mam' me. This needs sorting out. You're so aggravating, Paul!"

Paul put the book down and turned his face to the window.

"I make you good food, Paul. Everybody else likes it. Your sisters like it, and your dad likes it! So why don't you like it?"

Paul opened his mouth and started to pant.

"Look at me, Paul!"

Paul turned to his mother, but his eyes looked to one side of her.

"Dr Hardwicke said you've got to eat, and he should know – he's a doctor."

Paul didn't say anything.

"Well say something, Paul! Why won't you eat?"

There was a long silence and then Paul said quietly, "I just… I just don't want to, Mam."

"What do you mean 'you don't want to'? You can't give up eating because 'you just don't want to' – what's wrong with you?"

Paul turned away and said nothing.

Mrs Parnaby changed her tone and said with some urgency, "Is it me, Paul? Is it me that you don't like?"

"No, Mam!"

"Well what is it then? Why won't you eat?"

"It's just that…"

"Yes?"

"It's just that I don't like animals getting killed."

"You don't like animals getting killed? But that's what they're for, you soft ha'porth!"

"Aw, Mam – are you sure?"

"Aye, as sure as death! It's all down there in black and white in the Bible – animals are for killing and eating. The Bible's always right, Paul. That's why it's the Bible!"

"But animals are like… they're like little children, and you don't kill little children, do you?"

"No they're not – they're not like little children! They haven't got souls."

"They haven't got souls?"

"That's right, Paul! That's why you can eat them."

"Why haven't they got souls?"

"Because they're like Protestants – they don't go to heaven!"

"Where do they go then?"

"Well, when they're bad, they go off to the knacker's yard and that's the end of them, but when they're good they go straight into our bellies where they belong."

Paul didn't know what to say. His mother was all there was, all he ever trusted, but this time, she was wrong. Why didn't she know that animals were like friends? You don't eat friends! Then after a while he said, "I'd like an animal, Mam. I would. I'd like a dog, maybe."

"Don't talk daft, Paul."

"Dogs are my favourite."

"It'd be just another mouth to feed!"

"I'd feed it, Mam."

"You feed it? How could you feed it, when you can't even feed yourself?"

Paul said nothing; he was thinking. Then he asked, "What does your soul look like, Mam?"

Mrs Parnaby moved closer to him and whispered, "Your soul's in your heart, and it's as big as your chest."

Paul opened both hands and put them on his chest.

"It's white like satin and it's in a kind of hoop."

"It's in a hoop?"

"Aye, and it's got wings on either side of it."

Paul was listening intently.

"And when you do something bad, like when you tell a lie or you're greedy or you don't do what you're told, then a dirty stain appears on the clean satin and by the end of the week your hoop looks dirty and filthy and all stained. And that's why you've got to go the Monastery and confess your sins so you can get absolution, and when you get absolution all the dirt and the germs are washed out and your hoop's all clean again."

Paul was still listening.

"And when you die, your soul flies to purgatory and it's looked at. And if you've just been to confession and you've died in the street, right there – you're stone dead on the pavement outside the Monastery – your hoop's spotless and you go straight to heaven, but if you've not been to confession they find that your hoop's all dirty and filthy and all stained, and then…"

"Then you go to hell, don't you Mam?"

"Then you go to hell, Paul, where they do awful

things to you. My God, it'll be more awfuller than you've ever known, you'll be punished, and you'll be in torment forever and forever for being a dirty, filthy little sinner."

Paul stared straight ahead for a long time before turning to his mother and asking softly, "What's it like in hell?"

"Oh, it's awful, Paul. When I was at school the nuns made me look at a picture of it on the wall. It was awful. Everybody's got no clothes on. Everybody can see your bits, all the dinky-dos and everything. There's no hiding them, you know."

Paul had heard all this before, but he needed to hear it again and Mrs Parnaby needed to tell it again. His jaw opened. He stared round the room, and he began to pant.

"Not only that, there's fires and boiling pitch that you get pushed into with hooks and packing knives and there's... there's demons with pikes and spikes and beaks that bite, for ever and ever, demons with beaks biting and cracking your face, your ribs and fingers and everything."

Paul looked round the room. Was this right? Things were not things. Words were not words. Names were empty. His thoughts began to drift to the blind dog in Pine Street who loved him. He remembered the butterfly fields in books, and the pigeons pecking bread on the rec. He thought about his dreams, about George and the Dragon, the lion and the lamb and those dreaming hours on the coal shed roof. He listened for the waves breaking on purple shores, and the heavy heartbeat of hammers in the yard. The sound of hammered steel turned to pounding in his ears, a dull pulsing of blood deep within the skull. The fires in his flesh were like the fires of hell, and his eyes filled with tears. He looked his mother full in the face and said softly, "Mam, Mam – please – is my hoop dirty?"

"Of course it is! What do you expect? You're wilful and you won't eat meat, that's why you need to go to confession."

There was silence; then Paul reached out his hand. "Mam, please don't let them bite me. I'll go to confession. I will, Mam, I promise – honest to God, I will. I promise!"

"Promise! Promise? Promises are like piecrusts, Paul."

"What, they're dead hard, you mean?"

"No – I mean they're made to be broken!"

"I'll go, Mam. I will."

"All right! See that you do!"

Paul gazed around the room. "It's just that I don't like going sometimes. I don't like talking about some things. I don't like telling them things and then being told I'm bad when I'm always doing my best to be good."

"You don't understand, Paul."

"How can I understand then?"

"Well, you can start by saying your prayers."

Paul looked down at the bedclothes. For several minutes he just looked down. Then he crossed himself quickly and said in a whispered monotone, "O my God, I am heartily sorry for having offended thee and I detest all my sins, because I dread the loss of heaven and the pains of hell, but most of all because they offend thee, my God, who art all good and deserving of all my love. I firmly resolve, with the help of thy grace, to confess my sins, to do penance and to amend my life. Amen."

Mrs Parnaby smiled and then said, "Right then, now do the 'Infant Jesus'.

"Aw, Mam."

"Say it!"

Paul closed his eyes, put his hands together in prayer and whispered, "Infant Jesus meek and mild. Look down on me a little child. If I should die before I wake, I pray to God my soul to take. Amen."

"There now – that'll do for now, but I want you at confession next Sunday. Have you got that?" She got up and walked to the door. Then she turned and stared at him. Paul stared back at her. There was a long silence; then Mrs Parnaby said, "Anyroad, what's that book you're reading?"

"It's called, *The Water Babies*."

"Oh aye, I tried to read that one once, but I can't remember much about it now. Is it any good?

Paul looked up and said, "It's a bit hard sometimes, but it's about a boy, a boy like me, who wanted to make things better."

Mrs Parnaby stared at him for a long time. "Is it?" She shook her head. "Make things better! Make things better? What are you reading about making things better for? You want to start making yourself better, that's what you want to do, Paul Parnaby! And you can start by putting something on your feet!" Then she went out.

Mr Parnaby was stitching cut-out patches of bicycle tyres onto the soles of Paul's old boots with strong twine. There was plenty of wear in them now. He couldn't let Paul go round with holes in his soles; it wouldn't be fair. He'd hammer some studs in later. That should do the trick. He'd do anything for his son. One son and two daughters – that's what he had. Paul was a bit thin and he didn't do much, but he could read and he was his son. The girls could read too, especially Beau, who was a real daddy's girl. Not that he wanted her at first. "What do you want, Frankie – a boy or son?" He'd heard that time and time again in the factory yard when Ellen was carrying their third child. But when the baby was born it was a girl. She grew up well though. Some girls were pretty and some were clever. Some were neither of course, but Beau was both. He couldn't have wished for a better daughter, but he'd wanted a boy. Girls are all right, but he had one already and he wanted another boy. Men want sons and Paul was his only son – and like any father, he'd do anything for his son. He mused silently about his lot and then he whispered, "And besides, you have to be a man to make a girl."

Paul came in.

"You've got some socks on, son!"

"Aye, Dad – Mam said."

"You'll be able to put these boots on an' all soon. I've nearly done with 'em."

"You've put bike tyres on again haven't you, Dad?"

"Aye, son – we can't have you going round with holes in your soles can we?"

"Aw, no! I don't want them on!"

"Why not, son?"

"You know why! They'll get me at school! They'll get me, Dad!"

"No, they won't. They way I've done them this time they won't even see them! Come on – don't worry! Come here, you daft ha'porth."

Paul went to his father and laid his head against his chest.

"Come on son, sit down here."

"You don't know what they're like. If they see you've got daft boots on, they'll rag you all the time."

Mr Parnaby stroked Paul's hair. "It's May Day on Monday. Why don't you help your sisters make the May Bower?"

"Have I got to?"

"Aye, it'll be fun and you might make some coppers out of it."

"They made something last year, didn't they?"

"Aye, they did and we got some good socks out of it an' all."

"Why do we do it, Dad?"

"Do what?"

"You know, go round the streets singing on May Day?"

"I don't know son."

"Not many people do it round here now, anyroad."

"No, son. May Day isn't the same now as it used to be. When I was a lad they used to dress up all the horses with flowers and rags and ribbons. They got all the brass buckles and suns and moons that horses wear and put them in bags of sand strapped to the wheels of their carts for days and days to burnish them up ready for the big day. Then they'd wash and comb the horses' tails and brush their coats – and they'd even put boot polish on to shine their hooves!"

"Did they?"

"Aye, and the night before, they'd stay up with them all night to make sure they didn't lie down and spoil themselves before the morning and when morning came, they'd ride out and the horses knew they were all done up nice because they'd lift their legs all fancy like and step out like thoroughbreds on their way round town."

Paul had gone into a dream. They lay in each others arms for a while and then Paul said, "I like horses, Dad, a dead lot."

"I know, son. I know."

"I wish I could wash a horse and ride him round."

"I know, son. I know."

"I wish I could wash a dog an' all and run with him all round the streets."

"Aye, son, but you'd have to put your boots on first!"

"If I had a dog, Dad, I'd wear my boots all the time, honest to God, I would."

"What about the kids at school?"

"A dog's worth a good thumping, Dad."

Mr Parnaby looked into Paul's face and said, "I'd like a dog an' all, but your Mam won't let me get one. Aye, I've always wanted a dog."

"Have you, Dad? Why?"

"Ever since my little brother got one."

"Uncle Ernie?"

"Aye, your nana and granddad got one for him, but they never got one for me."

"What was Uncle Ernie's dog like?"

"He was a little black one. Aye, he was a good little dog an' all. He did tricks and he was good at jumping. You should've seen him!"

"What was he called?"

"Bob."

"Bob? That's a funny name, isn't it?"

"Why, what's wrong with it?"

"Well, you know, Bob's a lad's name. It's not like a dog's name, like Laddy, or Rex or Bruce, is it?"

"Yes it is – there was a clever dog called Black Bob, wasn't there? He was in all the comics. That's where my brother got the name from."

"Do you think we'll ever get a dog, Dad?

"I don't rightly know son. I'll ask your mam again maybe."

Paul didn't move for a long time and then he said, "I'd better put my boots and socks on in case she says yes."

It was Sunday morning and Mrs Parnaby was clearing up the breakfast things. She was whispering to herself, "There's nothing like a cup of tea and a plateful of dip butties to put a smile on your face after Mass!" She put the plates in the sink and looked out of the kitchen window. Frank was in the yard with the girls. They were sitting on a rug making a bower of paper leaves for May Day. What a sight! Frank was so patient with them. She was blessed, so very blessed. He was such a devoted father to his children. She watched him talking to Beau. She was looking at him intently, and listening to his every word. Frank was explaining something; Mrs Parnaby, watching the gestures he made, tried to guess what it was he was talking about. Whatever he was saying was making Beau smile and then giggle. Molly looked up from what she was doing, and her face too lit up with joy. Frank stroked Beau's hair; then he picked her up and sat her on his knee. What a pity Paul wasn't there to enjoy all this with them – but he was up in the bedroom polishing his foreign coins with Duraglit and an old cloth. Polishing foreign coins! She shook her head and pushed her tongue between her lips. At least he'd been to confession that day, and that was good. She sighed. "I only hope his soul is as shiny as his precious bloody coins."

There was a knock at the door. Mrs Parnaby got up and opened it. It was Madeleine Ellis and her boyfriend Jimmy Kidd. Jimmy was holding a brown canvas shopping bag. "Oh, it's you, Madeleine! We weren't expecting anybody today – it's Sunday! Jimmy was grinning under his thin black moustache. "Guess who it isn't, Ellen!" He pushed past Madeleine, stepped over the threshold and kissed Mrs Parnaby on the lips. She turned away and said, "Come on in, Madeleine, Jimmy, and make yourselves at home!" Madeleine went in and sat down. Jimmy moved Mr Parnaby's slippers and cigarettes. "Frank won't mind me keeping his chair warm for him will he, Ellen?"

"Oh, no – no, you're all right there, Jimmy. Sit down. Do you want a drink of tea?"

"Aye, Ellen. Go on then."

"You, Madeleine?"

"Aye, go on then – two sugars."

Mrs Parnaby went into the kitchen, banged on the window and beckoned to Mr Parnaby to come in. In a short while he appeared in the doorway, smoothing some of the creases out his collar. He didn't know Madeleine and Jimmy that well. They were Ellen's friends really, and when they came round he didn't know what to say to them. Ellen had got to know Madeleine years ago when she had come across her wandering the streets in the rain without any shoes on. She was crying. Jimmy had just 'gone on his holidays' to Strangeways, after some business involving the theft of a bike and a large amount of mercury from Avro's factory in Chadderton. Mrs Parnaby had taken Madeleine in and looked after her until she'd felt able to go back home. And when Jimmy came out of prison, Mrs Parnaby's brother, Joseph, had got him a job as a porter at Smithfield Market. Since then, the two of them couldn't do enough for the Parnabys. Madeleine was something high up in Lewis's, and she could get bits and pieces like vests and socks dirt cheap and without coupons. She once sold them a pink eiderdown for Paul, when you couldn't get hold of eiderdowns. It was cheap because there was blood on it. Madeleine said that one of the girls in the bedding section had cut her finger when she was packing it. Mrs Parnaby was really pleased. The blood didn't matter – after all, a good eiderdown was a good eiderdown. Jimmy brought them fruit and vegetables and sometimes, cheap meat. He got them cigarettes too, and once sold Mr Parnaby a cigarette lighter and some packets of flints to go with it.

Mr Parnaby stood there fiddling with his fingers and smiling like a child. Mrs Parnaby turned to him. "Well sit down, Frank, sit down!" He sat down on a stool, and Mrs Parnaby went to the kitchen to put the kettle on. Jimmy felt in his pockets and pulled out a packet of cigarettes. He seemed to have gold rings on every finger. He opened the packet and offered one to Madeleine and then one to Mr Parnaby. He took one himself and put it between his lips whilst he felt in his pocket for his lighter. After lighting Madeleine's cigarette and then Mr Parnaby's, he snapped the lighter shut before flicking it into flame again and lighting his own. "Don't want to be third time unlucky, do I?" He looked across at Mr Parnaby. "How are you doing, Frank?"

"Oh you know, Jimmy, Fairfield to Middleton."

"And how's work?"

"Well you know, Jimmy – I'm a worker. When I'm not working at Tether & Armley's, I'm cleaning windows."

"Aye, Jimmy – he's a grafter right enough. He has to be."

"Aye, I know that, Ellen. I've heard." He turned to Frank. "And er… how are you doing for fags? You see, er, I might have some Kensitas on the cheap like, if you fancy them."

"How much?"

"Ninepence for a packet of twenty, Frank. How many packets do you want?"

Madeleine nodded. "That's dead cheap, isn't it, Frank?"

"Oh, er, can you get me ten packets then?"

"Aye, all right, Frank. Just for you, Frank. I can stretch that far for you."

"I'll pay you back at the end of the week when I get my wages."

"I'll let you have ten packets now, but I want paying Saturday morning, all right?"

"Right oh then, Jimmy. Saturday morning."

Jimmy opened his shopping bag and rummaged in it. Then he brought out some packets of cigarettes. "Now, they're slightly bent, but they're all right. It's just that I accidentally sat on them on the bus."

"I hope they're not bent in another way, Jimmy. I don't want no monkey business!"

"Bent? Ah, you're a right comedian, Frank! You're a comedian right enough."

"I don't want PC 49 coming round here to get me."

"Frank! You know me! It's just that they're seconds, just seconds – there's a slight flaw in their size, that's all and you won't notice that when you've a pint in your hand now, will you?"

Madeleine nodded. "And think of the money you'll be saving."

Mr Parnaby took the cigarettes. "They look like they've been bent round a corner."

"Oh, they'll soon straighten out now, Frank." Jimmy took a packet and tried to straighten it between the palms of his hands. "There you are, as good as new. It's just that the packet's a bit crumpled, that's all. Inside the packet, they're as good as new."

Mrs Parnaby came in with a tray full of mugs and a teapot. "Oh, so you've brought us some cigarettes, Jimmy? You are good to us."

"Aye, Ellen. You know me – I do what I can."

"I know that, Jim! You're one of the best!"

Jimmy offered the packet of cigarettes. "Do you want one, sugar?"

"No ta, Jimmy. I don't smoke."

Aw, go on. It'll clear your lungs and keep you slim."

Madeleine nodded. "Go on! Have one, Ellen – he thinks it's dead swish to see a younger woman smoke a cigarette!"

"Oh, go on then, Jimmy. I'll have one."

"That's the ticket, Ellen!"

Jimmy took a cigarette out of the packet and gave it to Mrs. Parnaby. He lit it. She turned away and blew smoke out shyly.

"There you are Ellen. You're just like Betty Grable in that film, you know, *Pin Up Girl*!" Everybody laughed. Mrs Parnaby smiled and drew heavily on the cigarette.

Madeleine changed the subject. "How's the girls doing, Ellen?"

"They're all right, Madeleine. They're both doing all right at school. Beau is top of the class. Mr Benfold says she's a little belter!"

"Does he? That's good!"

"Aye, and Molly's all right too. She reads a lot though and she's a bit, a bit... quiet, if you catch my drift."

"Quiet? What do you mean?"

"Well, you know – sometimes I think she feels better off with books than with people."

"Tut, tut, tut, do you reckon?"

"Aye, give her a book and she's off in a world of her own."

Mr Parnaby joined in: "She'll grow out of it, Ellen. It's Paul I worry about. When he's not sitting on the coal shed roof with no socks on, he's on the railway embankment."

"On the railway embankment?"

"Aye, it's not right that, is it?"

"Bloody 'ell! He doesn't want to go there, he'll catch fever!"

"Aye, I don't like him going there. He's been there again ever since we came back from Mass! And there's nothing on him, Madeleine. You should see him. Dr Hardwicke says we've got to get some meat inside him."

Madeleine stared into space. "He's got dead nice eyes though."

"Whatever we give him tripe, scrag end of neck, ribs, you name it, he won't touch it!"

"Why not?"

"Not a scrap and now, the poor little bugger – well, he's all skin and bones."

Jimmy looked amused. "Have you tried him with

liver and onions? He'll eat that! Everybody likes liver and onions."

"He won't touch it, Jim."

Jimmy thought for a moment. "How about rabbit then?"

"Erm, do you know, I've never tried him with rabbit!"

Mr Parnaby put the palm of his hand against his face. "I like rabbit."

"So do I!"

"We've not had rabbit for a while, Frank. Shall we try him with some?"

"Aye, we can, but can you still get hold of it?"

Jimmy smiled. "I'll get you some rabbit meat, Ellen – a mate of mine skins them and he sells them dirt cheap."

"Does he? How cheap is cheap?"

"Pennies, Ellen, just pennies and er… no coupons."

"No coupons?"

"Aye, you get a good parcel of rabbit meat and some carrots and that to make a rabbit stew. It's dead cheap!"

"How much is 'dead cheap', though?"

"Er … big or little?"

Mrs Parnaby looked at Mr Parnaby.

Jimmy cleared his throat. "You'd better get the big parcel, Frank if you're all going to have a bit each."

"Aye, all right then, Jimmy – we'll have a big one."

"That'll be… er two and six, then."

"Two and six? That's not flippin' cheap…"

"It's for Paul, Frank. You're going to do your best for Paul, aren't you?"

"Aye, Ellen. I'm trying to do my best, anyroad."

"Right oh then Jim, get us a half-a-crown parcel then. We'll find it somehow, we'll find it."

"Right oh, Ellen. I'll bring a big parcel round when I come for my money on Friday!"

"You mean Saturday."

"Aye, I mean on Saturday."

"All right, Jim. You're on."

"Leave it to me. You know me. I never let you down."

Madeleine shook her head. "I wonder why Paul won't have meat, Ellen?"

"Oh he says he doesn't like killing animals or something."

"That's a bit daft, isn't it? You've got to kill them before you eat them, haven't you?"

"He just won't listen."

"You'll just have to knock it out of him then, Ellen!"

"How, though? How?"

Jimmy smiled. "I know – all you have to do is some reverse psychiatry."

"Reverse psychiatry?"

"Aye."

"What's that when it's at home?"

Madeleine touched Mrs Parnaby's hand. "He doesn't half come out with these things, doesn't he?"

Jimmy was enjoying the moment. "Well you know what the butchers on the market do don't you?"

"What?"

"When they're teaching young apprentices how to slaughter the animals?"

"No, what do they do?"

"Well, they get a sheep in a field don't they? And then they give the lad a blade and tell him to kill it. They just say, 'Right, cut it there, right across the neck.'" He made a slicing movement across his neck with a finger. "If the lad does it, he's all right, but if you get some Nancy boy who won't do it, you know what they do?"

"No, what?"

"They let the sheep go and tell the lad to get his jacket off and run after it and catch it!"

"What for? What good does that do?"

"Well think of it – if you've been chasing the sheep round and round for an hour or two, when you do catch it, you'll be only too happy to stick the ruddy thing!"

"Does it work?"

"Oh, aye. It always works. That's why you should think about getting Paul an animal."

"An animal?"

"Aye, it's reverse psychiatry."

"Why, what do you mean?"

"Well, if he's got to look after an animal all the time he'll soon change his mind. If he's got to feed it and clean it and do for it and all that he'll soon change his mind about animals. He'll get tired of it, won't he? And then he'll start to see it for what it is. It's just an animal. That's all it is, and then he'll lose all his daft ideas about killing them, won't he? It stands to reason."

"Aye, I get it now! Then he'll eat meat and he'll start putting weight on!"

"Aye, that's it, Ellen. That's it!"

"That's dead crafty, that is!"

"It's reverse psychiatry."

"He told me he wants a dog."

"Aye, he told me that an' all."

"We don't want a dog though, do we, Frank?"

"You know me – I've always wanted one, but you never let me have one."

"It'll be just another mouth to feed though, Frank, won't it?"

"Aye, but Paul said that if he had a dog he'd put his socks and boots on."

"Did he?"

Jimmy leaned forward. "It wouldn't be another mouth to feed, Ellen. You'll just have to give it plate scrapings, cold tea, bits and pieces and all that out the kitchen. If it's a small dog it won't eat much. That's why small dogs are the best."

"Oh, I don't know…"

"We could get him just a little one, then it won't eat much will it? And it'll be good to see Paul wearing something on his feet!"

"I can get you a small dog, Ellen."

"Could you, Jim?"

"Aye, I've got a mate in Tib Street. He'll get you one out of a litter for you."

"Well, I don't know."

"It'll just be a small one – just an ordinary dog. If you don't like it you can send it back."

"Send it back?"

"Aye, and he'll even dock its tail for you, so you don't have to get a dog licence."

"Oh, I didn't know that."

"Aye, do you know how he does it, eh?"

"No, how?"

"When they're a few days old, he just gets them and bites their tails off one after another – gomp, gomp, gomp – and then he dips their stumps in treacle!" He laughed.

"Oh, bloo-dy 'ell!"

"Treacle? What does he do that for?"

"Aye, treacle, so they'll all lick themselves better afterwards!"

"Bloo-dy 'ell!"

"Aye, you should see 'em! Eh, but you won't tell Paul that though, will you?" He laughed. "He might come and get me!"

There was silence and then Mrs Parnaby said, "What do you think, Jim?"

There was silence and then Mr Parnaby said suddenly, "How much will it cost, Jimmy?"

"Oh, not much – I can get you one for a… for a quid."

"How much?"

"One pound, Frankie boy!"

"A pound? I'm not made of it you know. First the

cigarettes, then the rabbit meat and now a pound for a dog! I'm not ruddy made of it you know."

"Frank!"

"I can't afford all that, Jimmy!"

Everybody went quiet and then Jimmy said, "I'll tell you what, Frank – you're a good pal of mine – so I'll tell you what we'll do. Save your money and you can have the cigarettes, the rabbit meat and the dog if you'll clean my mate's windows for five months."

"Five months?"

"I can't be any fairer than that now Frank, can I?"

"That's a good offer, Frank!"

"For five months?"

"Just five months and then that's it. You won't owe nobody nowt.

Mr Parnaby put a hand to his face and then looked at Mrs Parnaby. "What will we do, Ellen?"

"Well, I mean five months isn't very long and we can always take the dog back if we don't like it, Frank."

"And I'll fetch it some dog meat every so often an' all – and all for nowt!"

Mr Parnaby perked up. "Go on then, Jimmy! You're on. Five months. I'll do it."

Jimmy held out his hand. "Here's my heart, here's my hand, Frank." They shook hands.

"I knew you'd do it, Frank. You've got the cigarettes, so I'll bring the rest next week."

"When?"

"Saturday morning – one big rabbit and one small dog! One big, one small – that's how to remember it!"

"Make sure it's a dog and not a bitch, Jimmy. We don't want puppies everywhere, do we?"

"Aye, right oh then, Ellen! Leave it to me."

"Ta, Jimmy!"

"What are you thinking, Frank?"

Frank didn't reply for a long time, and then he said, "Oh, I'm thinking of calling him Bob."

The sun was shining. Paul was lying on the railway embankment with his face resting against the coarse grass. He'd been there since he'd come back from Mass, just lying, just being what he was, just dreaming about this and that. Black Fives had clanked by with wagons full of coal and coiled wire and rusting metal, and lit with deepest red fire from their fireboxes. Engine drivers had looked out and had seen him or missed him, but without showing any interest in him whatsoever. Paul had looked at insects in the roots of pulled-up sods. He'd watched butterflies, left this time to their own pure white traces of light and not chased on ragged wings by boys with coats and jam jars full of cabbage leaves. Even when it rained he hadn't moved. He'd just laid there as damp as soil, smelling tangled roots and pitch and listening to the waters rilling through the gullies. He was interred in earth, interred in the stony ground that clutched his flesh and held him close to itself and preserved him in life. And there he'd lain listening to the world in all its tragedy, the sucking earth and the throbbing in his ears, where he'd felt the dull ache of something cloying in the brain: something seeping through its soft tissue in tears of ruptured blood. He'd lain there in pain and full of sorrow and he'd prayed because he'd felt so alone.

Beau looked over the railway sleepers that made up the fence by the cutting and saw Paul in his usual place, lying by the gully near the red and white signal. She lifted the mug of milk onto the top plank and then climbed the fence and stretched her leg to meet the metal bolts driven in as footholds on the other side of the sleepers. When she was halfway down she reached for the mug and then stepped onto the railway embankment. She held the mug with both hands and made her way slowly down the bank towards her brother. She came close to him and called his name softly: "Paul. Paul it's me, Beau." Paul didn't move, but just lay there still, as still as death. Beau called again and Paul opened his eyes. "Paul it's me, Beau. I've brought you some milk. You need something inside you." Paul closed his eyes. Beau knelt down besides him. She put the mug down and picked him up like a mother nursing a child, like a comrade holding a fallen friend, like a lover at a death. She held her cheek close to his and whispered, "Beautiful brother – I've got a love for you. I've got a love I can't even tell you about. I'd die for you, but I don't want you to die for me." Paul opened his eyes and looked up at her. He was panting. Beau stroked his hair. "Have some milk, Paul." She tilted his head and lifted the mug to his lips. She held it there, listening to the gentle gulps as Paul drank. "That's it, Paul, get it down, get it down, love." She put the mug down and held him, cheek to cheek, and gently rocked his thin body backwards and forwards. "Oh, I can feel your ribs, you silly boy, you silly bugger."

Paul looked at her. "I feel a bit poorly, Beau."

They stayed there a long time and then Beau whispered, "Paul, our Mam's going to get you a dog."

Paul moved. "A dog?"

"Aye, Paul – just a little one."

Paul's eyes rolled. "A dog, a little dog!"

"Aye, Paul. You'll be able to play with it and take it for walks and everything."

They lay together. The sun came out and a restless wind began to blow. It blew their hair and they were joined in spirit, a brother and sister wedded together in eternal love. Beau drew up her knees and rested Paul's head in her lap. She stroked his hair and listened to him breathing heavily. After a while she reached out to a dandelion flower and picked it. She held it by the stem at arm's length and turned it in the lustrous air. Then she smelled it and shoved it gently through Paul's wet and tousled hair. They lay together in silence until they heard their father's voice calling them from the fence. Then they got up slowly, awkwardly and in silence. Before they left they looked along the railway line and saw Gez Molloy walking into the far tunnel with a black cat under his arm.

It was Friday night and The Bessemer was full. Mr Parnaby emptied his glass and wiped his mouth on the back of his hand.

"Don't do that, Frank – it's common!"

Mr Parnaby looked at Mrs Parnaby. "It's only the froth off the head on it. Chester's always has a good head on it!"

"I don't care what it is, Frank – you're out with me and what will everybody think? Look – young John Clements is over there with his smart navy uniform on. Have you seen him?" She smiled at young Clements, and he lifted his glass in return.

"Doesn't he look handsome, Frank? Curly hair and that lovely uniform."

"Aye."

"He's been to India and China, you know."

"Aye, but I bet he missed his home comforts."

"And look at his shoulders."

"Aye."

"And those teeth."

"Aye."

"He's a lovely brownish colour isn't he?"

John Clements winked at her and Mrs Parnaby turned away.

"I've gone all funny now he's done that."

"Done what?"

"Never you mind, Frank."

"Anyroad, I've got shoulders, I've got shoulders an' all."

The door opened and in came Jimmy Kidd. He saw them right away and came over to their table. "Eh! Guess who it isn't?"

"Oh hello, Jim!"

"Hiya, Ellen!"

"What brings you in The Bess?"

Jimmy leant across the table and kissed Mrs Parnaby on the lips.

"Business, Ellen, just business. I'm here to meet a mate of mine a bit later on."

Jimmy pulled up a chair and sat down. "Eh, Frank, guess who's had a bit of luck on the gee-gees, then? Tee hee, bloody hee!"

"Have you, Jimmy?"

"Aye, I have!"

"You jammy so and so..."

"Let me get you a pint in."

"Er … I'm all right, Jim."

"No, what's that? 'Fighting Mild' is it?"

"Aye, it is."

"The same in yours, Ellen?"

"Oh thank you very much, Jim, I'm sure."

Jimmy sauntered over to the bar, nodding at people sitting to the right and left of him as he went. He seemed to know everybody.

"Mrs Parnaby's eyes flickered. "He does look after us, doesn't he Frank?"

"Aye, I suppose he does, but …"

"He's such a nice bloke, isn't he? He really is."

"He's …"

"He's a fine man. Madeleine's so lucky."

"She's…"

"She's got one in a million there."

There was a silence and then Mrs Parnaby rounded on Mr Parnaby. "Frank, are you listening?"

"Aye."

"I hate it when you don't listen!"

"I was…"

"Oh, you're so aggravating sometimes!"

Jimmy came back with a tray. "Here you are, Ellen. Here's your gill and here's your Chester's, Frank and I'm treating myself to a wee double whisky and... here's three dinners!" Jimmy produced three packets of crisps and tossed them on the table.

"Ta, Jim! What a nice surprise!"

"Just to celebrate like, you know – aye, all my lovely winnings."

"What was the horse called, Jim?"

"Oh, er... it was er... Dusty Carpet."

"Where was it running?"

"York, no Aintree, it was."

Mr Parnaby opened his packet of crisps.

"Can I have your salt, Frank?"

"Er ... aye, all right then Jimmy, you can have it."

"You can have mine an' all if you like, Jim."

"Ta, Ellen. If put three lots of salt on my crisps I'll get more thirstier and then I'll be able to drink more!"

"Good idea, Jim."

"Crafty, aren't I?"

Mrs Parnaby opened her crisp bag, sorted through the crisps with her finger and pulled out the blue twist of salt. "I call them dolly blues!" She reached across the table and laid both her hands on Jimmy's hand. "Are my hands cold, Jim?"

"No, they're lovely, Ellen. They're as warm as your heart is beautiful."

"Aw!"

Jimmy slid the wraps of salt across the table and emptied each one into his packet of crisps. Then he licked the blue salt papers and made a show of holding the crisp bag at the top and giving it a good shake. His rings glittered. He took clutches of crisps and ate them hungrily one after the other. Mr Parnaby took one crisp and ate it slowly. After a while, he moved the bag to one side. Jimmy downed his whisky in one gulp and licked his lips. "How's your

Paul now he knows he's getting a dog?"

"Oh he's dead pleased, Jim. He looks like a different lad, he really does."

"Is he any better?" Without waiting for an answer, Jimmy examined his glass and stood up. "I'm just going to get another one. I won't be a mo." He sauntered over to the bar.

"Eat your crisps, Frank!"

"I don't like them without salt, Mam. They've got no taste to them!"

"Get them ate!"

Mr Parnaby reached for a crisp and then began to eat it slowly. Jimmy came back with another glass of whisky. He sat down and took a big gulp of it. "Don't you want your crisps, Frank?"

"Er… I'm not all that hungry, Jimmy."

"Give them over here then."

Mr Parnaby passed the packet to Jimmy, who took a big clutch of crisps and ate them quickly. Then he pulled a bent packet of cigarettes out of his pocket. "Here you are, Ellen. Have a gasper!"

Mrs Parnaby took a cigarette. Here you are, Frank. Mr Parnaby took a cigarette. "Ta, Jimmy." Mr Parnaby picked up his box of matches and shook it. It was empty. Jimmy took a big gulp of whisky. Mr Parnaby looked at him. "Have you got a match, Jimmy?"

Jimmy smiled a sly smile and put his hand in his pocket. "Aye, Frank, I have!" He looked down and shook his head. "Your face and my arse!"

Mr Parnaby looked hurt. Mrs Parnaby laughed.

"It's all right, Frankie boy. I was just being funny! I didn't mean it! I was just being funny, that's all!"

Mrs Parnaby reached out and touched Jimmy's arm. "Oh, you are! You're dead funny, you Jim!"

Jimmy flicked his lighter and lit everybody's cigarettes. He blew smoke out and then took a gulp of whisky.

Mr Parnaby still looked uncomfortable. "I'll get some matches when I go to the bar then, Mam."

"Oh, are you going to the bar, Frank?"

"Well… er."

"I'll have a neat little double then, Pal."

Mr Parnaby stared at him. "No you won't, Jimmy. You'll have Chester's like the rest of us. I'm not ruddy made of it, you know."

"Aye, all right, Frank. All right, there's no need to get shirty is there?"

"I wasn't." Mr Parnaby got up, lifted the waistband of his trousers and went over to the bar.

Jimmy turned to Mrs Parnaby. "What's up with him? He's got a face like a dog's arse."

"I think you've upset him, Jim."

"Oh, I was only pulling his leg!"

"I know, Jim. I know. It's just that he's a bit, you know, touchy about things at the moment, what with his work. He never stops and he's a bit skint and there's Paul, an' all."

"Why? What's wrong with Paul? Is he still acting daft?"

"He's not been well, Jim, the poor little mite."

"Aw, you're too soft with him, Ellen. You need to discipline him a bit. I would!"

"How can I, Jim? He's such a gentle lad and he's been poorly, hasn't he?"

"They say 'spare the rod and spoil the child', Ellen – that's what they say."

"Oh, I don't know, Jim.

"Tell him that if he doesn't eat like a normal lad, you'll put him in a home and see what he does then."

"Oh, I couldn't tell him that – honest to God, I couldn't."

There was silence and then Jimmy said, "Eh, Ellen. Did you hear about the Irish lad working on the building site in Manchester?"

"No, what about him?"

"Well, he sent his dad a telegram. It said, 'No mon, no fun, your son.' And his dad in Ireland sent one back saying, 'How sad, too bad, your dad!'"

Mrs Parnaby put her hand over her mouth. Mr Parnaby came back with a tray. He rattled a box of matches and dropped them on the table before lifting down two gills of Chester's for Mrs Parnaby and himself and then a pint for Jimmy. Jimmy got up. "I'm just going to get a bottle of barley wine to drop in this beer."

Mr Parnaby sat down and poured the gill of beer into his pint pot. "What's he been saying, Mam?"

"Oh, nowt, Frank. He's just been saying about the dog he's going to get us, and the rabbit meat. He's such a nice man."

"Is he?"

Jimmy came back with a bottle of barley wine and a glass of whisky. He took a gulp of his beer and then started to pour the barley wine into the pint pot. "The Lord Mayor of Manchester taught me this trick."

"Did he?"

"Aye, he's a good pal of mine."

"Anyroad, Jimmy – who is this mate you're meeting?"

"It's Lonz Webster – you know Lonz don't you? He's a big lad, a boxer, funny nose, arms like legs."

"No… er."

"He's the lad who works in Tib Street."

"Tib Street?"

"Aye, you're going to clean his windows for him aren't you, Frank?"

"Clean his windows in Tib Street?"

"Aye, that's what we agreed."

"But Tib Street! It's … that's bloody miles away!"

"Frank!"

"Aye, I know, but you've got a cart haven't you?"

"Aye, I know, but I don't want to push ladders on my cart miles and miles through all that traffic every month, do I?"

"Every fortnight, Frank."

"Every fortnight?"

"Aye, it's a shop, and shops need doing every fortnight, don't they?"

"Oh, bloo-dy 'ell!"

"It's worth it though, Frank. It's worth it for you as well as Paul – cigarettes, one big rabbit and one small dog – it's worth it all right!"

"Aye, I know, Jimmy, but I didn't expect to have to go to Tib Street, that's all."

"We'll cope, Frank, won't we?"

"I'll do my best, Mam."

Jimmy lifted his pint pot. They watched Jimmy's tongue extend grotesquely down the side of the pot as he gulped down the beer. He put the pot down and wiped his mouth on the back of his hand. "I've got all throff round my mouth."

Mrs Parnaby smiled fondly at him. "Chester's always has a good head on it, hasn't it, Jim?"

Jimmy downed the rest of the pint and felt in his pocket for his cigarettes. He took one out and lit it. "Aye, one big rabbit and one small dog – that's the way to remember it!" He picked up an empty crisp bag, blew into it and then burst it with clapped hands.

"Hey up, here comes Lonz!"

They looked across to the door. Jimmy got up. "Lonz – let me get you a pint in. I've had some luck on the gee-gees!" A cheer went up from the women in the corner of the room. Jimmy took a step towards the bar and then turned and kissed Mrs Parnaby on the lips. "So long, Ellen. I'll see you in the morning."

"Right oh then, Jimmy."

Jimmy looked mischievous and then he said, "Eh, Ellen, after I've seen Lonz I'm going home to take Madeleine's knickers off!"

Mrs Parnaby put her hand over her mouth and feigned shock. Mr Parnaby looked at his boots.

Jimmy laughed and pulled at his crotch. "I've been wearing them all day and they're bloody killing me!"

Mrs Parnaby shook her head and laughed. They watched Jimmy as he ambled to the bar to meet Lonz Webster. "What a lovely man, Frank! He's full of surprises, isn't he?"

"He's full of shit!"

"Frank!"

"Well… he…" John Clements came over with a cigarette in his hand. "Hiya, Mrs Parnaby. Hiya, Mr Parnaby. How are you both?"

Mrs Parnaby looked at him, standing there, handsome in his navy uniform – fine broad shoulders, curly hair, white teeth and brown skin. "Oh I'm wonderful, John! Really wonderful!"

John turned to Mr Parnaby. He flicked the cigarette between his fingers and looked down at the box of matches. "Have you got a match please, Mr Parnaby?"

Mr Parnaby stared at him intently. "Aye, John, I have – my face and your arse!"

It was a sunny day. Paul was sitting on the pavement outside his house watching Molly and Beau and the other girls skipping in the street. Their faces were expressionless as they sang in a flat monotone: "Charlie Chaplin went to France, to teach the ladies how to dance." The beat of the rope on the cobbled setts was like the beating in his ears. He looked at his boots, his great black boots that he'd polished earlier. He'd done what his dad had told him. He'd used a hot spoon to melt the polish and then he'd buffed them to perfection in the hope that somehow that would make the dog arrive earlier. And now here they were: black and heavy on his feet and shining in the sun.

The sun was too bright for Paul and he narrowed

his eyes to see the children who were playing with the rope. He could make out sugar frocks, roses and lace, straight faces, dull voices, clipping shoes and the warmth of familiarity. And all the time, the girls were singing with sweet intimations of heaven and earth. There he was under a sky haunted by the swollen faces of the dead. There he was sitting by a damp cellar that kept at arm's length the smell of minerals and gas. And all the time, the girls were singing with sweet intimations of life and death: 'Raspberry, gooseberry, apple jam tart, tell me the name of your sweetheart.'

Paul turned his head to see who it was who was walking towards him. It was Gez Molloy and his little brother, Paddy. A black cat was sitting on Gez's shoulder. Gez always had cats. When he was younger he used to catch them in a cardboard box and then put them in his backyard. He never knew what to do with them then, though, and he just let them go. Gez and Paddy stood in front of him. Gez stared down. "What are you up to, Paul?"

"I'm just sat here, Gez. I'm a bit ill in my ears and throat, that's all."

"You're ill?"

"Aye, it's in my ears and head and that."

"Have you still got all those sores on your arms?"

Paul rolled up his sleeves.

"Jeez you have! We can't have that now, can we? We'll have to try and make you better."

"My dad knows how. He's getting me a dog."

"A dog, is it?"

"Aye, it's a small one called Bob. It's coming this morning!"

"That's good! I hope you'll like him."

"I will. I will."

Gez looked at Paul's polished boots and whispered out of the side of his mouth to the cat,

"Will you look at those boots now, Eamonn? They're shone to perfection, aren't they? The man who wore them before him would've been proud, don't you think? Ah, but it's a shame about the cut tyres and studs underneath!" Paul moved his feet. "All right, Gez! Pack it, will you?"

"It's all right, Paul. I'm not like the others! I'm not going to rag you just for that. There's plenty in our family that have had tyres hammered to their feet."

"I know they're no good, but they're better than nowt."

"Oh, they're much better than that, Paul. My da used to say that holey soles belong to holy souls. You see if you died now, Paul, those boots would wing you straight up to heaven and no mistake."

"I hadn't thought of that."

"And also, they're both the same colour!"

Gez lifted his boots one at a time for Paul to see. One was brown and the other one black. There was silence as Paul surveyed Gez's boots.

"Anyroad, thin man, I've got a present for you. Give him the blade, Paddy."

Paddy fumbled in his pocket and brought out a long steel blade."

Paul looked at the blade. It was bright like silver. "Where did you get that, Gez?"

"I made it!"

"You made it?"

"Aye, it was a good new six-inch nail before it got flattened by a train on the railway line."

"Aye, I saw you in the cutting the other day – you and Eamonn."

"That was us right enough. Eamonn always comes with me when we go on the line, don't you Eamonn? We put pennies, nails and bolts on the line and when the train's gone over them, we sharpen them up on my da's grinder and we make spears and blades and arrowheads. You can have this one, but be careful now, it's sharp."

Paul took the blade carefully in both hands and stared at it. "Thanks Gez. Thanks Paddy. I've never had a blade before."

"I know you haven't."

"Ta, Gez, it's a belter."

"You use it carefully now, Paul."

"I will, Gez."

"Anyroad, I'll be on my way."

"Right, Gez."

"I hope the blade will make you better." He turned and walked off. As he passed Molly he said, "Hey, Molly – you should feed your brother Paul something. The poor little bugger looks like he's been in the potato famine."

Beau glared at him. "And you look like you caused the potato famine!"

Gez patted his belly and then he adjusted Eamonn on his shoulder and walked away.

Molly called after him. "You spoiled our May Queen with your daft Molly Dancing, you fat pig!"

"It was only a bit of fun!"

"You made such a din with your black faces and clanking pans!"

Gez pulled a face and sang in an inane falsetto voice, "Molly Dancers, Molly Dancers, kicking up a row, kicking up a row!" He adjusted Eamonn on his shoulder. "How much did you get, anyroad?"

"I'm not telling you."

"Don't then. See if I care." He laughed. "We made seventeen shillings."

"Seventeen shillings! We would have made more than that if it hadn't been for you!"

"You might say that we molly-crushed you then?"

Beau smiled. "Aye you did, but that's better than being Molloy crushed, you fat bastard!"

Gez feigned shock: "Ooooh! – the language on her!" Then he flicked a 'V' sign at Beau and went on his way.

Mrs Parnaby had got up early to do the best room. She'd cleaned the windows, swept the carpet, dusted and then polished the furniture and brasses. She'd finished by eight o' clock. Mr Parnaby stayed at home too. He hadn't been out on his window cleaning round. He wanted to be there when Jimmy came so he decided not to go. They'd waited all morning for Jimmy and Madeleine to arrive, but they never came and they passed time by making pots of tea and smoking. In the early afternoon, Paul had come in. He wasn't well and he'd asked again and again when Bob was going to come, but they didn't know and they couldn't tell him. Mrs Parnaby thought he was getting worse and she suggested that he went upstairs and lie down. She'd tell him when the dog arrived.

At half past three, there was a knock at the door. Mr Parnaby opened it. It was Jimmy. He was on his own and didn't look well. "Let me in, Frank, will you?"

"Aye, Jimmy, come in."

Jimmy came in. He had a large cardboard box. He put it on the floor carefully and sat down. "Make us a drink of tea, Ellen, will you?"

"Aye, Jim, course I will. Are you all right?"

Jimmy opened a packet of cigarettes, took one out and lit it. "Just a bit hung over, that's all, Ellen. I finished up getting a bit tipsy last night. Dear God!"

"I thought you were necking it a bit, Jimmy."

"Aye, I was. It was that Lonz Webster. He can't half sup that lad."

Mr Parnaby pointed to the box. "Is that Bob in there then, Jimmy?"

"Well it can be."

"What do you mean 'it can be'?"

"Well we've had a bit of a mix up, Frank. It's all

that Webster's fault."

"Why, what's happened?"

Jimmy paused and took a long drag of his cigarette. "Well I told him, I bloody told him, but as usual, he got it all wrong didn't he?"

"Why, what's he done?"

Mrs Parnaby came in with a tray with mugs on it. "Shall I pour yours, Jim?"

"Aye, Ellen, go on then."

"Well I told him: get one big rabbit and one small dog.'"

"That's the way you remember it, isn't it Jim?"

"Aye, but the silly bugger got it the wrong way round."

"What do you mean?"

"Well he's only got me a big dog and a small rabbit."

"What, he's got us a big dog?"

"No, he brought me a big parcel of dog meat didn't he?"

"Is that what's in the box?"

"No our Buster's already had that."

What's in there, then?"

Jimmy put the cigarette between his lips, squinted his eyes and then went to the box. He opened it. "In here... there's one... small... rabbit." He brought a small rabbit out. It was dappled brown. "This is Bob, if you want him."

"Bob?"

"Aye, if you want it to be."

"Bloo-dy 'ell, Jimmy!"

Jimmy put the struggling rabbit back in the box.

"I had my heart set on a dog, Jimmy – not a flamin' rabbit."

Mrs Parnaby looked indignant. "Just a mo, Frank. The dog wasn't for you, it was for our Paul!"

"Aye, I know, but I wanted a dog!"

"I know what you wanted, Frank."

"And there's a principle at stake here, an' all!"

"Principle! Principle? Paul can't eat principles, can he, Frank? Anybody with any sense knows that!"

"You can't eat a rabbit, neither!"

"Oh aye, you can, that's why Jimmy was bringing the rabbit meat, wasn't he?"

"What about that meat, Jimmy?"

"Our Buster's had it. Dog meat's no good for rabbits. They eat carrots and that, don't they?"

"So let's get this straight! You want me to push my cart five miles through the streets every fortnight for five months so I can clean windows for a bloke in Tib Street for cigarettes I've already smoked, for meat your Buster's already had, for a dog that never came and for a bloody rabbit? Well you can just... just... sod off!"

"Frank!"

"Don't be unreasonable now, Frank. We made a deal!"

"Aye, we did, but you've broken it!"

"Broken it?"

"Aye, you'd had a skin-full and... "

"It wasn't my fault, Frank! It was that Webster's."

"Like my dad used to say: 'You should never do deals in pubs!'"

"All right, all right, Frank! I confess – I might have been a bit confused at the time, but..."

"Confused! Confused? You were pissed!"

"All right, all right – so I might have been a bit..."

"Glad to hear it!"

"So, I'm sorry!"

"That's not good enough!"

"Look Frank, don't be such a wet rag."

"I'm not being a wet rag. I'm just sticking up for myself, that's all."

"Frank! I'll tell you what I'll do." Jimmy collected himself. "I'll cut the window cleaning by a month!"

The door opened and Paul came in. He was

trembling. "Has he brought Bob, Dad?"

"Aye, son, he has, but Bob's…"

"What?"

"He's going back!"

"Frank!"

"Going back? He's only just come."

"Well, you see son, Jimmy here has made a right mess of things."

"Why, what's he done?"

"Well Bob's not really a dog, he's a…"

"What?"

"He's a… a rabbit."

Paul looked at the box.

"A rabbit?"

"Aye."

"Is he in there?"

"Aye."

"Can I see him?"

Aye, er... Jimmy, get him out."

Jimmy lifted the rabbit out the box. "There he is, Paul."

Just then the door opened and Molly and Beau came in. "Oh, look at the rabbit!" They went across to the rabbit. Paul went with them. "Oh, he's so cute!" They stood round Jimmy, each stroking the rabbit's soft fur with a gentle finger.

Paul stared. "He's a nice rabbit, isn't he?"

"Aye, but he's not that nice and he's going back!"

Paul stared. "Can I hold him?"

Aye, son. Here you are."

The rabbit struggled. Paul held him awkwardly and started to stroke him. "He's dead good, isn't he, Dad?"

"Er."

Paul put his cheek against the rabbit's fur. "Hello, Bob."

"Don't get too fond of him now, Paul – remember, he's going back!"

Molly said, "Aw, look at him, Dad! You can't send him back!"

Jimmy was getting agitated. "Keep him, Frank. Keep him. I'll sort something out."

"Paul held the rabbit closely to his chest. "Let me… oh let me, Dad. Please let me keep him!"

"I'd like to keep him, son, but he's… "

Beau went up to the rabbit and stroked it. The rabbit struggled in Paul's arms. "Go on, Dad. He'll be no trouble. Let's keep him."

Jimmy turned to Mr Parnaby. "This is daft! I'll tell you what, Frank. Keep the rabbit, for Paul's sake. I'll bring the meat on Wednesday and I'll cut the window cleaning by two months! The room went quiet. Everybody looked at Mr Parnaby. Jimmy held out his hand.

"By two months, Frank!"

"Two months?"

"Aye, and if it doesn't work out you can send him back then, can't you?"

Everybody looked at Mr Parnaby for what seemed like a long time; then he shook Jimmy's hand. Mrs Parnaby went up to the rabbit and held its head in her hands. "Welcome to our house, Bob!"

Everybody cheered. The rabbit struggled in Paul's arms. It legs clawed madly, and caught Paul's arm. Paul let the rabbit drop to the ground. It righted itself and sent a jet of wee up Paul's leg. Jimmy caught the rabbit, and Mrs Parnaby went to look at Paul's arm. It was bleeding. "Come on Paul, let's get this under the tap."

"It's all right, Mam! He didn't mean to. He was just scared, that's all."

She looked hard at her dear boy and whispered. "Aye, son – he's got reason to be."

Mr Parnaby was sitting in the tin bath with a mug of tea in his hand. He took a gulp and pulled a face. "I bloody hate tea with no sugar in it!"

"What we haven't got Frank, we'll have to do without."

"Aye, I know, but I need some sugar. It's good for my nerves."

"So they say. What are you having a bath for, anyroad?"

"A compressor blew its gasket in the fitting shop and we all got covered in sump oil. It's all in my hair and everywhere."

"So what have you done with the rabbit?"

"I put him back in that cardboard box."

"Fair play to you. Will he be all right in there?"

"Aye, he's all right for the time being. I'll put him back in the bath when I've finished."

"We need a rabbit hutch."

"Aye, Bren says he's going to make one at work, but I don't know."

"What don't you know?"

"Well I still think we should send the ruddy thing back. It's bitten Paul three or four times and it keeps scratching him."

"Aye, it's a little monkey, that rabbit."

"And it piddles at him an' all."

"He loves it though, doesn't he?"

"Aye, I know and he's taken to wearing his socks and boots again."

"And he never leaves it alone when he comes home from school."

"I know. He'd never forgive you if you sent it back, Frank."

"But if we don't, one of these days it's going bite him and give him fever, or something bad like that."

"I know, but I can't fathom out what we're going to do."

"We could get Jimmy to bring us a small dog instead."

"But that won't stop him missing his rabbit. He

loves that rabbit."

"I don't know what we're going to do."

"I don't know, neither."

It had been a hard day for Paul. The pounding in his ears had gone on all day and he'd had a dull headache. It was a heavy, sickening headache that made his eyes feel hot and his head unbalanced. His mouth was dry, so dry, and he couldn't understand why it was that way. But when he was going home, he tried to forget about it the best way he could, and he thought about Bob. He knew that Bob could bite and scratch and wee, but that it was just because he was scared, especially when they put him in the tin bath with an old back door over it to stop him getting out. He wasn't doing bad things so much now, though. Paul was sure that Bob was beginning to recognise him and trust him. It was as though they were friends. More than that, Paul felt that Bob was his salvation; his friendship somehow helped to make sense of things. Bob was what mattered. Nothing else seemed certain. When Paul held Bob's thin body and looked at him, it brought a kind of dignity into the way they were. They shared the air, the time, the place, the anxious winds that smelt of gas. They each affirmed the futility of their lives – but together, they were somehow exalted over all the earth.

Paul opened the backyard, door and went out to the bath. It was empty, and the old door that usually covered it was leaning against the wall. Paul looked behind it, and in the coal shed and under things, and round the yard again and again, but there was no sign of Bob. He went inside the house and found his mother and father sitting in silence. They were calm and they had strange, expressionless looks on their faces.

"Where's Bob?" There was silence. Paul became

angry. "What have you done to Bob?"

"He's… he's… all right, he's all right."

Paul was trembling. "Where is he?"

"He's just gone away, Paul, but he's all right where he is."

"Have you sent him back?"

"No, Paul! We'd never do that would we?"

"Where is he then?"

"You see Paul, Bob was… he was biting you and scratching you and…"

"He doesn't bite any more! He's stopped…"

"He could bring fever here, Paul!"

"He never would!"

"We're not having fever here."

"So what have you done with him?"

"We've given him away."

"You've given him away?"

"Aye, son – it's the best thing."

Paul's shoulders convulsed and he began to sob silently.

"Aw, Paul – you can still see him! You can still see him every day if you like."

"Where is he?"

"We've given him to Mr and Mrs Shaw down the Terrace. They've got rabbits already and they know how to keep them."

"Oh!"

Mrs Parnaby got up and went to Paul. "Hush, hush now, Paul. He'll be safe there. They'll look after him. He doesn't have to live in the tin bath anymore. He's got his own rabbit hutch now. He'll be with other rabbits and when you go and see him, you'll be able to see all the other rabbits an' all."

"I don't want all the other rabbits – I just want Bob!"

"You can still see him … and you can talk to their Marlene, can't you?"

"I don't want to talk to Marlene!"

Paul struggled free from his mother's arms, and went unsteadily out of the door and up to the bedroom.

There is no pain like the pain of separation. No pain compares to the loss of love. It's a hunger that goes beyond hunger. It's everything you don't want. It's never what you do want. That organic yearning buckles the knees. It twists the bowels and gnaws at the brain. It lifts the veil and summons memories of earlier times, earlier loves and earlier losses – each one an awful imitation of the last. Loss is never simple. It allows no mercy. It reeks of pretence. A loved one's betrayal is beyond all forbearance. Paul lay there in the railway grass and wept.

"Where's our Paul?"

Mrs Parnaby put a hand to her face. "He's gone to Shaw's to see Bob."

There was a silence and then Mr Parnaby said, "Bob's better off there, anyroad."

"I know, but what about Paul?"

"But Bob was biting him all the time. You must've seen his arms!"

"Aye, I've seen 'em."

"It was getting out of hand."

"I just can't help worrying though."

"Aye, I know."

"I wish I knew what's in store for the lad."

"If only we could do something."

"When he came home from school, Frank, the first thing he did was to take his boots and socks off."

"Oh, we're back on that are we?"

"And he didn't want nowt to eat neither. He's running me ragged, he really is."

"The poor lad's taken it badly, hasn't he?"

"Have we done the right thing, Frank?

"Course we have, Mam. We couldn't have gone

on like that, could we?"

"I just don't know any more."

"Have we done the right thing, Mam?"

"I don't know, Frank. I really don't know."

"I'd better go after him."

"What good will that do?"

"It's as much for me as it is for him."

"What do you mean by that?"

Mr Parnaby took his wife by the hands and looked at her intently. "Sometimes Ellen, I feel as lonely as he does." He pressed her hand to his cheek and held it there before hurrying off.

Paul walked as quickly as he could. The stone setts in the back entry were smooth and cold under his feet. Nobody seemed to be about, but a radio played music somewhere and a dog was barking a long way off. He looked at the cracked brick walls and backyard doors and then at the dandelion leaves he'd brought for Bob – good clean leaves pulled out of a drainpipe.

He got to Shaw's backyard and he knocked at the door. It was quiet. A gentle breeze blew down the back entry and ruffled his hair. Nobody came. Paul knocked again. Nobody came. He lifted the latch and the door opened just enough for him to look into the backyard. Nobody was there, but he could see rabbit hutches stacked neatly on top of each other. He pushed the door open and went in. It was just like his own yard but much neater and it smelt of disinfectant. The rabbits moved as he went over to the hutches. His legs were trembling. He peered in and looked for Bob, but couldn't find him. He searched again, carefully this time, and checked each hutch in turn. He still couldn't find him. His searching became urgent. Where was Bob? He looked again. Then he stared at the window and the door of the house.

There was nobody who could help him. He turned and looked at the backyard door. He turned to it, his eyes opened wide and his jaw racked open. He looked and he saw, he didn't know what... he looked, and he saw, nailed on the backyard door, the stretched pelt of a dappled brown rabbit, crucified in its death. It was Bob.

Paul bent his head and let out a long guttural moan that stiffened his body with rage. He roared, "No!" He wedged both fists into his mouth and bit them hard and then slowly, he turned his head to behold the awful sight. Bob's head was gone. They'd cut his head off! All his feet had gone! Paul's eyes flashed green through tears. He ran to the pelt and tried to pull the nails out of it, but they had been driven hard into the wood and the nail heads sliced into his fingers. Blood flecked onto the pelt. He let go and stared at his hands. Then he ran to the house and hammered and kicked at the door. "You bad, bad, bad, bad people!" He went to the stack of hutches and punched them. One came down. Paul pushed a sack of coal over, kicked a box of glass jars and upturned the dustbin. Then he heaved up a bucket and threw it as hard as he could at the wall. Sawdust went everywhere. He stood there panting. His face trembled. He looked round the yard. How could anybody do this? The air became fleshed with fear and faces. Why had they done this to Bob? He crossed his thin arms over his chest and then slowly, and as though he were reluctant to do so, he went back to the pelt and rested his wet cheek against it. He stayed there for what seemed a long time and cried, silently.

After a while, he opened the yard door and looked into the back entry. There was nobody about, so he went through the door and hurried away. His body stiffened and he shouted with a trembling voice: "Bad, bad, bad, bad people!" He ran as fast as he could with his head held backwards towards the sky.

Mr Parnaby came into sight. "Paul, what's happened?" Paul fell into his father's arms. "What's happened to you, son?"

"Daddy!"

"Look at your hands … and you've skinned your knuckles!" Mr Parnaby kissed his son's face, his hair and his face again. Paul held his tear-streamed face closely to his father's cheek and whispered, "Daddy…"

"Have you been in a fight, son?"

"Daddy!"

"What son, what?"

"They've gone and skinned Bob!"

"You what?"

"Honest to God, Daddy – they have!"

"How do you know, son?"

"I've seen him, Dad. I've seen him!"

"Where?"

"He's skinned to the backyard door!"

"He's skinned to the backyard door?"

"He is, Dad, honest to…"

"Show me!"

"Aw, Dad, no…"

"Show me!" Mr Parnaby stood up and strode down the back entry towards Shaw's backyard. Paul ran after him. They got to the backyard door. Mr Parnaby lifted the latch and looked in. "What a mess…" He pushed the door open and went in the yard. "What's happened here, Paul?"

"I done it, Dad. I done it!"

Then Mr Parnaby saw the pelt nailed to the backyard door. ""For the love of… " He went across to the pelt and stared at it. Paul couldn't look. "Dear God! That's Bob! That's our Bob. The dirty…" He went to the backdoor and thundered on it. Nothing happened. He thundered on the door again. Then they heard footsteps and the sound of bolts being drawn back from the inside. It opened. Mr Shaw appeared. He was in his vest, khaki trousers and black wellingtons. "Oh, it's you, Frank." Then he caught sight of the mess in the yard and his expression changed. "What the...! Who's done all that?" He looked at Paul. "Have you done this?"

Paul looked at his feet. "Aye, sir. I done it."

Mr Shaw went over to the fallen hutch. He picked it up and lifted it back on top of the stack. He peered at the rabbits inside the hutch and then went back to Mr Parnaby. "All right, we all know that Paul takes after you, Frank. He's never been the sharpest knife in the drawer, but you tell me now why he's done this. Go on – tell me!"

Mr Parnaby's face twitched. He pointed to the rabbit pelt nailed to the yard door. "No, you tell me why you've done that."

Mr Shaw looked surprised. "That? That's nowt!"

"It isn't nowt, that's Bob, that is!"

"Bob? That's what you called it, is it?"

Mr Parnaby came up close. "Aye, it is! Why did you do that to him?"

"That's all you can do with them that bites!"

Marlene and Mrs Shaw appeared at the doorway. Mr Shaw saw them and jerked his thumb in Marlene's direction. "The little sod bit our lass twice, the vicious little ..."

"You could have given him back!"

"Not likely! It's worth more to me in meat."

"Meat?"

"Aye, that's where it's gone."

Mr Parnaby went straight up to him and pushed him with both hands. Mr Shaw fell amongst the tangle of boxes and jars and things in the yard. Marlene and Mrs Shaw screamed. Mr Shaw got to his feet. Paul saw the blue of his eyes, the shock in them and the blaze of anger. Then he watched with his mouth open as his father drove a brutal punch, and then another, into Mr Shaw's nose. A great bubble of blood burst from his nostrils and he went down. Mr Parnaby stood over him breathing heavily.

"That's all you can do with them that kill innocents, you... you Protestant bastard!" He went to the pelt and pulled at the nails. Mrs Shaw and Marlene clattered across the yard behind him. They swore and growled and thumped his back. Mrs Shaw took hold of a coal shovel and brought it down hard on Mr Parnaby's head. He turned, snatched the shovel and heaved Marlene and Mrs Shaw into the jumbled heap where Mr Shaw was lying. They lay there crying at his feet. Mr Parnaby went back to the pelt and used the shovel to beat the nails this way and that. After a few minutes, Bob's stiff skin was freed and he held it closely for a moment and then passed it to Paul.

"You take care of him, Paul. Come on. We're going home." He threw the shovel down and then looked at the bodies in the yard. "You touch any of mine again and I swear I'll kill you, you godless bastards." He went over to the backyard door and opened it. He glanced behind him, hurried back into the yard and pulled the stack of rabbit hutches over. Then he put his arm round his son and left.

Paul had been sent upstairs to bed in disgrace. He didn't mind being in bed and he didn't care about disgrace. He hadn't wanted to go to school anyway. That morning he'd pleaded with his mam to let him stay at home. He wasn't well. He kept telling her that he wasn't well, but she took no notice. She didn't believe him when he said his head was hurting. She hadn't noticed the narrowed eyes that couldn't bear the light of morning and the ears that couldn't bear the pounding of the steam hammer. She told him that he should simply face the fact that Bob was dead. "You can't run away from it forever, Paul. You've got to go forward and shine."

He lay there panting, ears burnt deep to the brain, a throat swallowing rose berries and lifting in chime, his skin as transparent as wax. He'd just been dreaming – dreaming of a monkey twisted in a tight leather belt, unable to breathe with the buckle shoved deep into its mouth. Next door in his parents' bedroom the clock ticked interminably. Tick, tock the grinding clock, time here, time there, one tear, one prayer. Paul knew where he was and what had happened. He could remember some of it, anyway. It had been awful at school. He remembered the noise in the playground. He remembered that he couldn't see much, but he remembered what he had seen when Gez Molloy came in holding something wrapped in a wet newspaper.

"I've brought something to put on the nature table, Miss."

"Oh yes, Gerard. What is it?"

They'd watched as Gez unwrapped the stained newspaper. Then he'd smiled and held something up for everybody to see. It was wet and black. Gez had twirled it between a finger and thumb, and then he'd rested it over his shoulder. Everybody groaned. It was something Paul had never wanted to see, and it was something he never wanted to see again. It took a few seconds to work out what it was and then it was obvious.

"It's a cat's tail!"

"Oooh, Miss!"

Paul had got to his feet and shouted, "That's Eamonn's tail!" Gez had nodded and smiled. It had been too much for Paul. He'd got to his feet and run out of the classroom. "You're all bad, bad, bad people!" He heard people calling after him, people who wanted to stop him, people who wanted to explain to him, but somehow he'd run home and had sat there upright against the front door crying in a daze until his mam had come home. She'd asked him questions he couldn't answer. He'd told her that he wasn't well and that he didn't want to go to school ever again and that he didn't want to be a boy any more.

His mam had laid him on the sofa, put cushions under his head and given him a spoonful of brandy. He didn't like it and had asked for a drink, so she'd made him some hot, sweet tea. He'd lain there until Molly and Beau came home and made a fuss of him, and Beau had put a wet flannel across his forehead and stroked his hair so gently, so very gently. He'd lain there for a long time with his eyes closed when he heard a knock at the front door. His mam had opened it and Paul heard a loud voice: "Eh, Ellen! Guess who it isn't!"

"Oh, hello, Jim! Come on in." Paul had heard the door close and Jimmy saying, "By 'eck, it niffs in here a bit, Ellen!"

"That's Paul. He's not been well you know. In fact he's proper poorly."

There had been silence and then the conversation continued softly: "Oh, is he?"

"It's his ears, you know."

"Oh, is it?"

Paul had wanted to say something, but he hadn't. He wasn't sure about things any more. And then he heard:

"Eh, I've brought something for you, Ellen!"

"What is it, Jim?"

"I've brought you Paul's rabbit meat!"

Paul had opened his eyes.

"It's just been butchered and so it's nice and fresh."

Jimmy had come up close to Paul and lent over him. Paul had felt his breath on his cheek. "Cheer up, matey! It might never happen!"

Paul had turned his stiff neck awkwardly towards Jimmy's face and croaked, "You've brought my rabbit's meat?"

"Aye son – yum, yum!"

Paul had struggled to raise himself on an elbow and hissed, "Grimes! You cruel bastard!" Mrs Parnaby had huffed and puffed, and she'd shouted when Jimmy had suddenly gripped Paul's face with a firm hand and said, "Now listen here, you little..." That's when Paul had opened his dry mouth and had bitten into one of Jimmy's foul fingers with all his failing might. Mrs Parnaby had slapped Paul's face and had ordered him up to bed. "I just don't know what this caper is with you! I just don't know." Paul had tried to get up; he hadn't managed it, but he had heard Jimmy say, "He's deranged, Ellen! You need to get him seen to – shock therapy or something!" As Jimmy nursed his finger, Molly and Beau had helped Paul to his feet and walked him with bent knees and lolling head across to the stairs. They had struggled with him, step by step, leaning against the walls and crying loudly. Paul could remember most of it, though somehow, it didn't seem to matter now. He lay there, ears burnt deep into the brain, a throat swallowing rose berries and lifting in chime. Next door in his parents' bedroom, the clock ticked interminably – pulses of time, pulses of time, like glass beads pulled through the heart's vein, until it glistened and closed.

Nobody was to blame. Nobody is ever to blame. Somehow things arise together like lilies in a briared wreath, breathing perfume and entwined, each one adding to the whole; breaths risen in the rainbow and now beyond time, beyond suffering, baptised by the hands of God into eternity: blameless, beautiful and full of grace.

Dr Hardwicke had gone. He said that it had been meningitis and that they should have sent for him far sooner. He said that they should all go downstairs and then stay in the house and that he'd come back again later that morning. Nobody spoke. Nobody could speak. There was nothing to say. Mr Parnaby stared upwards without expression. He just stared, his dull brown eyes fixed on the ceiling. Mrs Parnaby had one arm round Molly and the other round Beau. They were raw with crying. Father Edward Sollett came down the stairs and looked round the room. "Father Rack's still up there with him. He's just sorting one or two things out. He'll be down in a moment." He looked at Mrs Parnaby and the girls. "Come on now, Ellen, drink your tea. Dr Hardwicke said you should have some hot, sweet tea for the shock."

"I don't want it, Father. Sorry." Molly and Beau began to sob quietly. Father Sollett nodded at them. "Now then, this isn't the time for tears. You shouldn't be thinking about yourselves. You should be praying for the repose of that poor boy's soul."

"They're upset, Father!"

"I know they are Ellen, but we must think of Paul."

"How can we think of anything else?"

"He needs our prayers."

"We'll pray for him, we'll pray for him."

"His soul needs repose and God only knows if he'll be granted that."

"What do you mean, Father?"

"Did you not see it? He knew the time had come when his life was going to be judged and there was fear in his eyes."

"Aye, there was – we all saw that he was scared, the poor little mite."

"Perhaps there was good reason for him to be

afraid."

"He was a good boy, Father."

"Yes, he was, but I doubt if he was in a state of grace when he died."

"He'd been going to Mass and he'd started going to confession…"

"But when he did, his confessions were all too brief."

"What do you mean by that?"

"Well, we rather got the impression that he held quite a lot back."

"What?"

"There was always a certain reticence about the boy."

"Now's not the time to talk about that, is it Father?"

"We have to face facts."

"The facts are that he's not been himself just recently. He's been ill and he was upset about the rabbit."

"But that can't excuse his wrecking Shaw's backyard or insulting Miss Fulton and upsetting all those little innocents!"

"Father!"

"And then savaging Jimmy Kidd. Not that anyone would blame him for that – biting a rogue is one thing, but impugning the reputation of the Church is quite another!"

Father Richard Rack came in. "I've finished packing away the things now and oh, by the way, I found this under his pillow, Father." He held the sharpened blade against the palm of his hand. "It's unusual, isn't it? I wonder what he was going to do with it."

Father Sollett took the blade between finger and thumb and examined it warily. "You said he spent a lot of time on the railway embankment, didn't you, Ellen?"

"Yes, Father, he did."

"Well, this is a blade hammered on a tungsten anvil – it's a blade made from a nail flattened by the wheels of a train on a railway line. A boy at St Francis was stabbed with one such like not so very long ago."

"I didn't know he had that, Father! I swear I didn't!"

"No, no Ellen. I'm sure you weren't meant to know. It's a side of him that you wouldn't have known about."

Beau stood up suddenly. "And there's a lot you wouldn't know about him neither, Father!"

"Beau!"

"No Mam. I'm going to say it … he's got it all wrong!"

"What have I got wrong, child?"

"You've got no idea who Paul is, have you? You've got no idea!"

"Beau!"

"But he's supposed to be a priest, and he's not got the faintest idea."

"Beau, hold your tongue!"

"My beautiful brother was a lovely, gentle boy who… who just loved things. If you can't see that, what else can't you see?"

"Beau, Beau, please… show me some respect."

"Oh, Father, she didn't mean …!"

"I will, Father, when you start showing Paul some respect."

Father Sollett's face flushed and he got up. "Ellen, this is quite beyond the pale."

"We're upset. Can't you just leave it?"

"No, I won't leave it. The authority of the Church is sacrosanct and it should be observed at all times and in all circumstances."

"But Father..."

"I insist! You should all pray for salvation – for

your own as well as for Paul's, because it's clear that you're all in sore need of it!"

Father Rack cleared his throat. "Perhaps we should all settle for a moment while we call upon the good Lord in his mercy, at this difficult time, to bless us all."

Beau went to the door. "You lot can. I'm not." And she went upstairs. Mrs Parnaby said, "Do something, Frank!"

Mr Parnaby looked up. "Leave her, Ellen. Just leave her." He turned to Father Sollett. "I'm sorry, Father. I'll have a word with her!"

"Please do!"

"But I think you should go now."

"I think so too, but we'll come round tomorrow to sort out the arrangements."

"Yes, Father. We'll be here."

"I'll say goodbye then. God bless you all. Our prayers are with you."

"And ours with you, Fathers."

The door opened and the full light of the sun shone in. The priests went out to find children skipping in the street. "Mabel, Mabel, set the table. Don't forget the salt, mustard, vinegar, pepper, salt, mustard, vinegar..."

They walked down the street. After a while, Father Sollett turned to Father Rack. "How do you feel about that, Richard?"

"Oh, you know. It's always a bit disconcerting when you have to deal with a death and especially the death of a child, Father."

"Was this your first time?"

"Well no, I've had to deal with it often enough in Limerick, but that's before I was ordained."

"I understand."

"And it wasn't so different at home, Father. Death puts its own appearance on everyone."

"Yes, Richard, of course it does, but I'm sure you didn't have to contend with that degree of resentment at home."

"Oh maybe not, no, but the Parnabys are all right. There's always anger in the house when someone dies – people blame themselves, God, Uncle Tom Finn, everyone. That's no different."

"But can't you see that theirs was different?"

"In what way, Father?"

"What we saw wasn't just anger – it was resentment, resentment towards the Church. Can't you see that? Since the war ended it's been a growing problem round here. These are some of the poorest people in Manchester. They're poor in all senses of the word. And in some respects, they need the Church more than anybody else, but they are beginning to think purely in terms of themselves and not of the wider family of the Church. And you can see that in the ways in which they're beginning now to pick and choose what they believe, and which sacraments they'll observe. The rot has set in, and we have to do all we can to stop it."

"You think it's as bad as that, Father?"

"Well just look at the Parnabys. What a parcel of humbugs! They treat the Church with utter contempt, and yet they continue to demand our ministry. What hope have they got? What hope have the children got? They're all on the road to ruin. Frank's a simpleton; he's totally illiterate, so he can't read even the simplest of tracts I've given him – so how can he be an instructive father to his children? Molly and Beau are what you might call 'modern girls' – oh, they have plenty of confidence, but hardly any self-control and so they do exactly what they please. They don't even use their Christian names any more! I ask you, what's wrong with Mary and Bernadette? They're the names they were given at baptism! Ellen is a – well let's face it, she's a charlatan. Her mother was a protestant and an Irish protestant at that, and sometimes those reformist tendencies show in her, if you see what I mean. Father Corristan tells me that she's had a long history of trouble with the Church. Oh, yes. And I think her manner, 'yes, Father' and 'no, Father' and all that, is certainly not as genuine it seems." He paused and thought. "And then we have poor Paul, who turned out to be – not surprisingly, I suppose – a totally wayward child."

"Wayward?" Father Rack smiled. "Ah, but you know, Father, as they say in Ireland, 'Wayward children are never naughty, they're only bold!'"

"They might say such things in Ireland, Father, but in England we're rather more candid about such matters. We like to speak our minds plainly and with alacrity."

They passed the factory gates, and Father Rack said nothing.

They buried Paul in Gorton Cemetery with Dorothy and Theresa, the infant sisters he'd never known. Jimmy Kidd paid for the white marble headstone and the decorative stone chippings. And there, amid the sprawl of angels, the crosses and books and broken crocks, he paled in silence beneath the earth, beyond the plane, like a land baby touched by a dream.

First as Tragedy, Second as Farce: Frank's Story

It was raining again. Frank Parnaby was standing alone some way in front of the assembled men in the factory yard. Wind ruffled his hair. To the right of the men the Office door opened and Mr Mortimer Letchwith Fitch stepped out, followed by Mr Edward Worley and Mr Charles Spears, his under managers. Mr Fitch adjusted his bowler hat as he strode to the centre of the yard and turned to face the men. Mr Worley and Mr Spears arranged themselves on either side of him and adjusted their bowler hats. Mr Fitch surveyed the workforce.

"Now then, men. I've called you all here today to talk to you about an exceedingly grave matter, a matter as grave as I have dealt with in all my twenty years of service to this Company, and I can assure you that there has been none graver than this. As you all know, we're at war and it's our duty to serve our King and Country by becoming the engine of the war effort at home and abroad. We have resolved to conform to the highest standards. So far we have carried out our duties cheerfully, efficiently and without the slightest concern for ourselves. In England's darkest hour, we have rolled up our sleeves, tightened our belts, spat on our hands and put our shoulders to the grindstone for the good of the nation. England expects it; God expects it; and our God-fearing friends and neighbours, wives and children expect it too. It's our patriotic duty to work hard and without regard for our own comforts. It's the very least we could have done. We owe it to all those brave lads who, as I speak, are making the supreme sacrifice against the Nazi hordes, so that we might build Jerusalem here in England's green and pleasant land." He paused and tried to look patriotic. "And there's not a single man among us who would deny it – our call to arms and the beating of ploughshares into swords, pruning hooks into spears and knuckling under in order to work, work, work for the glory of God, England and Tether and Armley & Co. Limited. Nobody here would deny it. No one!" He paused and his expression changed. "All except for one, that is." He looked directly at Frank, raised his arm and pointed at him. "You see this man here?" He wagged his finger. "Apparently, he thinks otherwise. According to him, he's right and we're all wrong! Everybody is out of step except him. He's convinced of it! Now, you all know him. You can hardly miss him. Some of you say that 'he has a big mouth'. He's certainly got a lot to say for himself for just a yard boy, and a yard boy who can't even read or write at that, so he can't be that clever, can he? Mmm, wouldn't you agree? And you'll all know, too, that he calls himself a 'socialist' – a socialist in this day and age! But just recently, this man has gone beyond the pale and has been disseminating all sorts of political nonsense in the sheds. By so doing, he's been spreading alarm and despondency among you men. Alarm and despondency at a time like this! Anyone would think he hasn't realised there's a war on." He stared at Frank. "So this parade has been called to warn you about the damage idle talk can do, and to remind you that in time of war there is no room for insubordination in the workplace. What you do or don't do here has a direct bearing on the course of the war, and we owe it to our glorious nation to make sure that this bearing is a beneficial one. I hope you'll agree that socialist politics doesn't benefit anyone except the devil. So let's ignore it, turn away from it and get on with the job. Do I make myself clear?" He looked round the yard. "Before you go I'm going to ask Parnaby if he has anything to say to account for his behaviour. After all we're reasonable men – we're not Nazis – and he should be given every chance to make amends by acknowledging that in the past he has made errors of judgement and that at times, he has been somewhat, shall we say, 'overzealous' in his approach to things." He looked directly at Frank.

"Parnaby?"

Frank's head remained bowed, and the wind ruffled his hair.

"Parnaby, are you going to remain uncharacteristically silent or are you willing to say something – anything – about what I've just asked you to do?"

Frank was silent.

"Oh come on now, Parnaby! Surely the cat's not got your tongue!"

Slowly Frank raised his head. He stared directly into Mr Fitch's eyes, and said in a clear voice:

"*Hear this word... ye kine of Bashan, which oppress the poor, which crush the needy, which say to their masters, Bring, and let us drink. The Lord has sworn by his holiness, that, lo, the days shall come upon you, that he will take you away with hooks, and your posterity with fish-hooks.*"

The yard was stilled. Only the occasional distant hiss of steam issuing from the boiler room broke the silence. Mr Fitch whispered in a monotone, "Just listen to the voice of innocence! 'Crush the needy!' Crush the needy? You'll soon see the needy being crushed when the Nazis are at the gate!" The patience left him and he shouted, "You exasperate me, Parnaby! You exasperate me, sir! And it's not just your obtuseness that exasperates me – it's what you're letting loose within these walls. Walls have ears, you know!" He paused, and searched the faces of the men; then his voice took on a more moderate tone. "I appeal to you, men. Don't listen to him! You all know what socialism did for us in 1928, don't you, when mad-eyed revolutionaries like him set us all on the road to anarchy and ruin? If you listen to them again that's what'll happen. We'll all be ruined, the Nazis will march in and that will be the end of us all. Surely, that's not you want. Need I remind you that the other name for the Nazis is 'National Socialists'? Maybe he doesn't understand that his socialist cousins in Germany will probably be gloating over every sniving word he utters to undermine our morale and weaken our resolve. He's like a fifth columnist that's parachuted out of the sky dressed as a nun." There was stifled laughter. Mr Fitch became indignant. "Well he might not look much like a nun and he might not act like one, but he's just as dangerous!" He made an effort to calm himself. He looked round the yard. "Now this is a free country, and in England we're proud to enjoy freedom of speech and fighting hard to keep it that way. But on the other hand, I've been invested with certain responsibilities, and one of those responsibilities is to maintain order – order and efficiency. For that reason I'm not going to let any bolshevist talk get out of hand. If you give these people an inch they'll take a mile. So I'm going to nip it in the bud before it flares up and leads us down the road to heaven only knows where. If he continues to sap the morale of our workforce you can rest assured that I shall deal with him, and any others of his ilk, and I'll deal with them severely. So let this public reprimand serve as a warning to him, and a reminder to you all. Let it be known that the froth that this excuse for a man brings up is not worthy of brave men like yourselves. When all's said and done, he's a nobody whose only contribution to the war effort so far is to sweep our sheds, make tea and fetch and carry for the rest of us who are doing real work in this place. Remember that he's not content with saving his own skin by avoiding active service – he's now trying to endanger the lives of those who, thank God, have the guts and the common decency to defend our own people. The Government seems to think he's doing 'Essential Service', but I don't. Why should insubordination count as 'Essential Service'? I'm at a great loss to understand why. Maybe we should look into that. Now then, men, are there any questions?"

There was silence.

"Oh, come on now. Surely someone must have something to say!"

There was silence; then someone spoke from the back of the yard. "I've got a question, sir."

"Mr Fitch turned to Mr Worley. "Who is it?"

"It's McNally, sir."

"Oh, not again! All right, McNally. What is it?"

"My question is this, sir: what's brown and steaming and comes out of Cowes backwards?" There was stifled laughter. "Mr Parnaby thinks it's the Isle of Wight ferry. Are we right to believe him, sir?"

Mr Fitch went red. "Your attempt at 'braw' Glasgow humour is wholly out of place here, McNally. This is a very serious matter and it deserves to be treated seriously. Think of it: Frank Parnaby is part of a workforce that's making locomotives and tanks, guns and munitions to hurl against a foreign foe. If we let things get out of hand now, who knows what might happen? He might take it upon himself to persuade the workforce to start making bombs to hurl against the King and the Government. Socialist talk is dangerous talk, and I won't have it within these walls! I won't have it! Now, do I make myself clear? Good! Right! That's it! I've said all I'm going to say on this matter. You've wasted enough of my time over it already. So all of you get back to work, and let's not hear any more of this incendiary nonsense." He looked round the yard and searched the men's faces; then he adjusted his bowler hat, turned and strode off towards the Office, with Mr Spears and Mr Worley following on behind him. The men relaxed and began to disperse. Cigarettes were lit and they walked back to the Shops. Frank walked towards the Assembly Shop; then Bren Sherwood and Wren Owen came up on either side of him. Bren put his hand on Frank's shoulder and squeezed it gently. Wren smiled, and said in a low voice, "Well done, Frank. Well done, lad." And he ruffled his hair.

Mr Fitch closed the Office door and removed his bowler hat. Mr Worley and Mr Spears did the same. Mr Fitch was agitated. "I can't believe that Parnaby reacted so! There wasn't the least sign of respect or remorse about his manner. The man's either a fool or a madman!"

Mr Spears hung his bowler hat next to Mr Fitch's, on the hat stand by the door in the corner of the room. "If you ask me, he's probably both. He's an ignoramus!"

Mr Worley, in turn, hung his bowler hat on the stand. "A damned dangerous ignoramus!"

"I'm sure my public dressing-down hasn't had the slightest effect on the man. What are we to do with him, gentlemen?" They thought for a while; then Mr Fitch turned to Mrs Clumberbutt, who was sitting at her desk. "Mrs Clumberbutt, go and bring the rum and three glasses please."

"Yes sir." She got up and went into the anteroom.

"I still think you ought to sack him – Parnaby and all the others we know about – the likes of Urien Owen, Paddy McNally, that simpleton Sherwood and his chum, Smedley. They're troublemakers, all of them!"

Mrs Clumberbutt put three glasses on the desk and began to pour the rum.

"Thank you, Mrs... er... Clumberbutt. When you've poured those, would you toddle along to

Communications to collect the post?"

"Yes, sir, of course, sir." She went out.

"Sit down, Ed. Now listen to me. We've been through all this before. I can't sack him – I wish I could, it'd make life here so much easier for us all. But you know as well as I do that we've been told in no uncertain terms from on high that unless people are downright treasonable, we should do no more than keep a watchful eye on people expressing dissent. The Government is sensitive about these things, you know. There are all sorts of political considerations. How would it look in the papers if we started sacking people at the drop of a hat? How would it look abroad when so many of the partisan groups in Europe are socialists – not to mention the poor bloody Russians who are taking such a battering on the Russian Front? No, it wouldn't do. It wouldn't do at all. How do you think things would look to them, if we were seen to be heavy-handed with their so-called comrades over here? No, Ed, we simply can't do it. In times like this we have to remember what unites us, and not what separates us."

"He's right, Worley. There's the unions to think about as well. Their representatives have been quiet so far, and they're backing what they see as 'the war against fascism'. If ever we were to upset them, they might turn treacherous and we'd all be done for."

"You're right, Ed. They tried it on in the last lot, but it's not just that. You have to remember who we're dealing with. These are not pretty Manchester Grammar Boys you know – they're Gorton men. Many of them can't even sign their names. They're Gorton men, men of base metal who are driven principally by their appetites. To be of any good at all to the nation they need strong and educated leadership – our kind of leadership, or else they'll be gulled into doing whatever the nearest hothead demands of them in return for this or that gratification."

It went quiet; then Mr Worley said, "We could try to get them another way."

"What do you mean, Ed?"

"Well, we might not be able to sack them for talking socialist drivel, but we could get them for neglect, sloppy practice – anything that looks like incompetence, and dangerous incompetence at that, in a bomb factory!"

"You've been away, Ed. We've been trying to do that for weeks. The thing is, Parnaby's watertight: he's punctual, he works hard, he even misses tea-breaks sometimes. You can't fault him in that respect, really."

"And he's popular with the lads!"

"Yes, he is, and how much damage can he do sweeping up and brewing tea for the lads?"

It went quiet, and they thought about it.

"Well let's promote Parnaby then – to a job he doesn't like and couldn't possibly do."

"So he'd make a bloody hash of things you mean?"

"And then we'll be able to sack him without any comebacks!"

"Precisely!"

"Do you know, Ed, I think you might have it there! Yes, that's it. That's it!"

"We'll think of a job for him, and then watch every move he makes. And if we can find legitimate grounds... anything at all..."

"Then we'll do the dirty deed!

"Are we agreed, then?"

"Yes, unless anyone can think of anything better."

"No, let's do that!"

"In which case, this calls for another rum – and this time, boys, we'll down it in one just as we used to do at stand-down in 1915!"

Mrs Clumberbutt came in. She put the post on the desk. "Just the usual things, Mr Fitch – letters from the Ministry, bills, reminders, routine accounts and… oh yes, Mr Coltas in Communications wants you to see this – it's a parcel for Frank Parnaby!"

Mr Fitch looked at her. "A parcel for Frank Parnaby?"

Mrs Clumberbutt reached across and picked up a large parcel wrapped in brown paper and tied with string. "Yes, here it is: Frank Parnaby, Tether and Armley & Co Ltd, Gorton Lane, Gorton, Manchester 18."

"Let me see!" She handed the parcel to Mr Fitch. "What on earth…?" He showed it to Mr Spears and then to Mr Worley. "Mrs Clumberbutt, would you please go to the Assembly Shops and see if you can find Parnaby?"

"Yes, sir."

"Give him the parcel."

"Yes, sir."

"And, Mrs Clumberbutt."

"Yes, sir."

"Try and find out what's in it and who it's from, and why it's been sent to this address."

"Yes, sir."

"Find out everything you can – use your womanly wiles if you like. I'm sure he'll like that."

"I'm not sure I've got any of those left, Mr Fitch, but I'll see what I can do." She took the parcel and left.

"Right, I'm going off now to have a haircut. And by the looks of it, you two should consider going fairly soon as well. You know the old army rule: if it's long enough to get hold of, it needs cutting!"

"Yes, Mr Fitch."

Mr Fitch placed his bowler hat on his head carefully, adjusted it, licked his lips, opened the door and marched out into the rain.

It was Friday night, and The Bessemer was crowded. Frank was sitting with Paddy McNally, Harry Smedley, Madeleine Ellis and her friend, Margo Cuthbertson. Madeleine reached across the table and put her hand against Frank's face. "Paddy's just been telling us what happened this morning, Frank. We're right proud of you! That Fitch needed a proper telling, the silly little twerp!"

"Oh that? That's neither nowt nor summat."

"Oh, it was, it was – you're dead brave, Frank. I like that in a man."

"All I did was stand there and take it. We have to do that all the time, don't we?"

"Aye, I know, but quoting the Bible at him – that's dead clever, that is!"

"I bet he didn't even know it was the Bible."

"You must be a big reader, Frank."

"No, but I'm a big listener."

"Ellen will be proud of you. She's got a good man, she has. I always hoped she would get one. She's dead lucky, she is." Frank grunted.

"How she keeping, anyroad?"

"Ah, she's all right."

"And how's her brother, Joe? Is he still at Smithfield market?"

"Aye, he's doing all right at Smithfield."

Bren Sherwood and Wren Owen came across with a tray.

Wren said gently, "Get that one in you, Frankie boy. You deserve it!" He placed a pint of dark mild carefully on the table in front of Frank. Frank nodded and moved the glass to one side.

Madeleine leant forwards. "Oh, that's good. I like Joe – he's a nice lad! Eh, Frank, did you hear that I've got a new fellah – Roger?"

"Oh, aye, I heard that."

"He's doing well for himself, and he can get paint

dead cheap you know."

"Can he?"

"They've got funny names, though: sand, dark green, dark brown, duck-egg blue. Oh, and grey – he can get ocean grey an' all." She stared at Frank. "If you ever want some, Frank, just let me know."

"Right-oh, Madeleine. I'll let you know."

"Eh, Frank, he told me a story. It's about his mate Jimmy Kidd. Jimmy's in prison again and you know why eh? He was working at Avro's, you know, at Chadderton and he helped himself to all this mercury so he could sell it in the scrapyard. And you know what he did, Frank, eh? He poured it bit by bit into a bike frame and when he tried to ride the bike home it fell over! It was too heavy and he couldn't pick it up. He tried his best but it wouldn't budge and that's how he got caught. That's dead funny that Frank, isn't it?"

"Aye, that's dead funny, Madeleine – the daft sod."

"I knew you'd like that story, Frank. You're dead lovely you. Anyroad, there's Doris Bower over there. Come on Margo, let's love them and leave them and go and find out if she's been seeing that black American boy again. I bet she has – the little cow!" They got up awkwardly and gathered their coats and bags and started to make their way through the crowd to the other side of the room. "Bye, fellahs! Stay handsome and be lucky!"

McNally opened a packet of cigarettes and offered them round. Bren rubbed his nose with the back of his hand and then said to Frank, "What was Titch getting all het up about, anyroad? He had a bottom lip like a coal shovel, didn't he?"

Wren shook his head. "Well I don't know. We didn't come out with anything different from what we normally come out with, did we?"

Frank took a sip of the beer. "I don't know neither. I can't fathom it myself, unless it's got summat to do with you telling them mechanics about that German lad – what was he called, Wren?"

"Engels."

"Engels, that's the fellah. Wren was telling them that this German fellah came to Gorton a hundred years ago and he said Gorton was a right dump and that everybody was poor and then Wren said it's still a dump and we're no better off now!"

Wren smiled. "That could be it, but if it was why didn't they come for me then?"

"Because you're new Wren, like Paddy here, and the others. They went for Frank because he's an old sweat. They know he's not going nowhere. He's the devil they know, isn't he?"

"He's the devil they don't want to know."

"Aye, and they sure wish he was going somewhere."

"We dealt with it, though, didn't we, thanks to Frank?"

"Aye, but today won't change nowt, will it?"

"What do you mean?"

"It won't stop them coming after us, will it? They're going to be watching every move we make and if we put a foot wrong, they'll have us."

"Aye, you're right, Frank."

"They even sent Connie Clumberbutt across to see me."

"Ah, sweet Connie – I think she's got a soft spot for you, Frank!"

"You mean Frank's got a hard spot for her!"

"What did he send her for, anyroad?"

"Oh she just brought a parcel that had come for me and she told me that Titch wanted to know all about it."

"A parcel?"

"Aye."

"What was in it?"

Frank turned to face Bren. "Leos for meddlers –

all right?"

Wren looked across to Frank and winked at him.

"What did you tell Connie it was?"

Frank smiled. "I just gave her a load of guff, Bren. You should have seen her face!"

"You're in the firing line, Frank. If he's asking about things like that, it means he's out to get you."

"Aye, I know that, Harry."

"You'll just have to make yourself indispensable then, won't you?"

"How can I do that, Wren? I'm just a 'yard boy', aren't I?"

"We'll think of something, don't you worry, comrade!"

There was silence and then Bren said: "Eh, Frank, I bet you could have murdered Titch when hesaid you were just an excuse for a man. I bet you could have throttled the bastard!"

"No, I didn't care."

"Why not? Didn't you feel angry?"

"No, I didn't, Sherwood – honest."

"Why not?"

"You're new Bren. You've not been following, have you?"

"Following what?"

Wren looked to one side and then whispered: "Because for the last eighteen months, Frank's been shagging Fitch's daughter."

"Bloo-dy 'ell!"

"And if only he'd thought to ask her, she'd have been able to put him right about that, wouldn't she?"

Everybody laughed.

"Look at young Bren now – he's embarrassed! He's gone all red!"

"He's young, leave him!"

Sherwood rubbed his nose with the back of his hand.

"Itchy, Bren?"

"Aye, it won't go away."

"It looks like you're going to have a row with somebody then.

"'Appen it does, Harry. 'Appen it does."

It was early and Frank was tired. It had been a restless night and hadn't slept much. He had been troubled by dreams of early childhood; the father who was a sadistic bully, the mother who was suffocating, and yet who wasn't there when he needed her. The father who would stare at him and say: "You count for nothing in this house. You're just a snotty-nosed little kid." The mother who would look away and say: "Don't ask me to choose between you and your father because I'll choose your father every time." This was the father who was stripping wallpaper when his mother had taken Frank to school. And when she came back, this was the father who had robbed the gas meter and who had left them forever. This was the mother who had wept constantly and who had told Frank that she loved him and nobody else.

During the night, Frank had heard somebody running down the terrace. There were no words, no breaths, just the steady pounding of feet. It somehow sounded like how he had felt. In the dull loneliness of the hours, when fear rises into life, he'd wanted to run away, just as he used to do as a boy, to live under the railway bridge, or somewhere else where he couldn't be found. But he knew he could never do it. He was stuck with what he was and what he had. It was all he had. He opened his eyes and stared at his hands. They were scarred, rough and discoloured and they looked older than his years. He looked at the table: the bottle of milk, the flowery mugs, the cup of sugar, the tin mug of dripping, salt and pepper, the tea pot in its cover the white plate and the knife alongside it. What's the bloody point? Ellen was rattling about. She was making toast. She looked over her shoulder.

"Have you not poured the tea, Frank?"

"I will in a minute, love."

"You don't want to be late for work now, do you?"

"It was no good at work yesterday, Ellen. Do you know what happened?"

"Pour the tea, Frank."

"They called me out in front of all the men and said I was a trouble maker. They made out I was a Nazi and said I was an excuse for a man. That wasn't right, was it? It just wasn't right."

"It's always the same with you, Frank! You're always scuttling with the managers. I think you must enjoy it! Pour your tea."

"Anyroad, my mates were there and they were on my side."

"Did you go to The Bess with them all after work?"

"Aye."

"Was anybody in?"

"Aye, Madeleine Ellis and Margo."

"Oh Madeleine – did she say owt?"

"Only about her boyfriend."

"What about him?"

"Only that he can get paint cheap."

"Can he? That's interesting – we could do with some good cream paint for the front room, couldn't we? You'll have to get some off him if it's not too pricy. I'm sick of that green Walpamur."

"Aye, right-oh."

"Did she say owt about me?"

"No, I don't think so."

"Did you ask her about her mam?"

"No."

"Did you ask her about how things are at Lewis's?"

"No, I…."

"What did you talk about, then?"

"I don't know – we just talked."

"Pour your tea, Frank, or you'll be late for work."

"Aye, right-oh."

"What shift are you on next week anyroad?"

"Two-ten – so I'll be window cleaning in the morning."

"You never stop, lovey, do you?"

"Aye, I have to work, you know that. I'll do Casson Street."

Ellen got up and kissed Frank on the cheek. "You'd better get off now or you'll be late."

"Aye, I will. I'll take my toast with me."

"Go on then."

Frank got up slowly and took a cigarette out of its packet.. "Don't forget to post them letters on the table, will you?"

"I was wondering what them were."

"It's just that Wren's been helping me with my writing. He helped me with my tax form and a letter to Mam, to show her how I'm getting on – and there's another letter an' all, to go to *Picture Post*."

"You've written a letter to *Picture Post*? God help us! You'll be writing to the King next!"

"Aye, maybe." Frank lit the cigarette and then kissed Ellen on the cheek. He tied a scarf round his neck and went to get his coat. Ellen watched him put it on. "Don't forget your butties and your tea."

"I won't." He picked up the bread, which was wrapped in greaseproof paper, and pushed it well down into his coat pocket; then he picked up the white enamel canteen by the handle; and went to open the front door. He looked back and then left. The room was quiet. Ellen got up to take the plates and mugs to the sink. She stared into space. Frank was such a nice bloke: honest, decent, hard-working, full of high ideals and very, very sensitive. She thought about the way it was, the way he used to be when she first met him. She was working in the canteen at Crossley's at the time. Frank was just an errand boy in those days. He was so young, with black hair and good broad shoulders.

She remembered how he whistled a lot and made her laugh, and when she'd got to know him a bit better she found he was a modest, patient and accepting man. She felt safe with that kind of man; he was the kind of man you'd want as a husband. She turned to look at the photograph on the mantelpiece. There they were on the day they were married at the Monastery: two proud youngsters, smiling with joy. That was the day her dad had whispered that she'd got the best end of the bargain. She'd had no trouble believing him until she found out that he'd said the same thing to Frank. That's when doubt had set in. She knew that Frank wasn't her dad's first choice of husband for her, and she also knew that sweet as he was, Frank wasn't her own. But he was a husband, and a good one at that, and that was all that mattered. She was married, and was secured in wedlock. She tried not to pay too much attention to the fears that sometimes came to her in the loneliness of the night, or to those dark and distressing dreams. She was married now, and that was all there was to it. That's all there was.

Mrs Clumberbutt was typing when the door opened and Mr Worley came in. He looked at her and nodded. Then he went through his ritual, which Mrs Clumberbutt knew so well. First, he carefully removed his bowler hat and smoothed the nap of it lovingly with the sleeve of his coat. Then he lifted the hat and put it on the hook, before standing back and admiring it for a moment. Then, with just as much care, he took off his overcoat and scarf and hung them up too. Next, he smoothed his jacket with both hands, checked his collar and tie, cast a quick look at his shoes and then straightened up as though he were about to go on parade. Finally, he reached into his inside pocket and brought out a silver lighter and then a cigarette case. He opened the case, took a cigarette out and put it in his mouth. Then he turned to look at Mrs Clumberbutt. She looked away. Mr Worley lit the cigarette, and smoke streamed upwards in the light. Mrs Clumberbutt shifted in her seat.

"Forgive me, Mr Worley… I'm so sorry to ask you this… Do forgive me, I'd never ask you under normal circumstances, but… but would you be kind enough to let me have a small puff of your cigarette? I haven't had a proper smoke since Friday."

Mr Worley said nothing. He stared at her and drew on the cigarette.

"Certainly, Mrs Clumberbutt – I'll even let you have a cigarette all to yourself… if you'll do something for me." He smiled, revealing a row of even, browned teeth.

"Er… what's that, Mr Worley?"

"Oh it's nothing – just a little kiss, that's all."

"Mr Worley!"

He drew on the cigarette again. "Let's not make a big fuss about it. I only asked for a little, innocent kiss. Still it's up to you, m'dear. The offer's still there. Where you go with it is not my concern."

"What do you take me for, Mr Worley? I'm a respectable married woman!"

"Oh, I know that, dear Mrs Clumberbutt! Anyhow, have you typed that list of components I gave you yesterday?"

"I'm doing it now, Mr Worley!"

He moved nearer to the desk and looked at what she was typing. "Just a kiss – that's all."

"No!"

"Just one little kiss! No one will know."

"Mr Worley – I really must…"

"I won't say anything. What harm can it do? Just a

kiss, and then you can relax and enjoy your fag."

Mrs Clumberbutt said nothing, and carried on typing. Then she stopped suddenly and looked up at him. "Just a kiss... and nothing else?"

"You know me well enough by now, Mrs Clumberbutt. Just one kiss – one small kiss and the cigarette's yours." He put his hand into his inside pocket and pulled out the cigarette case; then he opened it and took out two cigarettes. Mrs Clumberbutt stopped typing, and looked at them and then at him.

"Look, I'll even throw in an extra one." He waved them in front of her. She stared at him.

"Stand up, Mrs Clumberbutt."

She got up slowly. Mr Worley put the cigarettes on the table; then he held her hands and pulled her away from the desk. She looked up at him. He put his arms around her; she put hers round his neck. He pulled her towards him and began to kiss her. After a while she pushed him away: "Your hands, Mr Worley! Your bloody hands! No!"

He chortled, and picked the cigarettes up and held them in front of her face. She stared at him. He laughed and then took the cigarette case out, opened it and put a cigarette back in it.

"You bastard!"

Mr Worley smiled again, and waved the remaining cigarette in front of her. The door opened and Mr Spears came in.

"What's going on here?"

"Nothing that would interest you, Spears – just lighting Mrs Clumberbutt's cigarette." He gave her the cigarette and flicked the lighter. She drew in the smoke, sat down quickly and started to look through some papers. Mr Worley picked up a file. "Just going over to the Plate Shed, Spears – won't be long." He went out. Mr Spears went over to Mrs Clumberbutt. "What on earth was going on then with that little stoat?" Mrs Clumberbutt laughed nervously. "Oh Charles, he was just being his usual creepy self, that's all."

"The swine – I say, he wasn't trying to take liberties with you, was he?"

"No, Charles! Oh, no!" She got up and put her arms round his neck, and they kissed. After a moment, Mr Spears broke away and looked at the door. "If he ever did that, I'd murder the toffee-nosed little swine!"

"Charlie, Charlie! It's all right. He was just being a pig, that's all."

"I know what he is. I served with him. You'll have to watch him, Connie. He means no good – no good at all."

"Oh, I can take care of myself, thank you, Charles!"

"I know that, but that swine rattles me. It's bad enough thinking about your damned husband with his paws all over you, but to think of Worley at it as well it... well, I just want to murder the odious little swine."

"He's nothing, Charles! I'm the dangerous one!" They kissed. "You know that! Once I've got my hooks into you there's no escaping!"

"I love your sort of danger! When can I see..." The door opened and Mr Fitch came in. Mr Spears went over to a filing cabinet. "Good morning, sir." Mr Fitch looked over to him. "Oh, good morning Charles! Good morning, Mrs Clumberbutt."

"Good morning, Mr Fitch."

Mr Spears took an armful of files from the filing cabinet. "I'm just going over to Finance to sort them out, Mr Fitch. They never do get it right, do they?"

"Jolly good. See to it then, Spears. See to it."

Mr Fitch went over to Mrs Clumberbutt's desk. "Er, Mrs Clumberbutt, have you done the Monthly Returns for The Ministry?"

"They're in the file on your desk, sir."

"Good. And the Iron Foundry Audit?"

"Mr Worley is dealing with it."

"Good – I'm glad he's doing something useful for a change." Mr Fitch looked round and then lowered his head. "And yes, Mrs Clumberbutt, did you er, did you manage to find out anything about Parnaby's parcel?"

"Well yes, sir, I did."

"Did you ask him?"

"Yes, sir."

"Well? What did he say?"

"He said the parcel was a delivery of armbands, sir."

"Armbands?"

"Yes, sir – red ones."

"Red arm bands?"

"For the men, sir."

"Good God! Did he really say that?"

"Yes, sir, he did."

"Then it's worse than I thought. He's a madman! The bugger is planning subversion!"

"No, it wasn't that, sir. He said he was going to start a revolution." Mrs Clumberbutt shifted uneasily in her chair and coughed.

"This is extremely serious, Mrs Clumberbutt. We must stop him. If anything else comes through for Parnaby – letters, parcels, telegrams – anything, I want to see them. Is that clear?"

"Yes, sir, I'll have a word with Mr Coltas."

"You do that, Mrs Clumberbutt. You do that. I'll soon put paid to his little scheme. You just see if I don't."

"Yes, sir."

The door opened and Mr Worley came in. "Come quickly, Mr Fitch – there's been an accident in the new Assembly Shop!"

"What?"

"Lifting gear has given way, and a wall and a

supporting beam has just come down, and it's piled into the inspection pit. It's a bally mess. There's debris everywhere and three men have been injured –Reynolds and Parnaby and another one quite seriously – Haines, I think it is."

"Oh, dear God!"

"Wetherby is putting jacks and blocks up against the ceiling, but you'd better come, sir! It looks like it's dangerous."

"Hold the fort, Mrs Clumberbutt, I'd better go and see what's happened. Hold the fort!"

"Yes, Mr Fitch."

Frank was in the yard just outside Assembly Shop 2. Somebody had propped him upright in a metal chair, and had draped a red blanket over his shoulders. His hands were swathed in red and white roller towels, and his hair was powdered with masonry and mortar. He turned his blackened face towards Wren, and drew deeply from the cigarette he held in front of his dry lips. Wren put his hand on Frank's back. "Just sit quietly now, Frank. There's some good strong tea on its way, and the ambulance will be here soon."

"Are you certain they're all right, Wren? Have they been seen to yet?"

"I'm positive – don't worry about them now, Frank. They've gone on stretchers to the Ambulance Room, and they're waiting there for the ambulance. It'll be here before you know it."

"Thank God for that! Thank God!"

"They're going to be seen to in the Infirmary, Frank, I promise you."

"I hope so, Wren. I hope so."

"You did bloody marvellous getting them out – bloody marvellous, it was."

"Honest to God, Wren – I thought they was dead, both of them. They just lay there, they just bloody lay there and Reynolds's leg was… you know, you could see the bone coming up backwards through his trousers – you could see it sticking out!"

"Well, he's being looked after now, Frank. He's all right."

"The poor little bugger, Wren – I could have cried for him. He's only a young lad and he's…" Frank's back arched suddenly and he began to sob.

"It's all right. It's all right, Frank. You're all safe now – look, here's Bren with a nice hot mug of tea for you!"

"Is Frank all right?"

Wren nodded, and then winked at Bren. He felt inside his overall and pulled out a half bottle of whisky. He beckoned to Bren, and they poured a good glugging measure into the enamel mug.

"Now take it easy with this, Frank. You don't want to spill it now, do you?"

"Thanks, Wren. Thanks, Bren." He took a gulp from the mug and coughed. "Jesus, it's…"

"It's fine, Frank. It's fine. Just let it do its work."

Harry Smedley and Paddy McNally came up. "Paddy's just told me what happened. Are you all right?"

"Aye, I'm all right thanks, Harry – just got a bit cut up, that's all." He raised one of his towelled hands.

"The ambulance is on its way, mate, and I've brought the first aid box in case it's needed."

"How's the other two, Paddy?"

"Well, they've been knocked about a bit but I think they'll be all right once the ambulance boys arrive. Bloody Wetherby's with them, though."

"Nobody's to tell Ellen! Do you hear me? I don't want her knowing about this."

"No, Frank – no danger. We won't tell her. We won't do nowt like that."

Mr Fitch appeared, followed by Mr Worley. He stared at Frank; then he and Mr Worley went into the

Assembly Shop. They walked over to the inspection pit and looked around. The place stank of hot oil, wet plaster and emptied bowels. Through the haze they could see men, angular and afraid, lined against the walls in stretched silence. Steel and concrete joists twisted up out of the inspection pit, along with an upturned tank turret and a heap of bricks, cables, framed metal chairs, plaster and overalls.

"Get more ceiling jacks and blocks up against that joist and that one, and under those doors, Ed. Get Crossley's or Hentey & Wilshaw's to give you all they've got, and get the men you don't need out into the yard. If this lot comes down we're all for it!" He turned and went towards the yard outside the main door where Frank was sitting. The men round Frank watched him coming. Frank looked up: "Mr Fitch."

"You're hurt, Frank. What happened?"

Harry Smedley got up. "It was that clown Wetherby again, Mr Fitch. He told them lads to fix a pulley to yon joist." He pointed inside the Shop. "He wanted to see if it would do to lower turrets onto a tank chassis. They told him it wasn't strong enough, but he just wouldn't listen – the silly bastard wouldn't listen, would he?"

Mr Worley came out of the Shop.

"Where's Wetherby now, Mr Worley?"

"He's with the injured men, sir."

"Tell him I want to see him as soon as the ambulance has gone."

"Yes sir."

Paddy McNally got up and stood close to Mr Fitch. "I saw it happen, Mr Fitch. Wetherby knew there was men in the pit. But he tried it and the beam came down. Those poor sods didn't stand a chance! But Frankie – Frankie was there to pull them out, wasn't he? He was the first one in. He threw his brush down and got in the pit, and dug them out with his bare hands."

"Remarkable."

"And there was oil in there, and live electric cables. It could have gone up at any time!"

"You're a brave man, Frank!"

Frank stared at him. "I just tried my hardest to get them out, sir."

"I've quite underestimated you, Frank. We'll... we'll just have to find some way of making up for that, won't we?"

"It wasn't just me, sir – we all did our hardest to get them out."

"Yes, I understand that, Frank."

"You could make up for it by just leaving me and the lads alone, sir. We're only trying to do our work."

"I can see that now, Frank – but then, I've got other things in mind for you."

Ellen had finished her early shift at the factory and had cleaned the fireplace, swept the rugs and polished the brasses. But now she was sitting at the table with a cup of tea and a cigarette and her father's Bible. She'd taken out the pressed lily that Wilfred had given her, and the photograph her father had taken that Whit in May a long time ago: the photograph of her as a girl. She stared at it. It was so long ago, so long ago – she was shy and gawky, and overdressed in things far too big for her, cradling lilies in the crook of her arm, and yet she was so pretty and full of life. She put a hand to her belly. She was full of life. She was full of life. She put the cigarette down and looked at her hands. They were hands that had held and been held in love. She turned them over. She was alive. She opened and closed them, and looked round the room. She was alive. She was aware of being able to breathe easily, and how her heart was beating steadily. She was easy with her thoughts and memories, and the quickness of being alive. She knew that being alive now would bring her to death, when people she didn't know would speak about her, and people she didn't know would walk through the streets, some far older than she was and some, perhaps, less deserving of life. There would be young people who would see and smell and touch and hear, and have what she would no longer have. There would be people who knew her but didn't care about her, and there would be some who had nothing to live for and who wanted to die. That would be then – but this was now, and she was full of life.

She looked at the brittle lily on the table, and reached out a finger and touched it gently. Dear Wilfred. The light in your eyes came from somewhere dark, but it lit my heart. It gave me life. What happened then? Did it really happen? What's happened now? Is it real? Is this the way it's meant to be? Dear Wilfred – precious man – come back to me. Please, I beg you, come back to me soon.

There was a knock at the front door. Ellen looked up; then she put the lily and the photograph back in the Bible and closed it. She got up, opened the door and looked out. It was Urien Owen.

"I beg your pardon, Mrs Parnaby, but you see there's been a bit of an accident in the factory. It's all right, Ma'am! It's all right. It's just that Frank's cut himself and I've been asked to bring him home. Come in, Frank." Frank appeared in the doorway. He stared at Ellen.

"Oh God! What's happened to you? You're filthy!" Frank held up his bandaged hands. Ellen hugged him and kissed his stained cheek. She stared at him, and then looked down at his bandaged hands.

"Oh, what have you done, you silly bugger? What have you done!"

Frank looked directly at her. I just got a bit of a cut on a steel joist, that all. It's all right. The doctor at the Royal put a few stitches in it."

"And he gave him an injection."

"Aye, and he said that I should have had a wash before I went to the hospital, but I had no say in it – they just took me there as soon as they could, with two other lads who were worse off than me."

"Oh, Frank come in – you too, Mr…"

"The lads called me 'Wren', Mrs Parnaby."

"Aye, you too, Wren. I'll put the kettle on."

"That's very good of you Mrs Parnaby, but I'll have to be getting back to work now I know Frank's safely home where he belongs." He turned to Frank. "You look after yourself, my good friend." The two of them exchanged glances; then Wren turned to Ellen and nodded to her. "Bye bye, Mrs Parnaby. I'll see you again."

Bye, Wren. Thanks for bringing Frank home."

Wren smiled and closed the door behind him.

Ellen hugged Frank. "You silly, soft, daft, stupid, lovely man! What are we going to do with you?"

"I'm all right – honest to God – I'm all right, Ellen."

"Come and sit down. I'll make a brew." She put the kettle on the stove and lit the gas. Frank sat down. Ellen sat next to him and held his arm. She stared at his tousled dirty hair, his oily overalls, dry lips and leathered skin, and the bloodshot whites of his eyes. For a long time she said nothing, but rubbed his arm gently; then she stood up and cupped his face in her hands.

"Frank, I've got summat to tell you."

Frank stared at her. He could hear his heart. It was bouncing like a rubber ball in a back entry. This was the face he loved. It was the loveliest face he had ever seen: those eyes, spectral blue, like the eyes he could imagine adorning some royal peacock's tail.

"Frank, I was at the doctor's yesterday."

"You was at the doctor's?"

"Yes. Frank." She smiled. "Frank, it's finally happened! I'm pregnant. I'm pregnant!"

Frank said nothing. Tears filled his eyes. He stared forward and then looked over her head at the far wall. A single teardrop ran down his cheek and made a line in the grime.

Ellen had helped him off with his overalls and stained clothes. She had taken the tin bath from the backyard wall and filled it with water boiled in the kettle. And there, in front of the fire, she had bathed his bruised body gently, and picked the plaster bits out of his hair. She had dried him with tender hands, rubbed zinc and castor oil ointment on the cuts and grazes on his arms and knees, and smoothed her own lilac talcum powder on his back; and he had let her, just as a child accedes to a proud mother. And all that time he had said nothing, nor she to him. The only sounds had been the splashing of water, the sparrows in the eaves and the steady thumping of the steam hammer in the factory yard. But now she had gone out to meet Madeleine, Frank climbed the stairs and went into the bedroom. He sat on the bed and put his hands over his face. They smelled of disinfectant. He sat like that for a long time and then he began to pray in an urgent whisper. He prayed about life and death and birth and sin, and above all he prayed for forgiveness. And then he wept into his useless hands.

It was raining. The men were lined up in the yard. The Office door opened and Mr Fitch came out, adjusting his bowler hat as he went. He was followed by Mr Worley and Mr Spears. Mr Fitch stopped and turned to face the men. Mr Worley and Mr Spears stood on either side of him. Mr Fitch cleared his throat.

"Now listen to me, men. You all know what happened here yesterday, and it's with regard to that I've got several important announcements to make.

First of all, I have to tell you that Mr Spears has just returned from the Infirmary, where he saw young John Reynolds and Colin Haines and their relatives. John is comfortable, but the doctor says he has multiple fractures to both legs, and he won't be rejoining us for a long time to come yet. Colin's condition is rather more serious, I'm sorry to say. He has broken ribs and a punctured lung, and other serious internal injuries. I have to tell you that he's on the critical list, and at this stage it's touch and go whether he's going to make it."

There was a low groan from the men. Mr Fitch held his hand up and then continued.

"Our thoughts go out to these men's families. We'll be sending them a small gift of fruit, and holding a collection for them later today and on Friday. This brings me to my second point. You will also know that Frank Parnaby risked life and limb, and led the charge to get those men out from the debris. He is injured too, but I'm pleased to see him here in the yard today. God bless you, Frank. You're a brave man. We owe you a lot."

There was a brief silence; then Mr Fitch started to clap. Everybody joined in. Frank bowed his head. "And we'll find a way of rewarding you. Please see me in the Office immediately after this parade." Mr Fitch looked at the men. "It might also interest you to learn that the Assembly Shop foreman, Mr Peter Wetherby, has been relieved of his responsibilities and has left our employ. He, more than anyone else, must bear responsibility for what happened yesterday, and he must therefore suffer the consequences for that event. He won't be troubling you again." There was a murmuring amongst the men. Mr Fitch continued, "In war we cannot and will not tolerate ineptitude wherever it occurs, and whomsoever is the cause of its occurrence. There's too much at stake. So please rest assured; where there is incompetence there will be retribution. We will weed these people out, I promise you that. Now then, are there any questions?" There was silence, and then Mr Worley said, "Smedley has his hand up, Mr Fitch."

"Smedley?"

"Aye, sir. The last time we paraded in this yard you said that Frank was 'an excuse for a man' and that he had no backbone, and now you've just told us he's a sort of er... a brave man."

"Yes, Smedley."

"Well he can't be both, can he sir? Which one is he?"

"Smedley – that was then and this is now. I've taken the liberty of modifying my views about Frank Parnaby in the light of recent events."

"Were you wrong first time round then, sir?"

"No, no, but perhaps I might have been, shall we say, a little over-zealous in reaching that conclusion."

"Does that mean you've been a little bit zealous about socialism an' all?"

There was muffled laughter from the men.

"Certainly not! That's just a red herring and you know that, Smedley. You men must never confuse bravery with morality. Achilles slew Hector outside the gates of Troy. He was brave and no one could possibly deny that, but he wasn't a socialist, was he? No, the *Iliad* tells us that Achilles was noble, strong, faithful, loyal and patriotic; in fact he behaved just like an Englishman. No, bravery and morality are quite different things. The two are not the same. Just think about it, you men. Think about it. You might learn something there. The two are just not the same. But in any case, your point is a good one, Smedley, because it leads me to my next announcement." He raised his voice. "Yesterday, you were all told by your foremen not to breathe a word of what had happened to anyone, and that does mean anyone whomsoever, outside these factory walls. I want to reemphasize that this morning. We don't want to allow the world to know the new Assembly Shop is out of action. That would be handing the Nazis valuable intelligence. Now, is that clear? Well? Is it clear?" There was an acknowledging noise from the men. "Not a word! And if any of you come within half an inch of breaking this edict, *I will do such things – what they are, yet I know not, but they shall be the terrors of the earth*! " He glanced left and right to Mr Worley and Mr Spears before continuing, "And not only that, but you'll lose your livelihood permanently, and find yourself in front of a magistrate. Now is that clear? Good! Right – now, are there any questions?"

There was silence; then Mr Worley said, "There's a hand up at the back, sir."

"Who is it?"

"Er, McNally, sir."

"Oh, God! What is it McNally?"

"Er sir, what's long and thin and covered in skin, red in parts and you shove it in tarts?"

And with one voice the men in the yard shouted, "Rhubarb!"

Mr Fitch closed the Office door. "Bring me the rum and four glasses right away, Mrs Clumberbutt!"

Mr Spears banged his fist on the desk. "The damned impudence of it! The sheer bloody cheek of it! You've got to stamp on it, sir! You must do something about it."

"I intend to do precisely that. I'll see to their impudence, Charles. I promise you, I will!

Mrs Clumberbutt came in and put the glasses on the desk where Mr Worley was sitting. "Pour three large ones please, Mrs Clumberbutt, and then leave the bottle here."

"Yes, sir!" She poured the rum. Mr Fitch gestured towards the glasses. "Just like the old days, chaps.

Down the hatch." They drank the rum.

"What are you going to do with Parnaby now he's become a right bloody hero?"

"Well you'll see in a moment, Ed, but mark me, his zenith will prove to be his nadir. You just wait and see if it doesn't."

"I hope so because, quite frankly, I'm getting browned off with all this."

"Me too. It won't do, sir. It's nothing short of insubordination in the ranks."

There was a knock at the door.

"This will be Parnaby. Mrs Clumberbutt, I'd like you to go to Communications and check the post."

"Yes, sir."

Mr Fitch looked at Mr Spears and then Mr Worley. He cleared his throat, "Come in!"

Frank appeared at the door. "Ah, Frank, Frank – do come in!" Frank hesitated and then went in."

"Close the door, old chap, and come and sit down. Get our Frank a chair, Mr Spears!"

Frank sat down.

"We're just going to pour ourselves a rum, Frank – you don't mind me calling you 'Frank' now, do you? Good. I hope not. It would be rather nice if you'd join us, Frank. Will you have a glass of rum? Go on, say you will."

"Is drinking allowed during work time, Mr Fitch?"

"Oh certainly it is on special occasions such as this one."

"I've never had rum before."

"No? Not even in the armed forces?"

"I never was in the armed forces, sir. I was too young... at the time."

"I see... Never mind. This rum's rather good. Pour the drinks, Mr Worley." Mr Worley got up and poured four good measures of rum. Mr Fitch handed one to Frank.

"Now then, Frank! First of all, I'd like to raise this

glass to a hero – a hero who saved two of our men's lives. I raise this glass to Frank Parnaby!"

"Er, yes. Cheers, Mr Fitch. Thank you, but…!"

Mr Worley stared at him and nodded. They drank the rum.

"And now Frank, I want to make a proposition. I've underestimated you. Yes, I have. It's no good denying it. What you did yesterday was exemplary, and I reward exemplary behaviour. So how would you feel about a spot of promotion?"

"Promotion?"

"Yes, by way of reward for what you did, you might say."

Mr Spears looked away. Mr Worley stared hard at Mr Fitch.

"Well, I don't really know about that, sir."

"Well let me make it easy for you, Frank. Those men are grateful to you. We're all grateful to you, and by way of gratitude we'd like to offer you promotion to Office Staff with immediate effect."

"Working in the Office? I don't rightly know about that. You've sprung it on me out of the blue."

"It'd mean a pay rise, Frank!"

"But that would mean leaving the lads – the lads in the yard!"

"It would, but you won't be fit for a long time to do yard work, will you? You might as well turn a necessity into a virtue and we can offer you an extra, an extra seven shillings and sixpence a week for your trouble – that's the very least we can do, Frank. Think about it. Drink your rum now."

"Sir, my wife and I could do with a nice pay rise just now, but there's summat you don't know about me that you should know, sir."

"Oh yes, Frank and what's that?"

"I can't… I have trouble with my letters and that, sir."

"I see."

"Owen's helping me write a bit, but at school I could never get the hang of it and now I just can't..."

"But Frank, Frank – we can see to all that. You'll soon get the hang of going to deliver letters and collecting the post and that sort of thing."

Frank looked down at his feet.

"And I'd benefit from your advice about things. You see Mr Worley and Mr Spears here, well we work as a team when we decide policy and that sort of thing, and you could be part of that."

"Seven and six a week?"

"And you'll be indoors out of the rain and in the warm."

"I just don't know."

"Well think about it, Frank. Why don't you come back first thing on Monday morning, after talking it over with your wife and doing the time-honoured thing by sleeping on it."

Frank stood up. "Thank you for the drink, Mr Fitch, and for the job offer. I'll come back on Monday and let you know."

"Very good, Frank. Let me shake you by the hand."

Mr Fitch shook Frank's bandaged hand gently. "Open the door for Frank, Mr Worley. I'm sure he is keen to think about the wonderful opportunity we have set before him."

Mr Worley opened the door. Frank went over to it, looked round the Office and left. Mr Worley sat down. Mr Spears became agitated. Mr Fitch, why on earth have you offered the scoundrel promotion?"

Mr Worley joined in. "I don't understand you sir. Weren't we all agreed that the man's a dangerous liability?"

Mr Fitch picked up the bottle of rum and poured three more drinks. "There's method in my madness, chaps. Isn't an Office boy who can't read or write his own dangerous liability? I think he might be!"

Mr Spears and Mr Worley relaxed. Mr Spears smiled. Mr Fitch got to his feet, "He who takes the King's shilling must do the King's bidding, won't he? And now, gentlemen, I'd like to propose a toast."

Mr Spears and Mr Worley got to their feet.

"And the toast is, 'To Parnaby's total bloody uselessness!'"

"To Parnaby's total bloody uselessness!"

They drank the rum and sat down.

There were more people in The Bess than there had been for months. Smoke clouded the room. The babble of talk merged with the clinking of glasses and pint pots, laughter and the clatter of dominos. Frank was sitting with Wren, Bren Sherwood and Harry Smedley. On the next table, the Kilpatrick brothers were busy tuning a fiddle and a low pipe. Frank looked up and saw Madeleine coming towards him, followed by Margo Cuthbertson. "Eh, Frankie boy – who's a bloody hero?" Frank put his hands under the table. Wren smiled, "But we all knew that before, didn't we, Miss?"

"We did, but saving men's lives is summat else – and on top of that he's been making babies, haven't you, Frank? You big dark horse, you!"

"Who's been making babies?"

"Frank has. Ellen told me all about it when I met her on Hyde Road this morning."

Harry Smedley looked at Frank: "You've kept that quiet, Frank!"

"I was going to tell you, Harry. I was... I was just waiting for the right time, that's all."

"Congratulations, my friend."

"Well, congratulations, Frank."

"Thanks, Paddy. Thanks Wren. I was going to tell you, honest to God I was."

"And I hear you've got a new job an' all! A posh one in the Office, haven't you, Frank?"

"Well, I've not really made my mind up about it yet, Madeleine."

"Ellen said you had. All this success must be in the stars! Oh, there's Doris just come in. Stay lucky, Frank. I'll see you again, darlin'."

Bren looked hard at Frank. "So you've decided to take that job then, Frank?"

"No, I haven't, Bren! It's just that Ellen wants me to – she says it's safer working in the Office and what with the baby on the way. She keeps saying: 'Needs is must, Frank. Needs is must.'"

"That's an odd expression."

"I don't know where she gets them from."

"She means that you need the money."

"Yes, I know. I know we do, but I don't know – I like working with you and the lads. You know where you are with the lads. And anyroad, I'd be no good in an office. Everybody knows that!"

There was a long silence. Wren lit a cigarette and gave it to Frank. Bren shifted in his chair. "Well, I don't think you should take it, Frank. I don't like the sound of it at all."

"Why's that, Bren?"

"Well, if Frank takes that job it'll be like... it'll be like he's with them and not with us. He'll have gone over to management and he doesn't rightly belong there, does he?"

"He'll only be an Office worker, Bren, that's all."

"No he won't! It'll be worse than that. He'll be like a class traitor – that's what he'll be like."

"A class traitor! You don't know me at all then, do you, Bren?"

Bren got up and walked over to the door. "If you take that job, Frank, I won't want to know you no more!" For a moment he looked back at where they were sitting; then he turned and went out the door. Frank looked down. Smedley looked at Wren and McNally and then said, "Bloo-dy 'ell!"

Frank exploded. "What's it got to do with him, the daft sod?"

"Frank, Frank – he's young!"

"Aye Frank, just ignore him – he'll come round!"

"He's just jealous, that's all!"

Wren held his hand up. "I fear not, lads! The fact is the boy's plain scared."

"Scared?"

"Aye, scared, because he knows what Frank could do if he becomes a poacher turned gamekeeper."

"They did say they wanted me to tell them about things – summat about policies."

"They want him to tell tales."

"He'd be in a good position to fleece us all, then, wouldn't he?"

"I'd never do that, Wren!"

"No, I know you wouldn't, Frank, but young Sherwood doesn't know that does he? He hasn't known you long enough – and besides, look what happened to Wetherby when he was made up. He was worse than all the rest of 'em put together."

"Aye, he knew all the tricks right enough."

Frank looked up. "It was a good job that we knew one or two tricks more than he did, though, wasn't it?"

Wren smiled. "Now that's given me an idea! Young Bren's gone and done us a favour!"

"What?"

Wren's eyes sparkled. "We could make them a present of Frank! He could be our Trojan Horse!"

"What – like our eyes and ears?"

"Exactly!"

"Like our cuckoo in their nest?"

"More like our thumb up their bum!"

Everybody laughed.

"So they want him to tell tales, do they? Well, we can surely see to that – can't we, lads? We'll give them some good ones then, won't we?"

"How do you mean, Wren?"

"We'll give them some good old fairy tales!"

Everybody laughed.

"Good old socialist ones! You take the job, Frank! Take what they offer you and grasp it firmly with both of your big beautiful bandaged hands."

Frank smiled. "Do you think I should?"

There were nods all round.

"Well you know lads – I think I will!"

Frank went into the bedroom and sat on the bed. After a while he put his hands together. Then he whispered:

"Oh – I'm dead upset, please help me. My heart's broken and I don't know what to do. I'm so lonely and as scared as 'ell an' all. I'm sorry. I'm so sorry. I know about the baby. I just don't know what to do about it. Sweet Lady, please help me. Saint Anthony come around. Something's been lost and can't be found. I'm sorry. I'm dead sorry. For pity's sake please help me. Oh, I'm no good at words and that. I'm sorry. I am – honest to God. My hands look daft with these bandages, and they're starting to smell a bit an' all. I shouldn't have to pray with smelling bandages, should I? Please forgive me. I beg you, but I'm lost, you see. I'm lost and I feel little, a little kid again. I want to find myself so I'll be all right. I'm lost and I can't do nowt about it. Christ! I'm in a right mess, what with the baby and the job and that, and Ellen says we need the money and she's right. I can't do nowt about any of it, can I? I know there's more to life than jobs. Wren knows that an' all, and he doesn't even believe in you. He just says the Church has made you up, and you're just there to make things seem all right when they're not. He knows a lot, does Wren. His union in Wales saw to that, but he's got no idea about you. Dear Lord, I'm a mess. It's my mess;

it's my own mess. It's my life, and I can't do nowt about it. I can't change what I am, but I suppose I can try and change the way I do things. Wren and the lads can't help me much with that, but you can though. You can, so please help me and keep me safe, and when I find myself again, I promise you… that then you'll be proud of me… and the world… all the world will be my lobster. Amen."

Mrs Clumberbutt smiled at Frank. "When have you got to go back to the hospital, Frank?"

"Thursday."

"To get your dressing changed?"

"I expect so."

"Are your hands any better?"

"They itch something terrible."

"That's them healing, then."

"Aye, maybe."

"Well we'd better go across to collect the mail."

"Have I got to go an' all?"

"Of course you do, you daft ha'porth. That's part of your new job isn't it? I've been told to show you the ropes. Right then – are you ready?"

"Aye, c'mon."

Mrs Clumberbutt opened the door and they went out into the yard. A dull drizzle wet their faces. Men in the Assembly Shop looked over at them as they walked across the yard. They got to the Communications Room and went in.

"Mr Coltas is in the back, Connie. I'll go and get him."

"Thank you, John."

Frank looked round.

"Have you ever been in here before, Frank?"

"Aye, but it was a long while ago."

Mr Coltas appeared. "Hello Connie, hello Frank. How's your hands?"

"Hello Mr Coltas. They're all right, thanks."

"The letters are in the pigeonhole. Oh, and Frank – there's a parcel for you in there too."

Mrs Clumberbutt emptied the pigeon hole and handed Frank a small parcel. Frank took it. He turned it over and said, "It's been opened."

"Oh yes, it was just by mistake, Frank. Just a mistake, that's all."

"What is it, Frank?"

"Oh, it's just some rose water from *Picture Post*. It's for Ellen's birthday, but somebody's opened it."

"The bottle isn't broken though, is it?"

"No, that's not broken, but who'd do a thing like that – open another person's parcel?"

"Forget about it, Frank. You can't have stuff delivered to an address that's not your own and not expect to have it looked at. There's a war on you know. Is everything in order, Connie?"

"But it was only rose water for Ellen's birthday…"

"I think so, Bob. Come on Frank. We'd better get back."

They went into the yard. There was a commotion near the new Assembly Shop with men going in and out of the main doors. Frank ignored it and said to Mrs Clumberbutt, "You know about this, don't you?"

Mrs Clumberbutt said nothing. Frank stopped in the middle of the yard and held her by the arm.

"You know about this so tell me! Who ordered it?"

Mrs Clumberbutt's lips tightened. "Frank I like you… very much, but I can't!"

"Who was it?"

"I can't tell you, Frank."

Frank held her jaw and stared at her. She gazed back; then Frank kissed her opened lips firmly.

He stared at her again. "Who was it, Connie?" They looked at each other.

"If I tell you Frank, do you swear you won't do anything daft?"

"Of course I won't."

"Or tell on me?"

Frank whispered, "Who was it, Connie?"

They looked at each other.

"It was Fitch. It was Fitch. He gave orders to Coltas to open anything that came for you!"

"Why? Oh, I get it now – you told him what I said about the arm bands, didn't you?"

"He was looking for bad things – orders, leaflets, bombs, I don't know…"

"Oh for Pete's sake!"

"I'm sorry."

"So it was old Titch, was it?

"He thinks you're trouble. He doesn't trust you, Frank."

"That's why he wants me in the Office! It was nowt to do with rewarding me, was it?"

"He wants to keep an eye on you."

"The crafty little bugger!"

"He wants to trip you up because you're trouble with the lads."

"Trouble, am I? Well, we'd better not disappoint him then, had we?"

"Frank, you said you wouldn't do anything daft, didn't you?"

"I won't, I won't!"

"As long as you know what he's up to…"

"Aye, I know what he's up to right enough. And I know which side's my bread's buttered on, but I'm still going to show him a thing or two. One way or another, I'll show him!"

"Oh, watch out, Frank. I don't want to see you get hurt, that's all."

Frank held her closely and kissed her. There was a cheer from the opened doors of the new Assembly Shop. Mrs Clumberbutt pulled away, and Frank waved to the smiling men. Then he took Mrs Clumberbutt by the arm, and they walked over to the Office and went in.

"Ah, Frank – there you are!"

"Mr Fitch, I've got my parcel..."

"Never mind about that, Frank – we've got a flap on. The traction engine that we sent into the new Assembly Shop to pull the beam out of the pit has broken down and we can't get it going again. Until we do we're at a standstill. Nothing can get out and nothing can get in. We're in something of a pickle."

Mr Worley scratched his head. "Well, if we can't use Crossley's engine until next week and Fothergill's shunter is down in Macclesfield, it's worse than being in a pickle. It's a bloody disaster."

"Are you sure we can't just strip and rebuild our engine?"

"We could, Charles, but it'd take far too long. We've got to keep up with the schedule."

"We're in for a damned rocket then, aren't we?"

"It looks like it, chaps."

Silence followed; then Frank spoke up. "When was promoted to the Office I thought you said you were going to ask me things about policy and that."

"This isn't policy, Frank, it's a matter of logistics."

"I don't know what that is, but I think I can see a way of helping out."

"You Parnaby? What on earth do you know about replacing a traction engine?"

"Steady on now, Ed. Let the man speak."

"Well, I think I can get it shifted, sir."

"Why, what are you going to do; Parnaby – bring in what's left of the Red Army so they can give it a bit of a push?"

"Or give us a quote from the Bible and thereby work a miracle?"

"Charles, Edward! Really! Let him speak."

"It'll take a day or two to sort out, mind."

"If we can solve this matter in a couple of days, our bacon will be saved and I'll reward you, Frank."

"Reward me?"

"I certainly will. This matter is critical, and if you can help us solve it you'll be fully deserving of a tangible reward!"

Frank thought for a moment and then said, "If I do this for you, sir… if I can do this, will you let me keep my rise but send me back to the lads in the yard where I belong?"

"The damned cheek of it!"

"That's plain bloody impudence!"

"Steady, Charles! Now listen to me, Frank. You are without doubt an avaricious little oik, but this is such a pressing matter… and if you can help us to solve it we might be able to offer you that sugar plum."

"You mean I'll be sent back to the yard?"

"If you succeed Frank, we'll certainly consider it."

"You won't go back on that, will you?"

"No, Frank, I won't – you have my word on it, but you also have my word that if this plan of yours turns out to be just another one of your barrack-room pranks, there'll be trouble. Is that clear?"

"Aye, sir – as clear as day."

"I'm glad we understand each other, Frank. Now what's your plan?"

"Well, I can't tell you about that, sir, until I've sorted it out myself."

"You mean, in a crisis of national importance you want me to put my faith in a plan you haven't already got?"

"Outrageous – I told you he was a damned ignoramus!"

"If we cannot see a way out of this, why should we listen to you – you're just a yard…"

"Ed!"

"I know what has to be done – I've just got to sort the details out, that's all."

"And you're not going to give us the slightest indication of what you have in mind?"

"Well, I can, sir. I can tell you that I'm going to need one or two things to get the job done."

"What – like a Crusader tank?"

"No, just one or two things that's rationed. That kind of thing."

"Now look here, Frank. Spit it out. What do you need?"

"Er, I need two gallons of petrol, er… a box of two score half-inch, used stainless steel ball bearings, er… a bar of hard soap, two buckets of dark ale, all the sugar cubes you can find – and oh, a good long hose attached to the mains water supply. That should do it, sir."

They looked at each other and then Mr Worley started to laugh. "Why not throw in a bell, book and candle while you're at it, Parnaby?"

"And perhaps a barrel of magic fairy dust? Come on – you're not going to take him seriously, are you, Fitch? The man's a madman."

"You're right, Charles – he couldn't do anything with that lot!"

"My patience is running out now, Frank. Do you expect us to take all this seriously?"

"Aye! I'm serious, Mr Fitch – honest to God, I am. I can shift that engine for you!"

There was a long silence; then Frank said, "Look Mr Fitch – do you want me to shift that engine for you or what?"

"I'll try anything, Frank, but if you don't succeed in shifting that engine and you make fools of us all, we'll shift you – right out the factory gates and down the lane!"

"At least I know where I stand then, don't I, sir?"

"And at least you know where I stand too, Parnaby!"

"Just get the things together, sir, and leave the rest to me." Frank looked round the room at each of them in turn. "I've got to go to the phone box on

Gorton Lane." Then he left the Office.

Mr Spears stood up. "You can't let him get away with that, Fitch – he's got no idea at all of how to shift that engine!"

Mr Fitch looked at Mrs Clumberbutt. "Go and get the rum, Mrs Clumberbutt and bring three glasses. What else can I do, Charles? I have no choice."

Mr Worley took his opportunity. "How can he shift an engine with a bucket of beer and a bar of soap? I mean, for pity's sake, Fitch. He's quite clearly mad."

Mrs Clumberbutt came back with the rum. "Pour three large ones Mrs Clumberbutt, and then go and see if there's any post in Communications."

"But I've only just been, sir."

"Do it. Thank you." She went out. Mr Fitch stared at the floor. "And yet he managed to get the men to shift close to a ton of steel and masonry with their bare hands, and save the lives of two trapped men! If there's half a chance he's got something up his sleeve, then we've no choice but to take it. Charles, get in touch with Crossley's again, and see if there's any change in availability. And check Fothergill's, to see if they can get a move on, and Ed…"

"Yes, sir."

"See that the lads keep looking at our engine to see if there's anything – *anything* – they can do to get the damned thing out of that Shop."

"Yes, sir!"

"I'll tell you chaps – I've got no confidence whatsoever in this, but I daren't do anything else."

"I just wonder whose side Parnaby is on, Fitch."

"I tell you, Ed – I'd rather be on our side than on his. If that unspeakable toe rag crosses me, he'll be in for a rude awakening and he'll be damned sorry. I'll show him the natural order of things! One way or another, I'll show him!"

Ellen walked to the railway bridge on Gorton Lane

and stopped. She looked down. There was the broken fence. There was the gulley, and the red and white signal. And there were the railway lines that rattled out the hours, and caught the shining light of souls in their steel. This is where butterflies danced in the sun, and where the dead lay ragged-backed and belching blood. This is where laden waggons hammered by at night when children slept, and where coal was scattered black amid the ballast and the dull, heavy sleepers. This is the place where they said there was hope, and where salvation was just around the corner. And this was the lifeless vein that ran its length through the heart of Gorton.

Ellen hurried by the terraced houses in Gorton Lane. Here, inside open doors and behind net curtains were things that made a home – sideboards, plaster figures and flower pots, chairs, crosses and bottle openers, cats, bread and milk, glasses of porter and mugs of sweet tea, and holy pictures with curling edges stuck in mirrors. Every parlour filled her with sadness. She was sure that somewhere in these rooms there were men who were becalmed by love, and women who had been made pregnant by warmth. She was sure they had children who had been raised without guilt. Why couldn't she have what they had? Why couldn't she have ordinary love, the kind of love you don't have to think about because you know it's always there? Why couldn't she have love you can talk about to anybody who wants to know? She arrived at the Monastery and went in.

Here were the familiar sounds and sights and smells that filled the senses and transformed earthly things into a dream. She genuflected, crossed herself and knelt down in the pew she knew so well.

And after a while she looked up at the Christ hung in its full misery. How many times had she gazed up at it? How many of her dead were still here? Her thoughts turned to Wilfred.

God please forgive me my sins. God bear my sins, for I can't bear them any more. God bless my baby. God bless Wilfred, wherever he is, and bring him to me safely so I can hold him again. He's mine. He's my husband. Why did you make him go away? Why did you make him come back to me? It was better that he'd stayed away with that woman, whoever she was. When he came back it was so nice. He gave me so much love – and now he's brought me more pain, and a baby, and I'll never be able to tell my baby the truth about what happened. I feel so guilty, so very very guilty. I've let Frank down. I've failed as a wife, and I'm going to fail as a mother an' all. But if Wilfred doesn't come back – please God, don't let that happen, please let him come back – if he doesn't come back, though, I promise I'll always love him, and I'll always remember him, and I'll always thank you for sending him to me. God forgive me. Amen.

Ellen reached for her handkerchief and blew her nose. She got up and started to make her way out of the pew when she heard a familiar voice.

"Ellen, Ellen, Ellen. How nice to see you." It was old Father Black. He smiled at her.

"I've been hearing all about your heroic husband! How you must be proud of him!"

"Oh, Father."

"Dear Ellen, you're crying. Sit down. Come on now, sit down here."

Ellen reached out and held his hand.

"Dear, dear. What's troubling you, child?"

Ellen sobbed. Father Black remained calm and stared at her. Then Ellen said, "Father – I'm wretched!"

"What is it, my dear?"

"Father, I've sinned."

"Who amongst us hasn't?"

"No Father. I've sinned against God, I've sinned against the Church and I've sinned against…"

"Why?"

"I've sinned against Frank."

"Why do you say that, Ellen?"

"Father I've been made pregnant."

"Well, now! Isn't that a wonderful thing?"

"No, it isn't, Father! And honest to God, I'm dead scared about it."

"Oh, Ellen – it's your first child and the first one often brings its own anxieties – you know that!"

"It's awful, Father!"

"There's no need to be afraid, Ellen. '*The Lord is my light and my salvation; whom shall I fear? The Lord is the protector of my life: of whom shall I be afraid*?'"

Ellen looked Father Black full in the face and said in a steady voice, "Father, you don't understand. You see the child is not… It's not Frank's, it's another man's."

Father Black sat down beside her. Ellen held his hand with both hers. Father Black frowned. "I see." There was silence and then Father Black said, "Ellen, does Frank know about this?"

"No, no, he doesn't."

"Are you going to tell him?"

"No, Father – it would break his heart."

"I see."

"I don't want to do that. I couldn't bear it. Please spare us both the pain of that, please."

"And what of the child's father? Is he local?"

Ellen stared at him. "No, Father."

"Mmm. So where is he now?"

"He's gone away. He's doing some sort of war work."

"What kind of war work?"

"He wouldn't tell me, but he said he had to go away and that it could be dangerous."

Father Black's eyes narrowed. "Do you think he'll be back?"

"I don't know, Father, but he did say he'd come back to me."

"And if he does, what will you do then?"

"What can I do, Father?"

"Will you tell him about the child?"

"Yes, Father! No! Oh, Father, I just don't know what I'll tell him."

"Do you love this man, Ellen?"

"Yes, I do, Father."

"And Frank?"

"Aye, I love him an' all. I could never leave him."

"You love them both?"

"In different ways, yes, I do."

He thought for a while and then said, "Then, *amor vincit omnia* – love conquers all things!"

"What does that mean?"

"It means that love is a mystery, Ellen, but because it is always of God, it always carries the redeeming power of God within it."

Ellen bowed her head and said nothing. Father Black continued, "You've stopped crying, Ellen."

"Yes, Father."

"That's good."

"You've given me something…"

"That's good, but let me ask you this: is Frank happy that you're with child?"

"Oh yes, Father. He's always wanted a child. He cried with joy when I told him."

Father Black bowed his head and said nothing; then he looked up at Ellen. "Then in the circumstances it might be kinder if we let Frank continue to embrace his joyfulness as he brings up the child."

"Do you mean I shouldn't tell him?"

"I mean if he's happy to love the child and bring it up in the light of God, then perhaps you should allow him to do so."

"And what will I do when the child's father comes back?"

"Oh, we'll think about that when the time comes."

Ellen stared at Father Black. "Father – Father, I've told you all this and I've been dead honest about it, and you're the only one that knows. But you won't think badly of me, will you, Father?"

"Oh, but of course I won't, Ellen."

"It was only the once with him, only the once. The baby was just an accident, that's all it is."

Father Black smiled. "Let me tell you Ellen – your baby is most assuredly not an accident. Nothing in this world happens by accident. Things happen through divine providence and not through anything else. Your child is the gift of God. You must always remember that."

Ellen looked at him and smiled. She lifted his hands to her lips and kissed them. "Thank you. I won't forget that, Father. I'll always remember."

"God bless you, Ellen."

"And God bless you also, Father."

Ellen watched as Father Black got up and walked away. She felt reassured at first, and then wondered whether she had done the right thing.

Mr Fitch gestured to Mrs Clumberbutt. "Have you got all the things that Parnaby wanted for his magic tricks?"

"Yes, Mr Fitch – it's all there in the yard."

"Good. We'll just have to wait and see what he intends to do with them."

"Oh, he asked for a handcart an' all."

"A handcart? A handcart! What's he going to do with a handcart?"

"And he also asked me to ask you for permission to open the main gates at 11.00 a.m. precisely, so two of his friends can get in."

"Two of his friends? Who are they? They could be anybody!"

"They're specialists, Mr Fitch. Apparently, he can't do the job without them."

"Is there no end to this fool's antics? But I suppose I have no choice. We've drawn a blank with the other three options and so I have no choice. Yes, I'll open the gates, Mrs Clumberbutt, but I want to see these people and talk to them before I'll let them anywhere near that engine, do you understand?"

"Yes, Mr Fitch."

Mr Fitch rubbed his eyes. "Oh, and Mrs Clumberbutt."

"Yes, Mr Fitch."

"Do we have names for Parnaby's little helpers?"

"Yes, Mr Fitch – they're called Phil and Lil."

Mr Fitch shook his head. "Dear God! Phil and bloody Lil!" He sat back in his chair and closed his eyes. "Bring me a large glass of rum will you, Mrs Clumberbutt?"

"Yes, Mr Fitch."

"I've got a feeling that this isn't going to be my day."

The doors of the new Assembly Shop were open and men were standing in the yard in little groups chatting, laughing and smoking. Mr Fitch was standing stiffly by the main gates with Mr Worley and Mr Spears. They were resplendent in their bowler hats. Mr Fitch looked at his pocket watch. It was two minutes to eleven o'clock. He snapped the case shut, put the watch back in his waistcoat pocket and nodded to Mr Spears. Mr Spears nodded to young Albert Bainbridge, who opened the main gates of Tether and Armley & Co Ltd. Everybody watched.

"Are you sure we should be doing this, sir? You know he'll make damned fools of us if you let him."

"Calm, calm, Charles. Let's just see what his friends have to say for themselves."

"But if this gets out of hand, were all for the high jump."

"It won't get out of hand, Ed – but you might. Poke your head round the gates, and see if anybody's coming."

Mr Worley went to the gates and stepped out into Gorton Lane. He looked both ways and then came back.

"See anything?"

"Not a thing, but I could hear some shouting. It was coming from Casson Street, I think."

Frank came up. "Good morning, Mr Fitch. Thanks for getting the things together for me and for getting the handcart an' all. I forgot to mention that."

"What do you want a damned handcart for, Parnaby?"

"To put the cans of petrol and the box of ball bearings on, Mr Spears."

Mr Fitch sighed. "Well do it then, Parnaby, do it."

Frank held up his bandaged hands. "I can't manage that just yet, sir."

"Spears, Worley – you heard what the man said. Load the cans and the box of bearings onto the cart!"

Mr Spears and Mrs Worley looked at each other and then went to load the cart without making any attempt to hide their irritation.

Mr Fitch put a hand behind his ear. "What was that?"

"What?"

"I thought I heard shouting. No it isn't – it's cheering!"

"That'll be them then, sir."

"What's all that commotion about, Fitch?"

"Apparently, Parnaby's chums are arriving."

"Open the gates wider, Bainbridge."

The gates were drawn back to their full extent, and a loud cheer went up from the playground of Tether Street School. Mr Fitch went through the gates and looked down the lane to see what was happening. Coming towards him was a man dressed in blue baggy trousers, a turban and a patterned jacket of Eastern design. He was followed by an elephant sporting a thick leather harness. Frank came out, followed by Mr Spears and Mr Worley. Frank smiled, "Oh aye – it's Phil and Lil, sir! Er… Phil's the bloke with the funny clothes on and Lil's the elephant, sir."

Mr Fitch's jaw sagged. "Well, I'll be damned! It's an elephant! An elephant and… a damned wog!"

"Good God, Fitch! You're not going to let a foreigner with an elephant rampage round the factory, are you?"

"They'll run riot!"

"Sir, he's not a foreigner – he's from round here."

"What?"

"It's Phil, sir. I know him. He works at Belle Vue. He goes to our Church. He says he's from Malaya. They're on our side, the Malayans are."

"All I know is that he's a foreigner and like any foreigner, Malayan or not, I don't trust him."

"Well said, sir!"

"You'd better trust him, Mr Fitch, because if you don't you'll never get that traction engine out of the shop this morning. Lil's good at pulling heavy things, but she won't do it unless Phil asks her to."

"Is that so?"

Frank went across and shook hands with Phil. "Excuse the bandages, Phil!" Phil whispered, "Eh, Frankie boy – what's all this, then, about playing the big hero?"

"Oh, that – that was nowt, Phil. Hello Lil!" Lil held her trunk to Frank's face and he stroked it.

"She remembers you, Frankie!"

"'Course she does. I remember her an' all – don't I, Lil? Oh, er, Phil come over here and meet the boss." They walked to the gates. "This is the boss, Mr Fitch, and them two are his understrappers, Mr Spears and Mr Worley."

Phil bowed. Mr Fitch cleared his throat, and in a loud voice and with expansive gestures said, "You think you shift BIG engine with elephant – savvie?"

Phil smiled and patted Lil's trunk. "That's a very interesting accent you have there, Mr Fitch. You must be from foreign parts – Senegal perhaps, or Donegal, or is it Bongo Bongo Land?"

"All right! Never mind all that!"

"Yes, good, that's fine and I'm quite sure Lil will do her best for you, Mr Fitch. Have you got all the stuff, I asked for, Frankie boy?"

"Aye, it's ready."

"Just a minute, just a minute!"

"Yes, Mr Fitch."

"How do I know I can trust you?"

"What d'you mean?"

"He means, how does he know that you and your elephant are not going to do us more harm than good?"

"Well I suppose, logically speaking, he doesn't."

"Why should we let you in, then?"

Phil thought for a while and then said, "Because if it ever gets out that you delayed production at Tether and Armley's, thereby endangering the entire war effort just for the sake of a couple of gallons of petrol, a box of marbles for my kids, a bar of soap to wash the elephant that would save your hide, and something for her to eat and drink following the safe removal of the engine – and all because the Mahout had a dark skin like all those other dark-skinned men in the British Armed Forces, including both my sons, who are, as we speak, fighting and dying for the

Allied cause in every theatre of war – then you'll be recognised as the nasty little prick that you really are, sir – that's why."

Mr Fitch glared at him.

"Now then, Mr Fitch, are you going to let us help you or not?"

Mr Fitch continued to glare. Phil waited, and then said, "C'mon, Lil. We're not wanted here." He began to turn her round and then Mr Fitch said: "Yes, all right, do your best then. Come in." He turned to the men in the yard and shouted, "Make way for the elephant!"

Phil followed Frank, and led Lil in. As they went he talked gently to Lil, and bowed to the men who were lining the walls on either side of the yard. Mr Fitch, Mr Worley and Mr Spears strode behind. Mr Fitch waved men aside. "Get on with it. Get on with it." They came in sight of the new Assembly Shop. Frank pointed to its opened doors and Phil led Lil in, talking gently to her as they went. Frank directed them to the traction engine. A crowd of men gathered at the doors. Among them were Mr Fitch, Mr Worley and Mr Spears, looking worried but important in their bowler hats. They came to the engine. Phil said something to Lil, who unfurled her trunk and touched the engine's boiler gently.

Phil waited a moment and then turned Lil round. Frank showed him where to anchor the chains on Lil's harness to the engine. These were made secure. Phil spoke gently to Lil. The heavy leather harness creaked and the chains went taut. Lil's body suddenly lurched forward. The massive bulk of her hind quarters convulsed towards her shoulders. Nothing happened. Lil was breathing heavily; then, without a word from Phil, she strained again. Her massive legs trembled. Frank heard strange guttural noises deep in the cavity of her chest, and then, bit by bit, the engine began to move.

At first it moved slowly, but as she continued it gathered pace and the men began to cheer. Phil waved to them and put a hand behind his ear. He waved again, and invited them to keep cheering.

Lil's tail began to swish, and carried on swishing all the way to the doors and out into the crowded yard.

"Would you pour each of us a large rum, Mrs Clumberbutt?"

"Yes, Mr Fitch. Thank you."

"Well, you've done it, sir! Engine and the beam out of the way, ceiling secured, rubble in the inspection pit cleared away and production readied to start again."

"I didn't do it, Spears. It was Parnaby who did it – Parnaby and his damned tame Sepoy! They were the ones who did it!"

"Does it matter who did it – after all, we're off the hook now?"

"Of course it matters, Worley. Can't you see? Parnaby's made monkeys out of us. The men can see that, even if you can't. We've lost the yard!"

"If we ever had it in the first place."

"The men thought he was a bally hero, and now they think he's a bally genius as well."

"They carried him shoulder high through the yard!"

"He'll think he's invincible."

"Especially since he'll be going back to the yard now he's managed to do the job for us."

"Ah, but he's not going back, Spears!"

"But I thought you said…"

"I said nothing of the sort. I only said I'd *consider* sending him back there – nothing more than that."

"Where is he, anyhow?"

"He's gone to the clinic to have his stitches taken out."

"That's the opposite of what should happen to him. Someone ought to stitch him up!"

"Leave it to me, Worley. Leave it to me."

Frank opened the door. "Mr Worley said you wanted to see me, sir."

"Yes, Frank – come in."

Frank came in.

"Sit down."

Frank sat down.

"How did you get on at the clinic, Frank?"

"I hate them places."

"But what did they say?"

"They said my hands was healing nicely, but I shouldn't do any heavy manual work for a month."

"I see."

"But I could do light yard work sir – you know – now I'm going back to the lads."

"Oh, I wouldn't dream of asking you to do that, Frank. We mustn't risk anything. A hero like you should be looked after. You need to be looked after, don't you, Frankie boy?"

"But I pushed the cart to Belle Vue for Phil and it was all right then."

"Yes, I know. Cans of petrol, no doubt destined for the black market."

"They were for Phil's motor bike, sir. He wants to see his mother."

"His mother?"

"Aye she lives in Liverpool. They've had it bad in Liverpool."

"Be that as it may, I'm not going to let you return to the yard. You'll stay in the Office and do light duties until I say so. Is that clear? And since it's only light duties, I'm putting you back on your old wages."

"That means you've gone back on your word."

"I run Tether and Armley's – not you."

Frank looked down.

"You see, I'm the boss, and I can do whatever I like. In fact, I'd like you to go and clean my boots – in the yard so you don't make a mess. And take my bowler and give it a good brushing."

Frank looked up and then said: "*Revenge not yourselves, dearly beloved.*"

"And what do you mean by that?"

Frank smiled. "Them as knows their own nose knows." Then he went out.

It was late. The sun was setting, and the sky was ablaze with shards of red and gold and apple green. Wren and Frank were walking slowly along the canal towpath by Walker's scrap metal yard. Wren shook his head. "Why didn't you tell him that you'd made a gentleman's agreement with him? Surely an agreement is an agreement, isn't it?"

"Because I didn't want to give him the satisfaction of knowing that I was dissatisfied, that's all!"

"Oh, Frank, Frank! But what did Ellen say about your loss of wages?

"She wasn't happy, was she? We need the money for the baby, you see."

"Why don't you ask for it back?"

"No, Wren. I've got my own ways of dealing with this, but for now I'll do well to bide my time."

"I'd strangle the old bugger."

"That's too good for him, Wren!"

"Well, what will you do then?"

"Don't worry, I'll think of summat. But he's out to get me. It's turned personal now. He's rubbing my nose in it. Now I'm on light duties he's got me skivvying as his batman. I've got to clean his boots every day, don't I? He knows I need the money now the baby is on its way. And once I'm fit and back on Office work he'll go for me. He knows I can't read all that good. Everybody knows that."

"I know, but you're learning."

"Thanks to you, but I'm not learning fast enough. Sooner or later I'll make a big mistake, and then he'll have me."

They passed the paint works and Slack's Brewery yard and the back of Grace's pie shop, and watched the seagulls crying like the dead, and wheeling on fixed wings beyond the factory rooves. The canal stretched before them, its purpled waters with its planks and reeds and paint pots and dead things turning into foam at the bywash. Wren peered into the water. "Do you know, Frank, even in all this shit there's still living things in here."

"I know – beetles, leeches, snails and there's still some tiddlers. I remember catching tiddlers when I was a kid, and keeping them in a jam jar."

"Aye, but it's a wonder that they survive in all that, right enough." He peered into the water.

"I've always found that funny about you, Wren."

"What?"

"You always see the wonder of things and yet you don't believe in religion, do you?"

"Religion has a lot to teach us, Frank. It's those who do the teaching who worry me."

"Oh aye? What has it ever taught you then?"

"*When Adam delved and Eve span, who was then the gentleman*?"

"What does that mean?"

"It means, Frank, that when your good Lord made the world he made people to live in it who were workers. There's no mention of him making bosses!"

"Who made them then – the devil?"

"No, no Frank – you can't blame the devil for that! For all his malevolence and love of pure evil, even he wouldn't stoop as low as that. No, Frank, the bosses have made themselves and that's why we must make ourselves, so we can stand up to them."

"You're going to go on about the revolution now though, aren't you?"

"By overthrowing them and running things ourselves – yes, that's how we solve the problem."

"We can't solve all our problems with a revolution though, can we?"

"Why not?"

"I know nowt, Wren and I'm not as clever as you, but I know this – after the revolution there'll still be things we'll still have to face up to, won't we – getting old, feeling scared, getting sick, losing people, being lonely – and all that? Revolutions won't shift that lot, will they? You might be able to do away with bosses and everything they stand for, but you'll never be able to do away with all our miseries and them things that make misery lose its grip – even for a short while."

"What, like fags and booze, you mean?"

"For some folk, aye! We all need some… some… you know… some way of getting by, don't we? But most folk need summat deeper – summat that tells them about the wonder of their lives even when they're living in shit like them poor buggers down there." He nodded to the water.

"Don't tell me, don't tell me – you're going to say next that after the revolution we'll all have to turn to God!"

"No, Wren, I'm not. What did you used to say? Aye, '*Now is the time*!'"

The Office door opened and Mr Worley came in and looked around.

"Where's Parnaby?"

Mr Fitch looked up from his desk. "Oh, I've sent him out to the Foundry. He'll be back shortly. Do you need him for something?" Mr Worley looked behind him and then closed the door. "Coltas tells me that a parcel has arrived for Parnaby. It's big and heavy – no rose water for his wife this time! You'd better come across and see for yourself."

Mr Fitch got up and went to the hat stand. "I hope this is it, Worley! I'll have that odious little oik yet!" He put his bowler hat on. "Damn it, Worley. I only had a haircut two days ago and now my bowler is tight again. Ernie mustn't have cut my hair short enough. I'll have to go again this afternoon. Damn it! I'm not made of money! Damn it!"

They went out and marched across the yard to the Communications Room. As soon as they reached the door Mr Coltas opened it. "I thought it best you should come across right away, Mr Fitch."

"Yes, yes – where is it?"

"There on the table."

Mr Fitch went across and examined it. "It serves to be forensic on these occasions." He picked the parcel up carefully. "Now let me see. About the size of a shoebox, heavy-ish, ordinary brown paper wrapping secured with parcel tape, ordinary parcel string well-knotted and sealed on the back with sealing wax. It's carefully put together, this... neat handwritten address... a Liverpool postmark... Liverpool, eh?" He examined the sides of the parcel. "Mmm... no sender's address. Have you a pair of scissors, Coltas?"

"Aye, on there." He pointed to the scissors on the table beside the parcel.

"You're not going to open it, Mr Fitch, after the way Parnaby reacted last time, are you?"

"I have to, Coltas – it's a matter of national security. Now then... if I cut along here..." He cut carefully along the line of tape, and then began to remove the brown paper wrapping. "Oh, it is a shoebox. It's taped at the sides." He cut through the tape. "Now we'll see what Parnaby's been up to! Now we'll see what his little game is."

"Come on, Mr Fitch – open it!"

Mr Fitch removed the lid of the shoebox. He stared at its contents.

"Good God!"

"What is it?"

"It looks like… it looks like shit!"

"Shit?"

"It is shit!"

"What on earth… ?"

"But that's not human shit, is it?"

"No, look at the size of it!"

"You'd have to be something big to pass that lot!"

"Close it up, Coltas."

"Wait – there's a little envelope tucked into the side."

"Get it out then, Coltas."

"Certainly not – I'm not putting my hands in there!"

"All right, Worley – you do it!"

Mr Worley pulled a face and looked at Mr Coltas. Then he went in carefully and removed the envelope. He turned it over.

"Good heavens! It's addressed to you, Mr Fitch."

"To me?"

"Yes, have a look!"

"By golly, you're right – it is!"

"Are you going to open it then?"

Mr Fitch took the envelope and opened it carefully. He pulled out a piece of paper. "It's got writing on it!" He read it and as he did his lips began to move. 'Dear Mr Fitch, But if you do not what you say, no man can doubt but you sin against God: and know ye, your sin will overtake you. Numbers 32:23'" What does that mean?"

"Who could have sent such a thing? It sounds like Parnaby!"

"I'm not certain where this comes from, Worley, but it's not Parnaby who's written it. Parnaby can scarcely write, and when he does his writing doesn't look like that. Besides, how could he have put a parcel together like this – his hands have been cut to ribbons?"

Mr Fitch turned to Mr Coltas. "Liverpool postmark, animal's droppings, they knew that we'd opened Parnaby's rose water? It's got to be Parnaby's chums – Ali Baba and his damned elephant – who've sent this! Don't laugh, Coltas – it's scandalous. They're making a mockery of us, the insubordinate little oiks! But I'll show them! I'll teach them to flout my authority. I'll soon get to the bottom of this!" Mr Coltas laughed. "I think you already have, Mr Fitch – it's an insubordinate elephant's bottom!"

Mr Worley joined in. "And one that's just delivered industrial-strength bowel movements!"

"Presumably on behalf of old Parnaby, who's not quite up to the elephant's standards yet!"

"In return for all the shit that Fitch has dished out just lately!"

"Worley! Coltas! You're not taking this seriously, are you?" See to it that this parcel is taped up securely and then presented to Parnaby. I want to know what his reaction is when he opens it."

"Smug delight, don't you know!"

Mr Fitch snorted and then hurried out of the door.

It was Bren Sherwood who came up with the idea. He was having a tea break with Harry Smedley in the Patterns Shop when it came to him. "I know, why don't we go and see Fitch and tell him that if he doesn't let Frank go back to the yard, we'll write to the Secretary of State for War, and other folks an' all – like the Bishop of Manchester and our MP and that – and tell them how badly Fitch has treated Frank after all he's done for Tether and Armley's." Harry Smedley's eyes shone.

"That's a beltin' idea, Bren, but I thought you'd fallen out with Frank!"

"No, not fallen out with him, Harry. I was just disappointed with him. It looked like he was betraying his class for money, but I can see now that he'd never do that."

"Course he wouldn't, Bren. He was just as reluctant as the rest of us, but what could he do with Fitch leaning on him one way, and his pregnant wife leaning on him the other way?"

"Let's just say I was a bit hasty, that's all. I'll make it up to him. You just see if I don't."

"We'll tell Wren about it. He's good with words, isn't he? He'll help us!"

"No, Harry! Don't tell Wren, or the unions or anybody else! They'll just take over and then they'll get all the credit, won't they? I want Frank to know that we did it and not Wren."

"All right, then. Start thinking about it in your head while you're working. I'll do the same, and then we'll meet tonight and try and write the letter."

"Aye, and when it's done then show the lads, so they can put their two penn'orth in it and sign it."

"Aye, all right, Bren. I'll see you in The Bess tonight."

"Aye, right-oh, then."

"We're going to change things, aren't we?"

"Aye – we're the ones who are going to find him out!"

The Office door opened and Mr Spears came in. "Well, has he opened it?"

"He has, but he took some persuading. I had the devil of a job!"

"Why was that?"

"Because he wanted to open it at home. I insisted, citing National Security, and he eventually gave in."

"Mmm. What did he say when he did open it?"

Mr Spears shook his head. "He just looked at it. Then he said he'd been expecting some elephant shit from Phil to put on his rose."

"On his rose?"

"Apparently he's got a rose growing in an oil drum in his back yard."

"But if that's true, why did Phil send it through the post? He would have been far easier to have just given it to him. No, that doesn't make sense. Old Sinbad knew we'd been checking on Parnaby and that we'd open the parcel! That's why he sent it to Tether and Armley's!"

"Along with the Biblical warning."

"Yes, I wonder what that was about?"

"I don't know, Worley."

There was a knock at the door.

"See who that is, Mrs Clumberbutt."

"Right away, Mr Worley."

She went to the door and opened it. "It's Brendan Sherwood and Henry Smedley sir."

"What on earth do they want?"

"They want to see you, Mr Fitch. They have a letter."

"A letter? A letter? – Oh, all right! You'd better bring them in, Mrs Clumberbutt."

Mrs Clumberbutt opened the door wide and gestured them to come in. Harry Smedley came in first. He took his cap off, nodded to Mr Spears, Mr Worley and Mr Fitch, and looked round the room quickly. Bren followed, staying close by Harry's side.

"Well, what is it, men?"

Bren glanced at Harry and then said, "We've come about Frank, Mr Fitch."

"What about Frank?"

"We want you to put him back in the yard where he belongs, sir."

Mr Worley turned in his chair. "Well, the damned cheek of it!"

"I'll deal with this, Worley."

"You see, sir, Frank – Frank's a hero, isn't he, saving them men's lives and that and getting the pit clear, and we think he deserves better, don't we,

Harry?"

"Oh, you do, do you? And what gives you the right to come to me and make demands about things that are of no concern to you?"

"We've brought a letter that explains why."

"Have you indeed?"

"Yes, sir."

"Is that it?"

"Yes, sir."

"You'd better give it to me, then."

Bren looked at Harry and then slowly held out the envelope. Mr Fitch took it quickly, opened it, took out the letter and unfolded it. He started to read.

"Dear Mr Fich",... He reddened. "Fitch has a 't' in it. You can't complain right if you can't spell my name right for heaven's sake!"

"Sorry, Mr Fitch!"

Mr Fitch shook the letter and started again. "Dear Mr Fich." He sighed and then continued, "We the undersigned workers of Tether and Armley and Company Limited of Gorton Lane, Gorton, Manchester 18 do hereby swear that Mr Mortimer Fich..." Mr Fitch looked up at them and then continued, "Manager at the above firm..." He looked up. "Manager at the above firm? Manager at the above firm? I'm not Manager at the above firm! I'm General Manager of the above firm! Is that abundantly clear?"

"Yes, Mr Fitch."

Mr Fitch shook the letter again and continued, "... at the above firm... has treated Mr Frank Parnaby very very badly indeed and even after he saved the lives of two men called John Haines who is critical and Colin Reynolds, who broke his limbs and he is only just a young lad after a very big heavy beam give way in the new Assembly Shop and crashed to earth and ruined the Inspection Pit and even after he got his friend Mr Hernandes to pull the beam out with an elephant just for some bolleys and some toffees for his children and some petrol for his motor bike and some soap to wash Lil with and some beer and some sugar lumps. We are very extremely adamant by how he has been treated and demand his immediate return to the yard forthwith."

"So you the undersigned workers demand his immediate 'return to the yard forthwith', do you?"

"Yes, sir – we do."

"But nobody's signed it!"

"Aye, but they will do, sir."

"Who are they?"

Bren looked puzzled. "All the lads in the yard, sir – plus me and Harry." He touched his chest and Harry's shoulder. "We're all going to sign it!"

"Are you quite sure about that?"

"And you see, sir, if Frank doesn't come back we're going to send it."

"You've already sent it, haven't you?"

"Yes sir, but no, we haven't yet, if you follow my meaning, sir."

"No, I'm not sure that I do, Sherwood."

"We've got a list, sir – a list of people we're going to send it to."

"A list of people you're going to send it to?"

"Not the same one, like – we'll only send copies to the people on the list, sir."

"Which people?"

"Have you got the list there, Harry?"

"Aye."

"Well give it to Mr Fitch, then."

Harry handed the list to Mr Fitch. Mr Fitch looked at it and then his face coloured. "List of Important People Who Will Get The Letter:

Father Black

Tommy Hanley in The Bess

Mr Margesson, the Secretary for State for War

Dr Hardwicke

The Bishop of Manchester... Are you mad? You can't sent this letter to the Secretary of State for War and the Bishop of Manchester!"

"It's not just them, sir. We've got some more on the list, haven't we?"

Mr Fitch shook the list and then returned to it. "Clifford Smith to give to all the Union Stewards. Mr Churchill... Oh, for Pete's sake!"

"What's wrong with that?"

"What's wrong with it? What's wrong with it? I'll show you what's wrong with it!" He put the list and letter together and ripped them into several pieces. Then he threw the scraps of paper into the air. "Now then – that's what's wrong with it! Now, I'm ordering you two scoundrels to get back to work. I don't want to hear another word about this. I run this factory and if you don't like it, there's the door! Do I make myself clear?"

"Yes, sir."

"Right, well, close the door behind you!"

They closed the door.

"The damned insolence of it!"

Mr Fitch sat down. "I don't trust them, Spears. How do I know they won't write another one?"

"You put the fear of God into them – surely they wouldn't do that now, would they?"

"Oh, but they might, Charles."

"What are you going to do?"

Mr Fitch stood up and took his bowler hat from the hat stand. "I'm going to have a haircut."

"What, again?"

"I know, but it still doesn't feel right. I'll apply my mind to the situation this evening, and then tell you my decision in the morning."

"Yes, it's as well to sleep on a problem."

"And if he's nothing else, Parnaby has certainly proved to be one big problem."

Mrs Clumberbutt was sitting at her desk typing.

The door opened and Mr Spears came in. He put his bowler on the hat stand and came across to her. "Don't you get up to say 'good morning' to me any more, Connie?" Mrs Clumberbutt carried on typing. She looked up briefly. "Good morning, Charles." Mr Spears turned her face towards him and kissed her. "Oh, do stop that, Charles!"

"I'm only kissing you!"

"Well don't! Is that all you think about?"

"That's all you used to think about – once!"

"What if someone sees us?"

"Who?"

"Well, what if Worley came in?"

"That little stoat! What do I care if he did?"

"Well you should care! Anyway, Ed's not a stoat!"

"Not a stoat? You've changed your tune, haven't you?"

"You don't know him like I know him."

"What do you mean by that?"

"Well I know he's a bit... you know... a bit of a Romeo, but he's not like that really. He's nice!"

"The man's an insufferable little..."

"No, he isn't, Charles. There's a side to him that's really sweet!"

"I don't believe you've just said..."

The door opened and Mr Worley came in. He looked across at them. "What the devil's going on here? Is he bothering you, Connie?" Without taking his bowler off he walked over to them.

"Oh no, Ed. We were just talking about Mr Fitch and what he's going to do with that troublemaker, Parnaby."

Mr Worley stared at them; then he took off his bowler hat and went to hang it on the hat stand. He came back, reached into his inside pocket and took out a silver cigarette case. He opened it and offered Mrs Clumberbutt a cigarette. She took one. He took one and snapped the case shut; then he put it back in his pocket and pulled out a cigarette lighter. He lit Mrs Clumberbutt's cigarette and then his own. "I know what I'd do with that repulsive tick!"

"What's that, Worley?"

Mr Worley came close to Mr Spears' face and hissed, "Men like that need gelding, don't you think, Spears?"

The door opened and Mr Fitch came in. "Good morning, everyone."

"Good morning, sir."

He looked at them.

"Well sir, what are you going to do with him?"

Mr Fitch collected himself and then said, "I'm going to send him back to the yard where he belongs!"

"But sir, you said…"

"I know what I said, Worley, but I've changed my mind. If he were to stay here he'd be a liability. If dimwits like Sherwood and Smedley can dream up such a potentially dangerous way of protesting as they have done, what do you think the likes of Urien Owen, the unions and even Parnaby himself are likely to come up with?"

"But they've not come up with much so far, have they?"

"That doesn't mean they're not going to, Charles! No, I can't take the risk. I'm sending that bad bugger back where he belongs and that's an end to it! Mrs Clumberbutt, Ed, please alert your foremen. Don't say anything about what I've just said – keep it secret – but tell them that there will be a parade of all personnel in the yard at 9.30 prompt this morning."

"Yes, Mr Fitch."

"And do it right away!"

Frank was sitting alone in the yard with a lighted candle and a hot spoon, melting black boot polish on Mr Fitch's boots. He had been ordered by Mr Fitch to sit in the yard, not so much as he had claimed 'so he wouldn't make a mess', but so the whole world could see him being made to polish the boss's boots. He put the boot and spoon down and looked at the bowler hat. A parade in the yard, was it? In which case there was a job to be done – and one that only a humbled boot boy would be able to do. Frank reached for the bowler hat and then looked round the yard. There were comings and goings, but nobody was taking any notice. He smiled and turned the hat upside down. He lifted the leather headband inside it carefully, looked round the yard, and then quickly went to work removing all the strips of newspaper he had hidden under it each time he had been given the task of brushing it. He stuffed the newspaper into his pocket; he would get rid of that later. He folded back the headband, and put the bowler hat to one side. Then he picked up a boot and began to polish it with all the innocence of St Crispin.

"Have they all been lined up?"

"Yes, sir."

"Well, we should go then. Make ready!"

"It's still not quite 9.30, Mr Fitch."

"I know that, but it'll take a couple of minutes to get to the yard. Worley – pass my bowler, will you, old chap?"

"Yes, sir."

"Have you got headwear, Parnaby?"

"No, Mr Fitch."

"Well you should attend to that forthwith. It doesn't do to comport yourself bareheaded nowadays, you know!"

"Yes, Mr Fitch."

Mr Fitch put his hat on and licked his lips. "At last, that's beginning to feel better. It fits far better than before. All right, men, follow me."

Mr Fitch opened the door and they marched out.

The men in the yard watched as Mr Fitch and his men made their way to the centre of the yard. As they strode out, Mr Fitch's bowler began to slip until it had reached his ears. He adjusted it nervously. Then it slipped again to his ears and flattened them. Mr Fitch stopped. Mr Spears and Mr Worley took their positions on either side of him, and Frank stood awkwardly behind them. Mr Fitch cleared his throat and addressed the parade.

"Now then, men, listen to me." There were murmurings amongst the men, and from somewhere at the back somebody started laughing. Mr Fitch tried to compose himself.

"I've called you all here today to give you some news."

The bowler tilted forward and obscured Mr Fitch's view; he had to lift his chin to see the parade. The men in the front row began to imitate the stance. Murdoch didn't try to hide his glee at what was happening. He stared at Mr Fitch, and through a gaping grin showed what was left of his teeth.

"It's come to my attention that our brave hero, Frank..." He turned to Frank and nodded, and his bowler slipped half way down his cheek. He righted it. "... has asked to return to his duties in the yard, having now... (he adjusted the bowler again, and lifted his chin so that he could see) ... completed his management training in the Office, and we have acquiesced to his wishes, and he will be returned to you on full pay – yard pay that is – with immediate effect."

The parade broke into applause. Cheers and laughter followed. Mr Fitch was taken aback by this reaction and turned to look at Frank, and with that his bowler hat fell off. The parade roared. Mr Spears retrieved the hat and passed it to Mr Fitch, who put it back on. It fell to his ears. The parade clapped enthusiastically. Mr Fitch tried to collect himself.

"Well, men, I can see that my decision to release Frank is a popular one!" He glanced quickly at Mr Worley. "And so unless there are any questions, I suggest you all get back to work, and on with the efforts of Tether and Armley's, to further our sterling contribution to the war effort." He lifted his chin and looked at the parade. "Any questions? No? All right. Parade is dismissed."

"There's a hand up at the back, sir."

"What?"

"There."

Mr Fitch strained to see. "Who is it?"

"Erm – it's McNally, sir."

"Oh, God, not McNally!"

"You'd better listen, sir."

"What is it, McNally?"

"Well, sir, you must have heard the expression, 'If you want to get ahead, get a hat'..." Laughter filled the yard. "But what we want... what we want to know is this..." He took a breath.

"Where did you get that hat? Where did you get that tile?" The parade joined in and sang. "Isn't it a knobby one. In just the proper style. I should like to have one. Just the same as that. Where 'ere I go they shout. 'Hello, where did you get that hat?'..."

At first Mr Fitch didn't move; then, at last, he reached up and removed his hat. The yard went quiet. Then, from the back of the parade, Bren marched forward, smiling as he went. He moved proudly and confidently, casting glances to right and left. He came to Mr Fitch's line of men, and went up to Mr Fitch. He stopped and then turned to look at the parade. They cheered, and the cheer became a roar as Bren grasped Mr Fitch's face in his hands and kissed him full on the lips. Mr Fitch staggered backwards and dropped the hat. Bren picked it up, faced the parade and held it up with outstretched arms. The men cheered, and waved their arms in the air. Bren bowed to them, and then went across to Frank. He held the bowler over Frank's head. Quietness descended on the yard as Bren brought the bowler down slowly on Frank's head. The men cheered loudly and moved forward. Mr Fitch, Mr Spears and Mr Worley hurried away towards the Office. Mr Spears glanced back and saw Frank, who was still wearing the hat, being carried on the shoulders of several men towards the new Assembly Shop.

Sometimes there was talk about whether that brief and irreverent moment of triumph in the factory yard had been Frank's finest. Some thought it was, but others thought it had been the day he'd pulled the men from the pit, or the 'day of the elephant'. One that was often talked about was the day of his wake. This took place two weeks after he'd fallen from a ladder in Tib Street. He'd been cleaning the windows of a pet shop owned by one of Jimmy Kidd's mates. He was hardly equipped for the job; his ladder wasn't long enough, and he had to stand on the topmost rung to reach the highest windows. He knew it was a dangerous thing to do, and he'd said so several times. Jimmy hadn't listened, though; he'd just told Frank to carry on regardless.

Frank's handcart had helped to break the fall, but he'd still been badly injured. They'd taken him to the Infirmary and after four days, following his request, the doctors had let him go home. Five days later, he died in the arms of his beloved wife, Ellen.

When news of Frank's death reached him, Jimmy tried to make light of it. He said that while doing the job Frank had overreached himself, and when it came to most things in life Frank usually overreached himself. That was a cruel thing to say, but there were more than a handful of folk in Gorton who were quick to agree with him.

Frank's body lay neatly in the coffin under the window in the parlour for two days. People came to pay their respects, and to gaze upon his stiffened ivory face. Mr Burntbrush, the undertaker, seemed to have done a good job; apart from a twist to his upper lip which revealed a protruding yellow tooth, Frank appeared to be at peace.

It was Jimmy Kidd's idea to have a private male-only wake for Frank. Ellen didn't really approve of it. She thought it was a daft idea, but she liked Jimmy and was grateful to him for offering to pay for the funeral and provide a headstone.

On the day of the wake they carried Frank's coffin to a duck-egg blue bread van Jimmy had borrowed from one of his mates. Jimmy decided to drive it, and Wren accompanied him in the front passenger seat. Harry Smedley, John Clements, Tommy Hanley, Phil Hernandes, Paddy McNally and Joe Molloy sat in the back with Frank's coffin. They drove to The Lake Hotel near Belle Vue, leaving Frank in the van whilst they went inside for a pint. After that they had drinks in some of the other pubs where Frank used to go: The Three Arrows at the bottom of Church Lane, The Shakespeare, The Steelworks and then on to The Vulcan.

They left The Bessemer to the last, and as they got out of the van Tommy Hanley said, "We can't just leave him here on his own."

Wren looked puzzled. "What are you saying, Tommy – that some of us should stay with him?"

"No, Wren, The Bess was Frank's local. We should bring him in."

"What about them inside?"

"Listen – I'm the Landlord of this place and I think we should bring him in!"

So they carried the coffin up the steps and went inside, and laid it across two tables near where Frank had sat after work with the lads. There weren't many people in, and the arrival of Frank's coffin was met with silence. Madeleine Ellis was sitting at the bar with some of her friends. She stood up and called out, "Come on, everybody – don't be shy! Let's give him a send-off to remember!"

Somebody left to tell the neighbours. Elsie wheeled the piano out. Tommy began to pull pints of beer and line them up on the bar. Madeleine and her friends came over to the coffin and pulled chairs round it. Tommy and his wife carried drinks on trays, and started handing them out. Tommy lifted his glass. "Listen, everybody! Three cheers for Frankie boy!" Hip hip…"

"Hooray!"
"Hip hip…"
"Hooray!"
"Hip hip…"
"Hooray!"

Elsie began to play. Everybody joined in. 'I'll be with you in apple blossom time. I'll be with you to change your name to mine. One day in May, I'll come and say, Happy the bride that the sun shines on today…' Madeleine and her friends came across and stared at the coffin. They sang gently and affectionately. At the end of the song, Wren put his hand out and touched the coffin.

"Last time in The Bess, Frank!"

McNally changed the mood. "How about making yourself useful for once, Frank?" He put his pint glass on the coffin lid. Everybody laughed and put their glasses on too. McNally knocked on the coffin and said in a loud voice: "The drinks are on you, Frankie boy!" Then Harry Smedley rested his cheek and a hand against the coffin lid and growled, "We all want 'Boddies', Frank! You can't beat the taste of good old 'Boddies'!" He licked his lips. Madeleine giggled: "Eh, you're dead funny you, Harry!"

Wren listened to all this and then held up his hand and said, "Boys, boys, behave yourselves! Let's have some respect. This is Frank – yes, it's Frank we're here to see off, isn't it?" Things quietened down for a while. Then people began to arrive in their twos and threes. They came to the coffin. They touched it, they kissed it; some crossed themselves. Women wept, and men looked away. Drinks were bought. Songs were sung. The day descended; beginnings and endings like changing tenses, coarse laughter and gentle words, close melded, into prayers for the dead. The litter in Taylor Street became its leaves.

Bren had fallen asleep. Harry Smedley looked at him and said, "Look at Bren – he's sleeping like a baby."

"He's had a skin full."

"He's had two skin fulls."

"We've all had two skin fulls!"

"Eh, do you remember that time in the yard when Bren crowned Frankie with Titch's bowler?"

"Aye, it was dead good, that."

"Eh, why don't we send Frank off with a bowler hat on?"

"Aye – why didn't we think of that before?"

"Aye, he deserved to have one on at the end."

Then Jimmy said: "Eh, it's not too late, you know! I know somebody who might be able to get a bowler for him." Wren groaned.

Joe Molloy pulled a face. "Course it is! How do you get a hat on Frank now he's screwed down?" Wren groaned again. Jimmy produced some change from his pocket. "Watch this!" He took a sixpenny piece and tried to unscrew a chromed screw in the corner of the coffin. He made several attempts at it and then gave up. Joe Molloy took the sixpence. "Give us it here!" He did his best with it and then threw it on the coffin lid and stood up. "Right, sod this! I'm going to get a screwdriver." Jimmy got up. "I'll go an' all – to see my mate round the corner and fetch a bowler hat." They left together. Phil looked at Tommy. "Have you got a whisky to get down him when the lid's open, Tommy – just for old time's sake, like?" Wren got to his feet and said: "Right, I've heard enough now, lads. No screwdrivers, no hats and no 'kin whiskey! Do I make myself understood? We're not going to open the coffin. We're going to leave Frank in peace now, aren't we?" He stared at each one in turn. "Drink up all of you, because we're going to take him back now." Everybody looked at Wren and then emptied their glasses quickly. Tommy woke Bren up and told him to clear the cigarette packets, ashtrays and empty glasses from the coffin lid. It didn't take long. When he'd finished, Bren cleaned it with the sleeve of his jacket. Tommy wiped it with a cloth. Wren stood up and tapped it. They lifted the coffin up and moved slowly towards the door. Some people in the corner clapped. As they went down the steps, Bren tripped and the coffin slammed down onto the pavement. A woman screamed and McNally swore. The coffin lay on its side. It was damaged on one corner, but otherwise it seemed to be sound. They picked it up and walked carefully to the van. Once the coffin was in the back and everybody had got in, the doors were closed and Wren drove to Frank's house in Gillingham Terrace with as much solemnity as he could muster.

They got out of the bread van in a reverential silence. Wren nodded, and they pulled the coffin out of the back and heaved it onto their shoulders. Madeleine rattled the door knocker. Then at Wren's word, they set off towards the front door. Just as Ellen was opening it, Bren tripped on the kerb and the coffin swung down heavily and finished upright facing Ellen.

Madeleine said, "We've brought your Frank back home, Ellen – here he is." Ellen stared at the coffin and said, "But you've got him upside down. He's standing on his head!"

Bren grinned. He looked directly at Ellen and sang, "Pa-na-by! He's no good! Chop him up for firewood! When he's dead, stand him on his head. Then we'll have some currant bread!"

Everybody laughed. Then they struggled to right the coffin and carry Frank inside. Ellen tried to keep her composure. After all, she had expected nothing less; it had been Frank's wake, with Frank's friends. And once, a long time ago, when things had been straightforward, she had been his wife.

Father Richard Rack's hair ruffled in the wind. He looked at the people standing by the graveside, removed a handkerchief from his trouser pocket and blew his nose. He looked up. "We've now laid Frank to rest. Frank, as he so earnestly entreated us, lies deep within his mother's grave and in sight of the grave of his little children, Dorothy and Theresa, and his beloved son Paul. And now it's up to us to support Ellen and the children in and through their grieving." He paused and looked around. The wind blew his hair. He swept it back. "But before we all go, I want to say something that's important to say." People muttered to each other, and Madeleine got hold of Jimmy Kidd's arm and pulled him back.

"Now we all know that Frank was, as they say back home in Ireland, 'a fine man for one man', and that he was an inspiration to us all at home and in the workplace." Father Rack looked directly to where Ellen, Molly and Beau were standing, and began again. "He's buried with his sweet mother now – we've seen to that. But what you might not have realised is that poor Frank was buried again and again throughout his short life." He paused and looked at Jimmy, who was wearing a black cloth diamond on the sleeve of his gabardine coat. The wind ruffled Jimmy's hair.

"He was buried by us. We saw to that. We buried him with our bigotry and lies; we buried him with our deception, deceit and cruel manipulations. He was buried with our wickedness, and with our lust and jealousy and downright treachery. And we've just buried him with our guilt." He scanned the pale faces; then he turned to adjust his black cassock. "Make no mistake, God is not mocked and as sure as death, we will be judged by our sins and throughout that time our salvation will be in doubt." He stared at the people; then he looked down at his feet. "That applies to all of us, you know, all of us, including dear Frank here. We're all sinners. Nobody is any better than anybody else. Sin is sin and you can find it everywhere. It's what human beings do. Accept it or leave it, that's what we do. But we can still repent our sins and pray for forgiveness, and resolve earnestly and with sincerity of heart to amend our lives. Sincere prayer is always heard. Our repentance is needed. Even prayers of repentance muttered with flat tongues and tight lips are heard just as readily as the prayers of a child whispered so soft as a butterfly's wings. Frank used to say, 'We will surely die, but our prayers can bring us eternal life.' Do you remember him saying that? When we leave this place, let us give thanks to God for Frank's life on earth, and ask him to forgive the ways we've been given to live our own. And let us give thanks for God's greatest gift of all, the gift of love, which, for brief moments, can make our troubled lives bearable. Amen."

There was silence; then, like breaths leaving a racked body, they passed and were gone.

Waiting for the Angel

Old Clem was born in this house. Life had been hard here, but the people he'd grown up with had made it seem all right. They had hearts that were warm enough to make things feel the way he wanted it to be. And they'd lived in this house, this dear house that sometimes seemed to be the only thing left of his life.

Memories drifted through his head like ghosts. He could still sense those people; he could hear them, and he could see them. In this room he'd snuggled in his mam's arms with his thumb in his mouth, and watched his dad snoring in the chair after he'd come back from The Bess. This is where he'd helped to wash his sister in front of the fire in a tin bath; it was where the family had played games at Christmas, and had stayed up late roasting potatoes on a coal shovel. And it was here he'd knelt by the chimneybreast to smoke his dad's Woodbines, and where he'd drunk his first gulps of stout from a flowery mug.

There was so much laughter in those days, like that time at Halloween, when his dad had blacked his face with soot and taken his teeth out to do the apple bobbing. His dad was like that. He'd once set fire to Mam's newspaper while she was still reading it. Then he'd come over all innocent, and everybody had laughed. Mam said he was a silly bugger who'd never change as long as he'd got a hole in his arse. But then, in the end, he'd had to. He'd cried on the day they'd made him redundant, and he'd never been the same after that.

And there were other things. Clem remembered his sister lying in the corner. She was so still. It'd been a blessing, because all through her illness she'd been unable to settle for long. She just looked up at the faces with fear in her eyes. And he could remember how his mam had looked at him the morning he'd left to join the navy. She was so proud of him, and when he came back on his first leave she'd told him that he'd gone away a boy and come back a man.

It was different now. Either way, there was no life in it. There was only the constant hiss of the gas fire, and the sound of cars passing in the street. The house was empty. But it hadn't always been like this; it used to have proper life in it. His daughters had opened Christmas presents in this room. He could remember the glass balls on the Christmas tree, and how they'd sparkled in the firelight. On Friday evenings, he'd drink Mackesons with a chum who played for Manchester City Reserves. And every Sunday, the whole family would listen to the wireless and eat bacon and eggs, with plenty of bread and margarine and brown sauce. And when the new television arrived, they'd roared England to victory over Germany in the World Cup, and they'd seen the Americans land on the moon. That was a long time ago. Things had changed. He had changed. His hands were old and he slept a lot. Sometimes he found it hard to breathe.

But it hadn't always been like this. This was the room where he'd first kissed the girl who became his wife – and where, when on leave, he'd loosen her hair and carry her upstairs to the bedroom. He'd been in his prime then – young and handsome, or so they said, working the great ocean liners and being paid to see the world – and she had been lovely and full bosomed, and full of life.

She was dead now. Her death had broken his heart. Things like that never really leave you. And sometimes, by firelight, he thought he could see her face smiling back at him in the mirror on the far wall.

He didn't look any more. The window was his mirror now. He could still look out. On winter evenings, he could see the streetlights coming on one by one. The light by the paper shop was always first. It stood near to where The Mission had been. He'd gone to Sunday School at The Mission; it was where the Church Lads Brigade would meet, and where he'd had his first Communion. It had burned down one Bonfire Night. The bonfires were lit on the waste ground just to the side of it: great fires, stacked with furniture, floorboards, tyres and railway sleepers that would burn for days. Houses were there now. It had been good fun, He'd watched Bonfire Night happen from this very window. There'd been well-wrapped mams with sweet parkin and toffee apples, girls who wrote names in the air with sparklers, and boys who got up to no good with penny bangers, and rockets launched from milk bottles. And once, he'd watched Ronnie Bradshaw do a snake dance when somebody had set the fireworks in his pocket alight. Everybody had got together on Bonfire Night; but not any more. They didn't have bonfires now. Everything was different. Everything – even the sound of Saturday nights was different. Gangs of lads going home didn't even sing.

Saturday nights in Gorton had always involved singing. Those long, noisy, smoke-filled nights in The Bess full of Gorton folk – the Bradshaws, the Coopers, the Parnabys with their lovely daughters, and the Molloys. Bess nights always ended with laughter, and people shouting for Elsie to play the piano. Everybody sang. It meant things, different things to different people, but mostly the singing was about love and the pain that surely follows it. *I'll Take You Home Again, Kathleen*. And sometimes, on the way home, you could hear music drifting over the rooftops. Sometimes it was a lone saxophone and distant cheers from Belle Vue, and sometimes it was voices singing in the terraces beyond.

And on long summer mornings the sun streamed through the window and into the room. The starlings were up first, and then the early workers on their way to the marmalade factory. In the old days you'd see the children going to school in twos and threes with their mams. You don't see so many of them nowadays, and they go in cars instead. And years ago, at dinner time, when the sun cracked the factory walls and the pitch bubbled up black as jet between the cobbled setts, he'd watch boys gather it up on lollipop sticks. Those were the days when the bears in Belle Vue Zoo would sigh in their pits, and motorbikes would roar round the speedway track by the railway bridge. And when the fair came in August he could hear the rock 'n' roll from the dodgems, and see youths going home with coconuts, and children with goldfish in little fish bowls held gently with both hands. Those were the evenings when there were such rich red sunsets that covered the sky. And when it got dark the firework displays from Belle Vue would begin, and stars of metallic green and red and silver burst over the terraced rooves, and dance bands would strike up the rhythm for the night, and there'd be singing.

But there was nothing now. It was just quiet, except for the buzzing of a fly against the window. He looked away and gazed down at the arm of the chair.

It was worn, and there were smooth black stains on it. That's where the old dog had rested her head when she was sleeping. The clock ticked. The fly flew in zigzags under the light bulb. Clem put his head on the arm of the chair and watched it. The clock ticked, his breathing became regular, and slowly he slipped into a sleep that lifted him gently into a dream lit by soft light. It was a light that brought pale pinks and greys to diamonds that framed clowns' faces and surrounded them with glass beads and light bulbs, and had them sing ancient lullabies. In the dream he saw the rooftops of old Shanghai, and in the streets below, the banners, rice dealers, tea houses, whore houses and smoking rooms, and his daft mates eating fruit. And through the clatter of trams and the shouts of street vendors, he heard the distant tolling of a ship's bell calling him home. The tolling became footsteps that got louder, until they marched like a brass band through the dark streets of Gorton. Then he heard a man's voice and the rattling of keys in the front door, and he was awake. He looked over to the door. It opened and there was his grandson, Graham. He was talking.

"Hello, son. Are you on your portable telephone?"

Graham nodded and carried on talking. "No, they've changed her dates and brought her forward. Yea, it's called 'La Lesh Express.' No, it's more to do with solid fuel indemnities. All right. Yea. Yea. Right. Yea. Laters. Ciao!"

"Were you on your portable, son?"

"My mobile, Granddad. It was my mate, Tony, on the mobile."

"Oh, it's a mobile."

"He's having trouble with his car."

"Is he? What's wrong with it?"

"It's dark in here, Granddad." Graham switched the light on. "Granddad, Mam said it'll be all right if I took that lampshade in the back there – you know, that twenties one with grapes on it."

"Oh, did she? Oh."

"Yea, it'll look a treat in the new bungalow."

"I suppose it will. Where is the new bungalow, son?"

"It's in Denton."

"Oh, Denton, oh is it? Er, do you want a cup of tea?"

"No, you're all right, Granddad, but if I can have a screwdriver I'll get the lampshade down for you."

"Oh, aye. There's one in the drawer. Should be in the drawer. It should be, anyroad."

"No worries, Granddad. Leave it to me. I'll fix it for you."

Graham went away to take the lampshade down. It'd always hung in the backroom; Clem's mam and dad had put it there years ago. When the light was on, the grapes glowed dark red. Clem and his sister had stared at them and played counting games. Sometimes the grapes had looked good enough to eat.

Graham came back. "Got it! It was a bit of a struggle like, but I've got it down." He lifted the lampshade by the chains. There it was, with its leaded greens, amber and cobalt-blue glass, and the clusters of ruby grapes that Clem and his sister had once thought so delicious.

"God, it's dirty, Granddad. It had loads of dead flies in it, and what looked like a piece of dried mistletoe! It's a right mess, but I've tipped it all out and left it on a newspaper on the side there."

"Aye, right oh, son."

Graham looked up at the light bulb.

"You've got a fly there, Granddad. Shall I swipe it?"

"No, son. You're all right."

"Are you sure?"

"Aye, son, leave it alone. It's done no harm… It's a bit of company really."

Graham's mobile went.

"Ye-llow! Hi, Tony. Yer. Got it. It'll look great when Julie cleans it up."

The fly flew in zigzags under the light bulb.

Graham laughed. "It's next Friday!" He turned to the door. "Granddad?" He looked at Clem and winked. "Oh, he's fine. The only trouble with Granddad is that he won't go under — will you, Granddad? No worries, Tony, he can take it." Graham switched the light off and closed the door behind him.

Old Clem listened to his grandson's footsteps fading away. After a while, all he could hear was the hiss of the gas fire and the ticking of the clock. Then, he sat in darkness and waited for the Angel.

I

74584551R00167

Made in the USA
Columbia, SC
06 August 2017